# Stand

T GEPHART

*Stand*

Copyright 2016 T Gephart
ISBN-10: 0-9944759-3-4
ISBN-13: 978-0-9944759-3-0

Discover other titles by T Gephart at Smashwords or on Facebook, Twitter, Goodreads, or tgephart.com.



Cover by Hang Le
        www.byhangle.com
Editing by Perfectly Publishable
        www.perfectlypublishable.com
Formatting by Max Effect
        www.formaxeffect.com

To the goodbye

I wasn't ready to say.

# THEN

**I**t was the calm before the storm.

Neither of us had spoken about it last night, both too caught up in each other to care what it all meant. He was irresistible and I saw no reason to fight the urge. No matter how many times we drifted apart, we always seemed to end up back together. Maybe it was sheer magnetism, maybe it was his amazing smile? Or maybe it was his delicious well-toned body that did amazing things to mine? It could have been any of those reasons, but mostly it was because of the way he made me feel.

Happy.

Some of my best memories featured the man sleeping soundly beside me. And it wasn't even about the sex, although . . . yeah, his talents weren't only restricted to the stage. There was just something about him. Something bigger than what he already was, and I knew living in the Bronx and working at Staples wasn't his destiny.

Sadly, neither was I.

International rock sensation Power Station had seen it too, signing up Black Addiction—Max's band—to be their support act for a huge stadium tour. They'd already wowed the crowds at Madison Square Garden, the other crowds would follow too and then the world would see what I already knew.

Max Reynolds was a rock star.

We'd taken a break from each other around three months ago. No messy break up, no drama—just our lives taking us in different directions. It wasn't a new thing for us, and in some ways, it just worked. But last night wasn't us getting back together; last night was something else entirely.

His eyes were shut tight as he slept, completely unaware as I watched him. His perfect lips parted just slightly as the air whistled past. And I knew this would be the last time we could do this; at some point we'd stop the revolving door.

"Hey." He slid open an eye, his trademark panty-melting grin not far behind. "You're awake. Feeling okay?"

"Yep, I know better than to try and keep up with you and your band." I couldn't help but smile back. "How about you? You had a pretty serious commitment with that bottle of Jäger." Don't know why I asked; I'd never seen him rocking the next morning regret like most of us did.

"Never felt better." He smirked, his fingers trailing up my side, tickling my skin until they reached my breast. His talented fingers palmed me, hinting that he had other things on his mind other than his lack of hangover. "And my only commitment last night was pleasing you. So, tell me . . . how did I do?"

God, he was smooth.

He had this uncanny ability to make you feel like you were the only woman in the room, like nothing else mattered, and even if I knew it was temporary, I loved it.

"I think you got all the confirmation you needed last night." I grinned as I nestled into his side. "If you want your ego stroked, you'll have to go elsewhere."

"That's not what I want you to stroke, Beth," he whispered into my ear, his voice loaded with suggestion.

"I should probably go." It's not that I didn't want to stay, but it didn't take a rocket scientist to know where this would end up. Sleep was not part of that equation.

"Why? Stay in bed with me." His muscular, inked arms caged me against his body, the heat between us having nothing to do with the temperature in the room. "I'm almost positive you won't regret it."

I wouldn't regret it.

I never would.

But in my heart I knew that this was the end of the road for the two of us. And as much as I wanted to keep going by his side, he had to walk it alone. How much longer could I stay? A week, a month, a year? He needed to be single. Free to do whatever he wanted to do when that spotlight finally hit him and not wonder if it would have been different without a girlfriend ball-and-chain. I wouldn't be the source of anyone's regrets, not least someone as special as Max. He was on the cusp of something great, and I cared too much to hold him back.

"You need sleep, you have a show tonight." My hands moved over his chest. "We both know if I stay, there will be no sleep." I tried in vain to free myself from his arm prison, my attempt laughable as he pulled me closer.

"Sleep's overrated." The words vibrated against my ear as I closed my eyes and remembered the moment. The one that would be the last time in his arms.

"You might not be dealing with a hangover, but you can't

outrun fatigue. Sleep and I'll see you when you get back in town."

It was a lie, an easy one to tell, knowing that when he came back things would be different. We would be different, and I think deep down he knew it was goodbye.

"Beth." His lips pressed against the back of my neck, my short black hair offering me little protection as his hot breath defied logic and gave me goose bumps. "We'll always end up like this, you and me."

*Not always, not anymore.*

I didn't dare say it. More because I didn't want to hear it even though I knew it was the right thing to do.

"You going to let me go?" I asked, his arms showing no sign of releasing me

"For now." He kissed my neck before loosening his hold and allowing me to sit up.

"You're going to do great on this tour; this is what you've been waiting for." I didn't have to even force the smile on my face, I was genuinely happy for him. "Your life is about to change."

"Whatever happens, happens." His arms flexed and anchored at the back of his neck. "I'm still going to be me, that won't ever change."

"Good." I fished my T-shirt from the edge of the bed and threw it over my head. "And I'll be your biggest fan." It was an easy promise to make; being supportive was something that I planned to continue. And something I could do even if it wasn't by his side.

"Just promise you won't get all weird and start stealing my underwear to sell on eBay." He watched me as I slid on my own and grabbed my jeans from the floor.

"So, I should put back the pair I have stuffed into my

purse?" I turned back to face him as I pulled up my jeans, batting my eyes seductively for effect.

I hadn't actually stolen a pair of his boxer briefs, but it was easier than the inevitable so-this-is-where-it-ends that needed to happen.

"Call me, Beth." He didn't hesitate, his eyes looking directly into mine. It was as if he already knew that I probably wouldn't but wouldn't push the issue either. It was a weird stalemate, so much left unsaid, but all those words not spoken completely understood.

"See ya, Max." I allowed myself one last look at him before scooping up my shoes and shuffling out of the room. The door closed behind me giving me a resting place for a second before I walked out of his house.

We both needed this. It wasn't just for him; this was for me too. Together neither of us would reach our full potential, and we owed each other that. I was more than just a bass player's girlfriend. I was more than a girl with tattoos, funky hair and a short skirt. If I stayed . . . he was too easy to fall in love with.

There was no sadness when I left; my heart wasn't breaking. I was excited about what the future held for both of us and while I'd miss him, someday we would both be thankful.

In time we would both move on, and hopefully when he thought of me, he'd remember good things.

I would always, when I thought of him.

# Max

## NOW

**"You know, I'm not sure why you waited so long to** make the move. Manhattan is where you belong." Her beautiful hazel eyes widened in satisfaction as she flicked her dark brown hair over her shoulder. Her lips settled into a grin as she leaned across her desk, the midday sun pooled through the massive glass windows of her high-rise office. "It's way past due."

"Well, I'm here now aren't I? You found me a place yet?" I eased back into my chair, wondering if she'd managed to find me a new address that satisfied the vague shopping list I'd given her. I wasn't Beyoncé, but I didn't want random fans knocking at my door. And an undercover garage as well, I didn't want to be street parking my '68 Corvette.

"Max, please." The laugh worked its way up her throat. "With your budget? I've found several." She turned back to her computer and gave her keyboard some love.

The lady in front of me was not only beautiful but also wicked smart, and working with one of the best realtors in NYC. In every respect, the kind of girl you'd be proud to have on your arm. But there was also a snowballs chance in hell I had any interest in her other than professional.

Ivy Shaw was the younger sister of my best friend Joey, which well and truly put her into the never-ever-gonna-go-there category. Not just because Joey would have my nuts if I even looked at her that way, but because I'd seen her grow up and she was the sister I'd never had. My brother, and only sibling, was still MIA and that's where I'd preferred the lowlife to stay.

Having Ivy take care of this meant I didn't have to worry about some asshole taking me for a ride. The money, the fame—it was still taking me awhile to get used to.

"So, do you have a preference to area? Tribeca? Upper East Side? Greenwich?" Her fingers tapped on the keys as she pulled up some prospective properties on the screen.

"As long as it has great security, my neighbors aren't assholes and it's bigger than a closet, I'm cool with wherever." Apartment living was going to be an adjustment and I'd rather not deal with some pain-in-the-ass pearl-clutcher who assumed I Satan worshipped.

"You know . . ." She kept typing without looking up. "There's a great place that has four bedrooms—"

"Ivy, four bedrooms? Overkill don't you think? It's just me. Three bedrooms is plenty. Then I can have a guest room and set one up as a mini studio." Hell, I'd even go down to two if I had to. The money was coming in, but I didn't want to spend more green than I needed on a bunch of rooms I had no use for.

"You know, no one could have predicted that my brother would be married with a kid. I'm just trying to keep your options open."

And here we go again. Ivy was a sweetheart, but she spent waaaaay too much time thinking about my love life. She'd been trying to set me up for a few months now so the angle wasn't new. I put up with it because she was harmless but that's where the interest stopped. I didn't need a matchmaker.

"And I appreciate that. Trust me, I'm open to doing all of that, but my options didn't exactly increase when my bank account did."

It had been awhile since I'd had anyone steady. And while I assumed I'd eventually do the love and marriage thing, currently it wasn't on my radar.

Girls weren't the problem. I had more opportunities than I ever did before—blondes, brunettes, redheads—take your pick. But as far as *keepers* went, none of them stuck.

"What do you mean?" She leaned forward in her chair genuinely interested.

"I mean, most girls see me as a meal ticket. Whether it's for money or to get their name in the paper. Most of the dates I've been on end up on Instagram. Not really wife material."

"Oh." She stopped typing as the penny dropped. Fame was awesome, but it came with a price tag.

"Look, I'm not complaining." I was genuinely okay with it. I was living a charmed life so the girl thing—or lack thereof— wasn't a big deal. "Seriously, it's a small price to pay for our Cinderella story, but I know that it's going to be harder from here on out, not easier. Just being realistic."

"Maybe you shouldn't be looking for someone new?" She shifted in her chair, her attention no longer on her computer screen. "Maybe you've already met *her*."

Well, there was a fucking revelation. It wasn't something that I'd thought a lot about, but every once in a while it got front and center on my current situation. So the *mention* wasn't some subtle hypothetical when we both knew who she was talking about.

Beth.

The girl who had been by my side for years and probably the last real girlfriend I'd had.

"Kid, I know you mean well, but you are wrong on that one." I was fairly sure the window for the two of us getting back together had closed. "It's been over four years since we last spoke. Hell, I don't even know where she lives anymore." She moved out of the Bronx, that much I knew. "Too much time has gone by."

"But I know—"

I didn't give her a chance to finish.

"Maybe, you find me a place and leave me to find my own dates. Or perhaps you'd like me to tell Joey about that stockbroker you're seeing?"

It was a dick move and one I'd never pull, but I knew one word of subjecting her new dude to Joey's rigorous screening would have her backing off the topic pretty damn quick.

"You wouldn't dare?" The death glare shot across her desk and chilled the room.

"Wouldn't I?" I smirked as I eased back into my chair knowing she wouldn't risk finding out.

"Fine, fine. I can take a hint and butt out, but I think if anyone is wrong, it's *you*. I'll just do what I'm getting paid to do." The sarcasm wasn't hard to miss but at least she was letting it go.

"Does this mean your commission just increased?"

"Yep, and you're taking me out to dinner tonight." Her smile returned as her eyes filled with mischief. "My Instagram could use some more action."

"You drive a tough bargain, Ivy Shaw."

"Yeah, I know, but you love me for it."

•••

"What do you think?" Her heels echoed off the wooden floorboards. "Three bedrooms, very secure, undercover garage." She rattled off my list like hostage demands. "Amazing location, great view . . ."

It had been exactly a week, and apparently Ivy had found what was going to be my next home. She'd woken me up, excited beyond measure about an apartment that I *had* to see. I'd assumed the process would take a little longer but was happy to get it wrapped up sooner than later. Everyone else had moved away and the house that Joey and I shared had been pretty empty since he'd left.

"Yeah, it looks good." I nodded as I walked around the empty space, the apartment huge by Manhattan standards. "Definitely ticks all the boxes. I'll make a mental note of all its virtues. Where to next?"

"What you mean next? This is *the* apartment." Ivy shot me a look like I was insane. Her hands out wide for good measure.

"So we're not even going to look at anything else? You know it's not about the cash. If I need to spend a little extra, it's all good."

I assumed that we'd poke around three possibly four apartments, and I'd ooh and ahh at all the right places and then pick out the least pretentious. Or at least that had been my understanding of how this property buying shit worked.

"No, Max. *This* is the best apartment in my portfolio." She shook her head unwilling to relent. "This is like the Hope Diamond. You don't get a penthouse like this open up for sale often. I'm telling you, I'm fighting with three other brokers for this. We walk away from this, it will be off the market by noon."

Not sure why she was putting on the hard sell, she knew that I wasn't wasting her time and a sale either today, tomorrow or next week was a sure thing. I was in the market, not wandering around empty rooms trying to make myself feel better about the size of my wallet. And the reason I'd chosen her—besides the obvious that she was kickass at what she did—was so I didn't have to deal with the shady agent trying to slip his hand into my back pocket and rob me blind.

"Ivy, we're not talking about a used car or a case of beer. There are a lot of zeros on that price tag." Sure I could afford it, but I hadn't woken up and completely lost my mind. Who the fuck bought property on a freaking whim? This wasn't a game of fucking Monopoly. No one was going to be handing me cash every time I passed go.

"It's the Upper West Side, trust me, it doesn't get better than this. This is the one. You need to buy it."

I should walk away.

I should tell Ivy to stop being such a hard ass and find me some other possibilities or at the very least sleep on it. Impulse shopping was one thing, but this—

Fuck.

Seriously, what's the worst that could happen? And it was only money right? When the hell did I turn into such a conservative fuck? If this shit all ended tomorrow and I wound up on someone's sofa, who the hell cared? Now was not the time for me to bring out the safety net, if I wanted to play with the big dogs then I had to start acting like it and a swanky new address would be a good start.

"You're sure?" Translation, if you're going to talk me out of it, now would be the time.

"Yes, positive. It's the best." Her big-ass grin proved she knew I wasn't about to tell her no.

"Fine, put in an offer." I pulled her into a hug, happy for her to handle all the extra shit, especially the paperwork it was going to take. Negotiations bored me to tears. Just tell me where to sign and hand me the keys, I wasn't interested in the finer details.

"Good, I'm glad you feel that way." She slowly eased away from me, a tight smile settling into place. "I negotiated it this morning; I'll have the contracts this afternoon."

"You put in an offer before I'd even seen it?" I couldn't help but laugh; she certainly had a pair of balls on her. "Jesus, Ivy. What if I'd said no?"

"I knew you wouldn't." She elbowed me and rolled her eyes; apparently I'd been a forgone conclusion. "Like I said, I had to fight three other brokers. You need to be here, Max. This is your new home."

"Well it is now, huh? You know I used to think your brother was cocky, but I'm seeing it's a family trait." I pulled her into another hug. "Fine, get me whatever needs to be signed."

"Will do." Ivy smiled against me. "Let's go downstairs and introduce you to the doorman. We're on a first-name basis now. I've sold three apartments here in the last three months. I think I'm his favorite."

There weren't a lot of people Ivy couldn't charm—myself included—so this little nugget of information didn't shock me. Besides, I had no plans so meeting the dude I'd probably be seeing on a daily basis, seemed like a good idea.

"Sure, no point me arguing anyway, you'll just pout until you get your way." I playfully pushed her toward the door.

"I don't pout Max Reynolds, I'm persuasive—there is a difference." Ivy grabbed the door and pulled it closed behind us.

As we walked to the elevator it hit me how much my life

had changed. It wasn't just the upmarket penthouse, but that I was essentially going to be living by myself for the first time in forever. I'd gone straight from my parent's place to the house I'd shared with Joey. Sure he'd moved in with his wife and new baby daughter five months ago, but the newly vacated spare room meant that every second night or so one of our friends would crash. Our place had always been a hangout, full of action. Even my piece-of-shit brother Phil had couch surfed a few times, but I hadn't seen him in months. Honestly, it was better for everyone if that part of my family tree stayed buried.

The asshole had fucked up royally. Of course his crowning glory was the reappearing daddy trick he'd pulled after initially deserting his kid. That it happened to be Rusty's—our guitarist and one of my buddies—girlfriend, well that was just the icing on the cake.

My parents were done with him too, which meant that short of committing a homicide, there wasn't much I could do to get on their bad side. Guess I had Phil to thank for that. They didn't even give a shit that occasionally some lowlife reporter hid in their bushes. Nope, they just took it in stride, called the cops and told me how proud they were I was making music and had followed my dream. Those two people were way better than I could ever strive to be. And between them and the band—well wasn't I just the luckiest son-of-a-bitch alive?

"You okay?" Ivy tapped me on the arm, my mental vacation noticed as I stared off into space.

"Yeah, just thinking about the old house. There were some good times there." The elevator doors opened, our short trip over.

"Trust me, you're going to like it here. Lots of good times coming your way." She was so damned pleased with herself I had to wonder if it was more than a hypothetical.

"We'll see, shall we?" We stepped into the foyer, the door-man we'd cruised past earlier giving us his full attention.

"Hi Ben, this is Max Reynolds," Ivy slipped into the intro without skipping a beat. "He's going to be moving into the penthouse on fifty. And Max, this is Ben Schwartz."

Mutual handshakes were exchanged as the dude gave me the quick welcome-to-the-building. All pretty standard. Ivy took the few minutes that Ben and I were engaged to give her phone some attention. The meeting with me had forced her to shove the device in her purse and she'd been no doubt going through withdrawals.

"Well thanks, man. Looking forward to moving in." Another handshake was exchanged with doorman Ben as I said my goodbyes, Ivy's head snapping to attention as the phone went back into her purse.

"Thanks Ben, I'll see you later." Ivy gave him a wave as she threaded her arm around mine, our feet moving toward the door. Her smile more than just a little familiar.

Ordinarily I wouldn't have paid it much attention. She'd already established she knew the guy, and the whole real estate gig meant she probably spent as much time apartment hopping as she did in her office. But there was something about the smile that got me more than curious.

"You have another client you need to come back to?" I held the door open as we walked out onto the street.

"No, not a client. A friend of mine lives here in the building." She looked uncomfortable as she adjusted her jacket.

"A *friend* huh? This wouldn't be the stockbroker you still haven't told your brother about is it?"

"Maybe, maybe not."

Sure, that wasn't obvious. Her omission was as good as a signpost as far as I was concerned.

"Wow girl, you are playing with fire. You don't think Joey might stop by and visit me at my new place? I'd say the chances of your little secret not staying that way for long are better than average."

Not to mention she was obviously really bad at keeping it under wraps. The only reason Joey hadn't clued in so far was because his wife and baby girl had his undivided attention, but the dude wasn't blind. And then the fireworks would start; definitely not playing it smart if it was something she wanted on the down low.

"My *friend* lives on the twenty-sixth floor, you're on the fiftieth. It's a big building, no need for anyone to see anyone." She waved it off like I was the crazy one. "Besides, it's complicated. We don't see each other a lot. Just occasionally here and there so it's not going to be an issue."

"What do you mean it's complicated?"

Giving her a hard time about this dude was one thing, but if this asshole was doing anything disrespectful then it wasn't going to be her who would be getting the third degree. She was family, and I'd do a lot more than have a friendly conversation with some guy if the situation called for it.

"Really Max, I have one big brother, I don't need another." She shook her head doing little to convince me that I didn't need to be involved.

"Well it sucks for you then because that's exactly what you have."

"It's nothing, really. Forget I said anything." She fumbled with her purse; doing everything she could not to look me in the eye.

"Yeah, not gonna happen. So start talking."

"Max, seriously. It's fine. I just wanted things to be different, but I understand why it has to be this way. It's probably for the best, I'm really okay with the way things are."

That shit did not sound like anything I wanted to hear. And she could tell me to mind my business as much as she wanted, but a sit down with this guy was happening. And so help me God if this douche wasn't deserving of her.

"What apartment?"

"Max, no. Don't be ridiculous." She yanked on my arm trying to pull me away from the door. "You aren't going there. There's no need for you to be involved."

"You can tell me what apartment or I can knock on every single one on the twenty-sixth floor. I've got nothing but time. It would be a great way to introduce myself to the neighbors wouldn't you say?" It would be the polite thing to do, and I wasn't shy in saying hi.

She had to know that I wasn't kidding because she suddenly stopped fussing with her jacket, purse and everything else that stalled her looking at me when her eyes snapped up to mine.

"I shouldn't have said anything. There is really no issue. None actually. We're fine. Nothing you need to involve yourself in."

It was a little late for her to be having regrets now. "So if there is *no* issue, what's the harm in me saying hello? I like to meet new people, think of it as me being social." Yeah, 'cause that's what it was about.

"If I tell you, promise me you won't lose your cool?" She bit her lip nervously and it wasn't an act either, she was genuinely worried about me and this asswipe meeting. And didn't that just give me the scratch.

"I'll be a model fucking citizen, I'm just going to go introduce myself."

"I mean it Max, promise me. Whatever happens, you cannot be angry."

"Cross my heart, you have my word." Beating his ass was still on the table and if she was looking for assurances that I wouldn't, she was SOL.

"Fine!" She huffed out a breath knowing that I would make good on my promise to acquaint myself with everyone on the twenty-sixth floor. "But don't do anything until after you move in. Okay? And remember about keeping your cool. You've promised."

"Jesus, Ivy." My fingers raked through my hair in frustration. What the hell was she doing with this guy in the first place? Whatever, I'd find out soon enough and fix it, promise or no promise. "Fine, now give me the number."

She hesitated a beat, the argument over as far as I was concerned. "Twenty six sixteen." The numbers said in a rush.

"See, that wasn't so hard, was it?" I'd just save that piece of information for later. I'd honor my part of the deal and not go door knocking until the place was mine, but I was paying cash and the apartment was empty; it wouldn't take long before I had my chance to do some investigating.

"I'm already regretting it." She blew out a breath, her feet moving restlessly on the sidewalk. She didn't bother trying to talk me out of it, or elaborate why things were complicated. Possibly because the damage was already done and like it or not trying to stop me meeting him was going to be a fruitless exercise.

"Everything is going to be fine." I pulled her in close and gave her a hug.

It wasn't an idle promise either; whatever was making her nervous was going to be sorted real soon. She could bank on it.

I wasn't used to hangovers anymore.

That horrible feeling of regret mixed with wanting to die. It had been a while and now I remembered why.

Ugh. I was probably going to puke.

It hadn't been my intention to get drunk last night. In fact, my intention had been to have a glass of wine or two and spend a nice evening finally having sex with the guy I'd been *sort of* seeing. I guess you could call it dating if you had a really wide definition but even then it was a stretch.

Stupidly on New Year's Eve—the last time I was drunk ironically—I'd committed to getting into shape. Yes, I know, save the eye roll, but it seemed like a good idea at the time. Jules—my roommate and co-conspirator in this stupid plan— and I had been drinking cheap pinot grigio straight from the bottle and eating nachos while sitting on our couch. Of course unless you counted an occasional sprint to the subway as a workout, we hadn't even attempted getting fit before, but surely it couldn't be that hard. It seemed like a solid idea, what could possibly go wrong?

Jules lasted exactly two weeks before she waved the white flag of defeat, while I continued defiantly more to prove I wasn't just another cliché. Enter the hot guy who ran beside me on the treadmill almost every single morning.

Yep, another freaking cliché.

Believing the gym gods were rewarding me for my diligent commitment, I flirted shamelessly with the hot specimen of man while I ran beside him. Like *Rocky,* but with less coordination and no theme song. He was stunning.

So, I took the flirting a little bit further and suggested we go out. I mean, I'd been seeing him for months, no rings, no jailhouse tattoos—what could possibly go wrong?

Unfortunately, it didn't start well with my promising night taking a nosedive the minute we met in front of the gym. He'd arrived late, picked a hideous restaurant and talked about himself for most of the evening. I should have heeded the signs, the ones that told me to say goodbye and find my good times elsewhere.

While usually I wasn't a one-night-stand kind of girl, I figured it didn't count because technically I'd known him for weeks. Technically, you could count our shared workout time as *dates*, right? And, my love life was in such a funk I thought what the hell. Besides, I was trying to remain optimistic and hoped there might be some redemption in between the sheets. A body like that looked to deliver promises of a good time and I didn't care it seemed shallow; surely everyone deserved a little no-strings fun? And he was my reward remember?

Let's just say that my *reward* came up a little short in the pants department.

As in, it was tiny.

Like, I wasn't even sure it had been inside me.

How I wish I were joking.

So after faking a terribly overacted orgasm, and trying not to make eye contact with his microscopic penis, I hightailed it out of his apartment and back to wine. I mean, *mine*. Where I consoled myself with *wine*. It took a while, which is why I feel like I'd licked the floor of a public bathroom. Oh, and now I needed to find a new gym as well. Which proved nothing good came of New Year's resolutions. And my alcohol tolerance had been substantially lowered in the last three months.

"Beth, did you die?" Jules knocked tentatively on my door, the sound of her knuckles against the wood making my head pound.

"Yes, I've perished," I mumbled, praying that if I kept my eyes shut the room would stop spinning.

"So I assume your night didn't go so well?" She ignored my corpse imitation and sat on the bed beside me.

Jules was not only my roommate but had grown to become one of my closest friends.

Deciding a few years ago the best thing for me was to get serious and leave my party-girl days behind, I moved away from my home in the Bronx. Not only did I finally get to use my college education for what it was intended, scoring a teaching position at a swanky elementary school in the Upper East Side, but I also gained a new BFF who not only taught at the same school but was also looking for a roomie. While her original place had been small—the second bedroom really just a glorified closet—we found a newer place with more room that was still in the budget. And the location was outstanding. Everything pointed to me making the right decision, and while I still loved seeing my friends and family from the old neighborhood, those parts of my life stayed very separate.

"*Not go so well* is an understatement." While his insistence that we only eat organic and carb free hadn't bugged me initially, it wasn't my stomach being left unsatisfied as why I was rocking a headache from hell. "It seems there is no direct correlation to the size of a man's body to other *parts* of him." I tried my best not to be unnecessarily crude. Not that there was any other way around it, his *fingers* had been more substantial.

"Whoa. Hold on a minute." Jules refused to let me wallow in my self-induced misery as she grabbed my shoulders forcing me to turn around. "He had a small cock? That can't be right, he was like seven feet tall."

"This *thing* wasn't a cock. I've seen cock, trust me, this didn't qualify." I dared to crack open an eyelid. "I'm assuming it's either steroid usage, or the reason for the rest of him being so big is compensation." I wriggled my little finger, "It's like it stopped growing or something. I even snuck a look at his ID while he was in the bathroom to make sure he wasn't a mutant sixteen year old and I needed to hand myself to the cops."

The fear had been real.

While the chances of him being a minor were remote, I wasn't about to end my career, face statutory rape charges and be fodder for the Mommy Mafia of my current work place. Thankfully, the crisis was averted with him being of legal age, but the experience drove me to drink. Heavily.

"I swear, it could only happen to you." Jules laughed, my misfortune being her morning entertainment. "Why don't you haul yourself out of bed and I'll make you waffles. Lots of syrup. It's either going to soak up some of the alcohol or put you in a carb coma, either way you're bound to feel better than you do now."

As unappealing as leaving the warm sanctuary of my comforter was, she had a point. My dinner of macrobiotic, organic, free range *whatever* hadn't been appetizing, which meant most of it stayed on the plate, another reason as to why the wine had done its worst. Last night had just been a disaster.

"You're so good to me." I marveled at how, despite my failures in the relationship department, I really did lead a charmed life. Finding Jules and my new job was better than I'd ever hoped.

"I know." She shrugged, "But you'd do the same for me, so we'll call it even."

She was right. I would totally do the same for her, even if I'd known her a fraction of what I'd known my other friends.

Jules didn't linger, making good on her promise to feed me and bring me back to sobriety with calorie laden breakfast food. And I decided to help the process along by trying to wash away last night's disaster under a spray of hot water and a gallon of shower gel. As much as moving made me want to hurl, getting clean did make me feel marginally better. Plus, I had smelled the cheap wine oozing from my pores when I'd lifted the comforter and if the hangover wasn't enough to make me nauseous, my own eau-de-wino surely would.

After toweling my body dry until it pinked, I pulled on a pair of sweats and a favorite unicorn T-shirt. The sweats were for comfort, not function, with my resolve to never step foot inside that gym anytime soon well and truly in place. And the T-shirt was my fave; the well-worn fabric hugging my body like a second skin. I also forwent the bra because . . . who the hell cared? It was Saturday morning and I had no one to impress.

"You almost look normal." Jules smiled, pulling out two plates and placing them on the counter. "I hope you're hungry, I made loads."

"Uh-huh." I picked up my juice and sipped it tentatively. I didn't want to get cocky; puking wasn't completely off the table.

The plates had just been loaded up with waffles, ready to be smothered with syrup when there was a knock at our door.

A knock.

Jules and I locked eyes as a surge of panic overrode the hangover.

"Does he know where you live?" she whispered, her eyes darting between me and the door.

"Even if he did, how did he get past the doorman?" One of the perks of living in our apartment was no danger of door-to-door salesmen or unwanted boyfriends banging on your door at three in the morning. Every visitor had to be signed or escorted in, with the concierge militant about the no-stranger rule. Unless someone vouched for you, you were left to chill on the sidewalk.

Of course the smart thing to do would be to open the damn door. Then we'd see who was on the other side, rather than deliberating if someone had been stealthy enough to get through the rigorous security measures. The second knock punctuated the point.

"We should answer it." Jules' head tilted toward the door, and by *we,* she meant *me.* She had made breakfast so I guess if we were going to get murdered by some random stranger, I should be the first one to go. It would be the polite thing to do.

"Fine, I'll do it." I shuffled to the door, regretting my decision to not wear a bra. Last thing I needed was the murderer checking out my rack before he went slasher on me. Seriously, enough with the fucking clichés.

I tiptoed to the door like an idiot, unsure of when I turned into a moron and pressed my eye to the peephole.

Oh.

My.

God.

"What the fuck?" I said it out loud as well as in my head, because my brain couldn't connect with what my eyes were seeing. My hands fumbled with the lock as I tried to open the door. *C'mon fingers, twist and pull;* the door flew open confirming who I'd seen through the peephole hadn't been a mirage.

"Beth?"

Standing on my threshold was Max Reynolds, the six-foot-three, dark haired sex god from Black Addiction who I'd said goodbye to years ago. And goddamn those years had been good to him. Sure, I'd seen him in magazines, on TV or the occasional Google search, but it was nothing compared to what he looked like in the flesh.

Wow.

Was I staring? I must have been, because he was looking just as confused as I was.

"Beth?" He said my name again, stepping forward without an invitation. Not that he needed one; he pretty much owned every room he ever walked in. Mine—was no exception.

"Max, what are you doing here?"

There were a million questions running through my mind, but what had brought him to my front door was probably the one that was screaming the loudest. Along with, "How did you get hotter?" and "Can you please take off your shirt?" Thankfully the last few were saved just for me.

"Whoaaaaaaaa, Max Reynolds, the bass player from Black Addiction?" Jules' voice reminded me I wasn't alone as she sidled up next to me, her eyes almost bulging from her head.

"That would be me." His lips spread into a huge grin and every memory of that smile and what it was capable of came flooding back.

That smile was dangerous and I was already having trouble fighting gravity today. The temptation to check if this wasn't some alcohol fuelled dream proved too great as I reached out and placed my hand on his chest.

Hard.

Even through the fabric of his T-shirt, I could feel the toned muscles underneath.

"Do you fondle all your guests or just ones you haven't seen in a while?" His brow rose as we both looked down at my hand. It seemed to have a mind of its own, wandering with reckless abandon all over his torso, as I stood there mostly silent.

"Crap, sorry." I yanked my offending hand away from his delicious body and reminded myself I still had no idea what he was doing here. It was also a safe bet I had no idea what *I* was doing either so I hoped he had a better handle on it.

"No apologies needed." Another smile.

*Don't touch him,* I reminded myself.

"Someone want to explain why Max Reynolds is at our front door?" Jules eyed us impatiently. "And why does it seem like you know each other already?"

"Because we dated. Extensively." Max's eyes stayed glued to mine despite it being Jules who was asking the question. "And I just moved in, figured I'd get to know my neighbors."

"You live here?" My mouth shot out, drowning out Jules'. "You dated?"

"Yes." He answered Jules before turning his attention to me. "The fiftieth floor. It has a nice view."

I wasn't sure what shocked me the most. The fact Max was here, standing in front of me in all his badass, sexy glory *or* that he apparently moved into my apartment building out of the millions—okay, possibly a slight exaggeration—of housing options in the city of New York.

"Soooooooo . . ." My brain fumbled with an appropriate response.

Yep, I've got nothing.

"Did you want to come in?" It was the best I could hope for given the circumstances. Considering we'd been lingering in the doorway, an invitation was way past due.

"I'd love to." He had always had an uncanny ability to make innocent words sound so illicit. The ones he'd just spoken were no exception.

"Dated huh?" Jules elbowed me in the ribs as we both stepped aside so he could walk past. "We are having some serious words later," she whispered as both of our eyes traveled the length of his back and settled on his very fine ass.

"Damn," she cursed under her breath.

"Uh-huh," I agreed. It had been awhile, but it was no less spectacular.

"So, this is where you ran off to?" Max turned around, either ignoring the fact we were ogling his ass or being too polite to mention it. "It's a nice place."

"I wasn't running, just chose a different direction." True it was a lifetime away from what he probably remembered, but I hadn't run. And this was exactly where I needed to be even if I was miles away from home.

"Very different." He moved closer and picked up a few strands of hair that fell against my shoulder. The black, short bob he remembered having been replaced by longer locks in my natural brunette color. "It looks good on you."

"Thanks, it's easier to maintain."

Was I really having a conversation about my goddamn hair?

"Well, I guess I'll make my own introductions, I'm Jules. You'll have to forgive Beth, she had a rough night." Jules held out her hand which Max returned with a shake. "Max." His part of the introduction unnecessary, pretty sure everyone in the city knew *exactly* who he was.

I really needed to get my shit together. Other than inviting him in, I had no game plan nor did I have any idea of what I was actually doing.

"Are you hungry?" *Why the hell was I so nervous?* "Jules made waffles."

"Starved." A sexy grin pulled at his outer lips as he glanced down at my unicorn T-shirt—the grin getting a little wider.

Yeah, that wasn't sexy at all.

"Greaaaat," I said with equal parts enthusiasm and hesitation. "The kitchen is this way."

This was not how I imagined my Saturday morning was going to end up. If I wasn't before, I was well and truly sober now. And I was seriously regretting my wardrobe choices this morning. Oh, and I was probably—it was too soon to tell definitively—never drinking again.

# Max

**I**vy Shaw had a lot to answer for.

*Best apartment in her portfolio,* my ass. And her *friend* was not the fucking douchebag she'd been dating; he probably hadn't set foot inside this building. Which is exactly why she made me promise not to fly off the handle three weeks ago when we'd signed the contract. It wasn't the occupants of apartment *twenty six sixteen* that she was worried about, it was her own ass.

It took me three seconds after the door opened to realize I'd been set up. Not that I fucking cared. Being pissed at Ivy took up mental space I no longer had available, all of it occupied by the woman I could barely take my eyes off—Beth.

She looked different from the last time I'd seen her, and it wasn't just her hair. The tight pink T-shirt gave me a sample of the kind of body she was rocking underneath and I very much liked what I saw.

Beth had always been beautiful, and able to get me from zero to a hundred with little more than a look. Curves in all the right places and she'd known what to do with them, but this incarnation was so much more. She was more toned than I remembered, her body tighter and more conditioned. You could tell she'd spent some quality time inside a gym, not that I gave a fuck how much she could bench press. Nope, my interest was a lot less virtuous than that.

As for her hands on me, well that was something she would never have to be sorry about. My dick was already jealous it hadn't been him.

Should I have done the hello-nice-to-see-you-again and left? Probably—the reunion obviously just as unexpected for her—but there wasn't a chance I was leaving and it had nothing to do with breakfast.

"So when did you move to Manhattan?" Beth placed a plate piled with waffles down in front of me as she took her seat at the table. If my reappearance had fazed her, she'd gotten her composure back real quick.

"Yesterday, it's still getting furnished." And not a moment too soon it seemed, my weekend getting exponentially better.

"Well if you need anything until you get all your stuff, let us know." She offered, her beautiful smile hitting me like a kick in the balls.

"Yeah, anything you need." Her friend poured me a glass of juice. "Cup of sugar, fresh towels, a bed . . . ouch! Don't kick me." She hid her smirk behind a coffee cup while she rubbed her shin with the other hand.

"My foot slipped." Beth shrugged, biting her lip.

"Sure it did." Jules glared, her face even less convinced than her tone. "I'll just go and enjoy my breakfast on the balcony. Less chance of bruising."

We watched as she grabbed her plate and moved away from the table, a wordless exchange passing between her and Beth before she left the room.

"So, yeah . . . whatever you need." Beth settled into her seat.

"Thanks for the offer, might take you up on that." And I wasn't talking about a cup of sugar. I was more than just a little bit pleased that now I had her all to myself.

Of course I had no idea what exactly was on offer, but I was more than just a little curious to find out. The idea of getting reacquainted sent a shiver right down to my balls.

Beth had been more than just an ex-girlfriend; she'd been part of my world for so long I'd just assumed she'd always be there. Deep down I knew she was saying goodbye when she left the last time, but part of me assumed we'd stay friends.

There had been no bad break-up, no hurt feelings—there never was with us—and even when we hadn't been a couple, she'd always been cool to hang out with. So I had been surprised to hear she'd packed up and moved out of town without telling me. She didn't call and I was too caught up in what I was doing to call her. Not even sure why I didn't to be honest, but before you knew it, the months stretched into a year. Then a couple more, and in time she just became a part of history. A really awesome part of my history.

Unfortunately it wasn't her virtues as my *friend* that had me currently juiced up and I had to remind myself that there was a lot of water under the bridge. And not only had it been years since I'd slept with her, the lack of conversation between us had been just as long. Oh, and I had no idea who or what was in her life right now. Getting up to speed on the particulars was suddenly a more pressing issue than unpacking boxes.

"I have to say . . ." Beth's eyes dipped down to her plate before coming back to where I wanted them. On me. "It's a strange coincidence that you moved into my building. I mean, what were the chances?"

She'd always been bright, and that million-to-one possibility was just a little too convenient. Of course, probabilities had a big helping hand.

"I'd say better than average when Ivy Shaw is involved."

The more I thought about it the more fucking obvious it had been. Ivy hadn't been that slick, I'd just been too freaking distracted to take notice. I should have known and yet there we were . . . surprise, eating breakfast with the girl who'd probably meant more to me than any girl ever. Oh and my it's-all-in-the-past bullshit that I'd convinced myself of was no longer valid. I was not about to go quietly into the night after our little reunion that much was for damn sure.

"You know, I always assumed she would have told you." Beth pushed her hair out of her eyes and gave me her full attention. "She's still one of my closest friends, and she was the one who helped me find this place . . ." She left her sentence trailing.

"Yeah, well I know now." And wasn't that the truth.

Beth Hart was not the kind of girl you could meet and go on with your life like she didn't exist. Lord knows I'd fucking tried. It wasn't just her looks—even though we'd established she was a knockout—there was something more. Something inherently good that I'd always found hard to walk away from. And seeing her now reminded me exactly what had attracted me to her in the beginning. And while I assumed our relationship had run its natural course—not pushing the issue—I wasn't so sure I'd made the right decision way back when. Amazing how quickly I could do a one-eighty, being indifferent to our initial separation and now knowing one way or another I was having her in my life.

I couldn't peel my eyes away from her, ignoring the uncomfortable silence between us.

"You've done really well for yourself." She was the first one to break the staring match we had going on. "The band has done great, and you look . . . good. I'm so happy for you."

"Come on, Beth. It's been over four years." My fingers reached out and brushed over her knuckles. If she didn't want me to touch her, she was going to have to say so. "I don't want to talk about the band or how I look. Why did you leave?"

"I didn't leave; I've been in New York the whole time." She shrugged but didn't pull her hand away. "I just needed more, Max, for both of us. It was just the wrong time and we needed to move in different directions. You had the world at your feet, and I didn't want to be left wondering what if."

There was no regret in her voice or her eyes. No hesitation. Just crystal fucking clear clarity that I wasn't sure I'd ever possess.

"I'm a teacher, Max." She kept talking, my mouth not opening despite the million thoughts churning through my head. "I have a wonderful group of kids and I love what I do. I love Manhattan and I love where I've ended up. Being with you was amazing, some of the best years of my life, but we weren't ready to settle. *I* wasn't ready to settle."

Had she always been this fucking smart? Obviously she'd been way beyond my league; my head had just been too far up my ass to notice.

"I'm glad you didn't settle." I pushed my plate away, no longer interested in anything that was on it. "And I'm glad you are teaching. It's what you always wanted to do."

"Seeing you follow your dreams, kind of gave me a nudge in the right direction." She moved her hand to cover mine. "We were good together, but we were also really good apart."

"This is so fucking weird." I couldn't help but laugh. I mean seriously, the whole situation was a fuck load of absurdity. Freaking sliding doors and near misses—the exact bullshit I would have expected from some asshole in a turban at a county fair. *Step right up folks, I'll read your palm for a twenty.*

"You think this is weird?" She screwed up her face in mock horror. "I'm the one sitting here in no bra or shoes and a blood alcohol level that is probably still questionable. Trust me, if anyone could have used the tip off it would have been me."

I tried to stifle my grin, but it didn't stand a chance. "Just so you know, the no bra thing isn't a problem." And not something I hadn't noticed.

"Yeah, yeah. Nothing you haven't seen already." She shook her head as a smile twitched at the edges of her lips. "I'm still going to kill Ivy."

FYI, I didn't care how many times I'd already seen her tits, it would never get old. My dick thickened just at the mention. So her thinking that because I'd already been *there*, I had no interest in being there again was crazy talk. Not that I was going to bring it up, we'd already superseded the level of awkward for one day.

Instead I turned my attention to the second part of Beth's statement and the pint-size brunette who sadly had a price on her head. I hope that stockbroker boyfriend hadn't gotten too attached. "I think it should be a team effort, I have a score of my own to settle."

"Agreed."

•••

There weren't a lot of reasons for me to stay in Beth's apartment. As it was, sitting down and eating breakfast had been a stretch. Sticking around playing catch up—I was almost positive I was outstaying my welcome.

Her friend came back, her time on the balcony exhausted, as I thanked them for the breakfast I didn't eat and made for the door. My head threatened to explode with the new development, the holy-shit-blast-from-the-past not what I had been expecting this early in the morning.

Fortunately for me I was almost positive that my best friend—and drummer extraordinaire from Black Addiction—Joey, would also be awake. A newborn daughter will do that to a guy, and Uncle Max had never been more pleased that Layla was an early riser. The call for him to meet me at my new pad happened before I'd even made it back to my front door.

"Nice place," Joey strode in, the tray of extra-large coffees balancing in one hand. "Ivy really is a genius when it comes to property, right?" His feet continued moving from my entrance-way into my living room, not needing an invitation.

"Yeah, it's not her *good eye* that I want to discuss." My head tilted toward the two armchairs that were seriously over-whelmed by the new space. Decorating was no longer a priority.

"Is this going to be a serious conversation?" Joey settled into one of the armchairs, grabbing a cup and handing the other to me. "It's okay if it is but I'm going to need to have coffee first." I grabbed the cup and took my seat as he continued. "I love my kid, but last night was brutal. Kenzie walked into the bedroom naked and it took me four minutes to notice there were tits on display. Now that's some industrial-strength fatigue, my friend. I didn't notice *tits.*"

It seemed we both had wandered into the twilight zone in the last twenty-four hours, for different reasons obviously.

"Well, drink up then because you'll never guess who's kicking it a few levels down. And when I say, you'll never guess, I mean what-the-hell-are-the-chances kind of odds."

"Dude, please don't make me guess. If I was too tired for tits, I sure as shit ain't up for a game of charades."

Yeah, I wasn't up for the game either.

"Beth."

"*Beth*, Beth?"

"The very same."

It's funny how no further clarification was needed, the one word enough.

"Are you shitting me?" He waited for the obligatory *nope* to come from my mouth before continuing. "Wow, I'm not even going to wrap my head around the one-in-a-million coincidence."

The one in a million would probably have been generous, except those odds had been stacked more than a little.

"It wasn't fate, unless fate stands about five three and shares your last name." There was no need to point out the obvious, we both knew who had been orchestrating the show.

"Wow, so you got the apartment *and* a side order of girl-you-used-to-date. I should have brought vodka; the coffee isn't going to cut it. How did it go?"

"Dude, I'm not even sure." I shook my head, replaying the exchange for the five millionth time. "I think I was able to string enough words together so I didn't sound like a complete moron, but it felt like someone had just zapped me in the balls."

Usually I was cool, calm and collected and hopefully that was the vibe I had given off, because underneath, my brain kept misfiring. And while Beth might have been slightly rattled at the start, she'd reined it in pretty fucking quickly.

"Fuck dude, was she mad?" He winced as he took another sip, the coffee really not strong enough for this conversation. "I mean . . . were you guys back together before we left?"

"No, she wasn't, and no we weren't."

Joey wasn't trying to be an asshole; the question was

completely valid. Of course most couples broke up and stayed that way except that with Beth, well we always seemed to get back together.

"You know what's funny, is that she seemed really okay with all of it. Happy even." Not too many girls you used to sleep with who'd be cool with a random knock on their door. Of course, my morning visit hadn't been planned but it would have been totally okay if she'd told me to fuck off or at the very least given me a lukewarm reception.

"Isn't that a good thing? You guys were close and even when you weren't dating, you were friends."

"Yeah it should be a good thing except that whole thing is driving me batshit crazy."

Because that made all kinds of sense. Things were all fine and dandy but that wasn't enough for me. Oh hell, no. I wanted to dissect it a little more.

"Dude, you must be in trouble if you are asking me for advice. You know that when it comes to smoothing things over I suck. Badly." Joey wasn't wrong, he wasn't the kind of guy who would do great in public relations.

"Yeah, I'm going to need to see her again."

There was no need to say it out loud; I think we both knew that was going to be my plan.

"Of course you are, she lives downstairs." Joey stated the obvious.

"No, not like that."

As Joey mentioned running into Beth would probably happen. Getting the mail, seeing each other in the lobby—all very possible. But shit had seen to it that we should meet, and I wasn't leaving anything else to chance. Nor would I be happy with a five-minute discussion about the weather when passing each other in a hall.

"Whoa, you're gonna try and date? After four years? Man, you got some big stones." Joey barked out a laugh, his hand slapping me across the back for good measure. And wanting to see her had nothing to do with the size of my stones.

"Possibly, although she hasn't given me any indication she'd be up for that."

At no time did she give off the vibe she was looking to hook up in any way romantic. She'd been polite, gracious even, but other than giving me a quick wax-on-wax-off across the chest, there'd been no hint that she'd even consider a date. Which with any other girl would have been my cue to say goodbye and head out the door. With her, unless I had it spelled out— and I do mean explicitly, word choice totally intended—I wasn't walking away.

"So of course you're desperate too." Joey shook his head, completely reading me like yesterday's news.

"Yep."

"This is probably going to end badly." The warning not something I wanted to hear, nor cared about at this point.

"And yet, I'm still going there."

We'd already established this was out of character. I hadn't gone after a girl in—well, not since Beth. Sure I'd been spoiled, even before the band got big I'd managed to get girls with very little effort. Maybe it was because the bass or guitar in my hand acted as a magnet, maybe it was my face—surveys were never handed out. I was never without attention when I wanted it, so chasing wasn't my thing. That shit was all about to change.

Whatever reason we had gone our separate ways, was no longer good enough. Of course I had come up with this assessment without her consultation but I was on a moving train I had no hope of derailing. And sure it was bordering on insanity that a short meet-and-greet had spurned this situation but regardless of my mental stability, I wanted to know her again. If I got to date her again? Well wouldn't that be the jackpot I was looking to win.

All of which should have been a tip off of how significant she'd been. And obviously I'd not seen it until now because I was either too stupid or a dumbass. Hindsight is great like that, proving what a complete dick you had obviously been. Not that it mattered; I was going to rectify that shit post haste.

"Just be prepared for that ship to have sailed." Joey slapped me on the back trying to play devil's advocate. "Like maybe there was a reason you guys could never keep it together."

"Thanks for the advice, but you're wrong, the ship has far from sailed." At least it hadn't until I gave it one last shot.

**"Start talking."** Jules yanked on my arm the minute Max had left the apartment. "All the details and don't leave anything out."

My eyes were still locked on the door that had just closed in front of me, trying to reconcile it all in my head. By some act of God—seriously, thank you Jesus—I was able to pull it together. My hands had also behaved themselves as I reminded myself why I put the distance between us in the first place. And what do you know, my mouth and body cooperated and I was able to act like a normal person. As opposed to the fruitcake I was currently acting like in my head.

"It was before they were famous. When I lived in the Bronx."

I knew better than to think this was going to be a three-minute conversation. Jules was going to want to know when, how, why—with a storyboard and cue cards.

"I don't care if they were famous or not, you slept with Max Reynolds. Did you happen to catch a look at him when he walked in here? He's not hot, he's like DAMN! Even if he wasn't famous, he was worth mentioning. At least a freaking footnote or something. I thought we were friends."

"Jules, it's not like I am going to run down my entire dating history. It's been a few years, I didn't think I would see him again so didn't think to mention it." More like happy to leave that part of my life in the past. "And of course we are friends, I'm not someone different because my ex-boyfriend ended up being a rock star."

"Don't be all *I'm still Jenny from the Block.* That's some big news, like huge. As in, should have been thrown out there. Hell, if I dated him I would be freaking signposting it. There's a Facebook group dedicated to his penis. His *penis*, Beth! Oooooooh, is it true? Is he really that big?"

Jules was easily excited. Part of the reason we became friends was because, despite our rather conservative workplace, she liked to have a drink or two and cut loose. See a local band at a bar, go watch some avant-garde play or spend hours dissecting less famous French impressionists. She was quirky, breaking into song randomly or scaring the neighbors with her own—and often randomly timed—Broadway show numbers. And while I had come out of the cocoon and left my former life behind, being with Jules anchored me to my inner true self. Besides, she was awesome and a great friend.

"I'm not going to tell you how big he is." I scoffed. Point blank, we were *not* going to be talking about Max's cock. But if ever there was one that was worth talking about, it was most definitely his.

"Why not?" She pulled back, absolutely horrified I wasn't doling out prized information. "It's not like you are still dating him. You had no problem telling me how *not* big gym guy was."

I guess on that she did have me. A precedence had been set which unfortunately pointed to me not having a problem with discussing *that.* But with Max, I just didn't want to share. Which was stupid because from all reports he'd shared the knowledge of his cock with many women.

Oh, and I knew about the group. Possibly even wandered in there a few times. Purely from a curiosity stand point. Okay, so maybe a little bit more than curiosity, part of me was somewhat smug to have insider knowledge. Yes, yes, I know how unbelievably conceited that makes me sound—I never said I was a good person.

"This is different." I maintained my stance, no comment remaining my rote response.

Her eyes widened, my silence fueling the rumor. "Oh my God, he's huge."

HUGE.

I was in no way a dick expert, but I'd seen a few. And none of them had ever measured up—and I am talking literally—to what Max was packing. Besides, it wasn't just the size—which ain't gonna lie, was *more* than substantial—it was what he did with it. And Max Reynolds knew what he was doing in a bedroom. Or a bathroom, kitchen, backseat of a car . . . I'm getting distracted, but you get my point. He was the master of his domain, wherever that domain was.

"You saying nothing right now is all the confirmation I need." She smiled smugly; content she had gotten the truth, the matter being far from over.

"Can we change the subject already?" I ignored her, turning my attention to clear the breakfast dishes. That was a more productive way to spend my time, cleaning not talking about Max's—yeah, now I wasn't going to be able to stop thinking about it.

"Sure, I'll let that part slide for now, but you still have told me nothing." She joined me in the cleanup, my reprieve short lived. "How long did you date? Why did you break up?" She continued the inquisition. "Obviously, it wasn't horrible because you were looking at him like a side of bacon."

"No, I wasn't." Oh God please tell me I wasn't. "I wasn't."

I couldn't be sure. Not one hundred percent. I had touched him and what my hands were making contact with was very pleasing. Which was ridiculous because I *knew* what he looked like naked. Probably why I had the need to get handsy in the first place.

Oh hell, I had looked at him like a side of bacon.

"Who you trying to convince?" She laughed, not like a little chuckle either, I'm talking a full bellied eruption to illustrate the hilarity of my refusal. "I'm surprised you didn't need to use your shirt as a napkin."

Once again, valid.

Perception was one of Jules' strong suits so as much as I wanted to dance around it all, eventually she would get it out of me.

"Fine, I'll tell you everything but you can't tell anyone." I threw up my hands admitting defeat. "Especially not people we work with."

"Please, it's in the vault. I'm basically going to listen, nod and then hate you because you managed to tap *that*." She motioned toward the door Max had not long passed through. "But I can't promise there won't be questions. They may or may not feature his cock."

She was only willing to concede so far, and I guess as long as her silence was assured—in my heart I hadn't needed her word, knowing she'd never intentionally gossip—I could deal with the millions of questions that were going to be coming my way. Whether I answered any would still be my call.

So with a huge—it seemed to be the theme for the

morning—cup of coffee we took up residence on the couch. She listened with wide-eyed wonder and I recounted the whole tale. Meeting him in high school, and being incredibly smitten. Then of course our first *break-up* happened when I went away to college, somehow always winding up back together whenever I'd be home on break.

And so started the merry-go-round—on again-off again—like a favorite pair of jeans you couldn't bear to throw out. I think most of my uncertainty stemmed from the fact there was never ever a conclusion. At no point—at any of those numerous times—did we say goodbye and end it. Nope, we just drifted until the current brought us back together. He was the tide and I was the sand, mostly moving together but sometimes moving apart.

"I don't know if that is tragic or beautiful." Jules clasped her hands dramatically. She really had missed her calling as an actress. "Possibly even tragically beautiful." The batting of the eyelashes was unnecessary; I realized how corny it all sounded.

"This is exactly why I didn't tell you." I tossed a throw pillow her way. "It's not something a lot of people would understand and I'd rather not deal with the sarcasm."

I didn't care about the judgment. No doubt those who had been around or heard the story would cast their conclusions. I had either been a doormat, so desperate to have a boyfriend I welcomed him back every time, or I was a groupie who slept with the guy because he was in a band and it gave me cool points. Neither of these were true. I loved being with Max, because I loved being with Max. Period. And people could think what they wanted; it wouldn't change what we had.

What I didn't want to deal with was the trivialization. The jokes. The bullshit people needed to tell themselves so that we made sense in their minds. They could say and think what they wanted, but I didn't have to hear it. It was my story and it wasn't up for review, which is why for the most part I kept it locked up tight.

"Hey." Jules stopped laughing, her face turning serious. "I'm sorry, I was being a dick. Honestly, it sounds epic. A love story I could only hope to have."

"It's fine, it's in the past." I ignored Jules' it's-the-most-epic-love-story-of-all-time. Besides, it was in the past and that's where it should stay. We had both moved on.

"Let's just forget the whole thing; I need to go back to dealing with this hangover." Which was totally a lie, because I had almost completely forgotten about it. "And go on with our day." Yeah, because *that* was a possibility.

Not going to lie, pretending was going to feature highly. Just because I wasn't talking about it, didn't mean I wasn't thinking about it. And Jules could sniff out weakness. So I was taking my happy self—big freak show smile plastered across my face—to my room, putting on some fresh clothes and possibly taming my hair into something manageable. Something I should have done *before* answering the door.

Actually I'm not sure how he didn't turn around and run when I opened the door looking the way I did. Best prediction without the mirror confirmation was: bloodshot eyes—fuck you, Sauvignon Blanc, hair like it'd been through a wind tunnel—not in a sexy way, and an outfit that was a cross between thrift store chic and homeless person. Ha. How was he able to resist? Screw you, universe! If we were destined for a reunion couldn't I have at least been wearing a bra?

Which brought me to another bone of contention—let's face it, I had a few this morning.

Ivy Shaw.

I'd known that girl almost as long as I'd know Max so it was going to be sad to say goodbye. We'd had a good run, but unfortunately I was going to have to kill her. The reason for her demise was twofold. One, she sold Max an apartment and directed him to my door and two, she hadn't warned me about either. At the very least a cryptic text saying "Hey make sure you don't answer your door looking like an extra for The Walking Dead." That's not too much to ask, surely.

So after de-zombiefying myself—at least I'd look good in the mug shots—I waved goodbye to Jules and Ubered myself to Ivy's front door. It had been tough getting away from my roommate. Her cries of if-you-are-going-to-see-Max-take-a-photo-of-his-cock rung in my ears as I hit the buzzer of Ivy's cute Greenwich Brownstone. Jules would be down for body disposal later, she was good like that.

"Hello" Ivy's sweet voice leached from the speaker. Good, she was home; the neighborhood would be spared my rampage.

"It's Beth, open up." I didn't bother with a *hello* or *good morning*, no point pretending this was a social call.

"Are you mad?" She giggled back through the speaker clearly knowing the reason for my impromptu visit.

"I've calmed down." Not a lie, I'd let her have some last words now, earlier I hadn't been so charitable.

"Then come up." The lock on the exterior door popped open. Ivy living on the second floor was convenient; it meant I didn't have to climb too many stairs before exacting retribution.

"Hey," She finger waved as she stood in her front doorway, all butter-wouldn't-melt-in-her-mouth. "I assume you met the new tenant?"

"Please tell me you didn't sell him that apartment hoping

we'd get back together, Ivy." I didn't even wait for the comfort of her living room, starting my rant as I crossed her threshold.

"Beth, it's a great building, the same reason why I convinced you to move in." She shrugged as she motioned me to the couch. Her sly grin hinted that her reasons had more to do with her helpless romantic nature rather than finding everyone suitable real estate. "I only want the best for the people I care about. Now, if two people I care about happen to live at the same address—and it's a wonderful address—then I'd say it's more efficient than anything else."

"This isn't a time to be cute."

I assumed that if he asked, she would have only been too happy to give him my address. I wasn't in witness protection and if he'd really wanted to know, I was listed in the good old white pages. But having him move in, where we would forever—well unless one of us moved—be sharing space, was a little more hint that she was hoping for more.

"Oh come on, Beth." She took the seat opposite me. "You know you guys were great together. Even if you don't end up a couple, don't you miss him as a friend? When was the last time you guys even spoke?"

She had a point. Which pissed me off. Max and I had been great friends, the best kind. And even in our separations we'd always kept in contact. So . . . exactly why was I angry? Ugh, I really hated logic.

"It wouldn't have killed you to at least give me a tip off." I huffed back convinced I should still be angry; at what, I had no idea. "He turned up on my doorstep looking fucking fabulous while I was a hot mess."

"Oh hush, you look great." A dismissive wave shot in my direction.

"This wasn't what he was greeted with this morning." I

waved my hand dramatically around my face.

*This* would have been okay. The combo of jeans, striped cotton tee and black blazer, perfectly fine. While I wasn't the mirror-mirror-on-the-wall-who's-the-fairest-of-them-all  kind of girl, when put together I could look pretty good. Key words there were put together, which this morning I hadn't been. Not only was my appearance a disaster, but my mind had been a crime scene.

"It couldn't have been that bad, I'm sure he's seen much worse." She laughed, the sympathy noticeably lacking in her tone.

"So not helping, and so not the point." The point, something I hadn't been clear of either, but I wasn't mentioning it. My tantrum not even close to being done.

"Is it possible that regardless of how you looked that it was just nice for you both to have seen each other again?"

Ahhhh. The point.

Just not the one I had been trying to make.

Bravo. I was an idiot.

"You're making it very difficult for me to stay angry, Ivy. I came here for a vendetta and I don't like having to change my agenda."

"Aw, you love me." She gave her famous I'm-so-innocent smile.

The vendetta would have to wait for another day, she was right. I was glad to see him and I was already hoping for another chance.

# Max

I had never been impatient. I didn't believe the *good things come to those who wait* BS, if you wanted something you had to go and get it. But there was a time and place for it and going in all guns blazing didn't always give you a favorable outcome.

So rather than go back downstairs all *here's Johnny* at her front door like a stalker, I decided my juiced up energy could be better spent. Namely with my real estate broker. Oh, happy days.

Joey needed to get back to being super dad—able to change diapers faster than a speeding bullet—which meant my what-the-fuck session with one Shaw had come to an end. And because it had been so freaking awesome I decided to Kardashian that shit—keeping it all in family—and share the love.

As luck would have it, the holy-shit wouldn't be reserved only for the early part of the morning, a double dose coming my way.

I'd barely parked my car, the engine still idling when I saw her walking down the stairs, the second time seeing her no less impressive than the first. Seriously, my head must have been firmly lodged up my ass when I let her go, a hundred percent knockout material. While she might have been rocking uptown girl with her new look, underneath the conservative threads was straight up sex. Clearly I liked it because she couldn't dress more PG and yet my dick was already hard.

So rather than sit in my car contemplating her outfit verses my erection, I killed the ignition and stepped out of my ride. I didn't even have to move, leaning against my car knowing she would have to walk right by me. Sure, the stalker tag I had been trying to avoid was now in danger of becoming a reality. And for no good reason either; I hadn't even been camping out at her door like I'd wanted too.

"I thought we agreed this should be a team effort?" I couldn't help but smile as she stopped mid-stride, her eyes flashing with recognition when they landed on me. "I should have known you'd go rogue."

"My visit was purely reconnaissance, she's still whole." Her lips curled into a smile. Nice. I liked that a hell of a lot. "And your accusation of me going rogue is ironic seeing as you're here too." She moved closer so she was standing directly in front of me. "I must have missed the *pistols at dawn* memo."

"Touché."

It absolutely killed me not to touch her. My hands having been on her so many times before ached to go back, but I knew I didn't have her permission. The last thing I wanted was for her to spook. So I kept my hands right where they were, chilling by my sides while she glanced over at my car.

"This is new." Her hand ran over the hood, my dick absolutely appalled it hadn't been him getting stroked. "You got rid of the Thunderbird."

"I did, do you like?"

The Thunderbird had more than just a lot of miles on the clock; it had a lot of history as well. Our first time together had been in the backseat of that car. Lots of good times, but I didn't need the metal box as a reminder. Had it all tucked away up in my gray matter.

"Yeah, it's great. I think it suits you." She gave me a smile of approval that I hadn't realized I wanted up until then.

"Thanks."

"I should head back." Her eyes darted to the road, the cars moving about their business without any concern for us. And I wasn't ready for the conversation to end as well. At least now, I had an excuse to prolong it without looking like creeper.

"Well, if you've already done recon and we aren't mission-ready on Operation Ivy, there's really no reason for me to be here." I tapped the door of my car. "I could give you a ride back."

She hesitated a minute. "You sure it wouldn't be any trouble?"

"We live in the same building." *Thank you, Ivy.* "I am literally going back to your place."

"Yeah, that would be great."

Without giving her a chance to reconsider, I popped open the door and let her slide in. My body took up residence on the sidewalk until she had her ass on the seat and was fastening her seatbelt. Then with an urgency I hadn't had a minute ago, I moved to the driver's side and hopped in. The rumble of the V8 roared to life as I buckled in.

"You good?" I asked for no particular reason other than it gave me a chance to look at her.

"Yep, ready to go."

We peeled away from the curb as the car inched into traffic. It was the one time I prayed for gridlock; the drive back wouldn't be long enough. Not unless I could find a viable excuse.

"You want to go grab a coffee or something?" The *or something* what I was mainly interested in.

"Sure, we could do that." She answered with little hesitation. "We can discuss strategy."

Hell, I was happy to discuss the migration corridors of geese if it bought me more time. Hopefully somewhere in there I could see where she sat on going out for dinner because I was an asshole who wouldn't leave well enough alone.

The rest of the ride was easy, as it had always been with her. Tunes played in the background as her eyes stared out the window, the need to talk not necessary. It could have been awkward, but it wasn't, and I was glad that at least that part of what we'd had stayed the same. The unspoken ease the same as it had always been.

I parked the car on a side street not far from the coffee house I'd recently discovered. I still preferred my java old school—coffee pot to cup—with the whole over-priced-fancy-shit-in-takeaway-cup making me eye roll. But inviting her back to my place for a *coffee* sounded about as innocent as asking her to hold my dick while I took a piss. Even if my intentions were on the level, it would look shady. Which meant I had to outsource, the ma and pa operation of Beans a palatable compromise.

We exited the car and took the short walk. I couldn't help but hold back a few steps and admire the view, the sun catching her hair in just the right way so that the ends looked like they were on fire. She was so fucking beautiful I wasn't sure how she'd ever ended up with the likes of me. I had definitely been punching above my weight.

Pulling my head out of my ass long enough to open the

door, we strode inside of Beans and placed our order. Americano for me, and some toasted caramel macchiato for her. I even reserved the eye roll when she ordered it, the drink losing its douchebag status simply because she wanted it.

With drinks in hand we snagged a booth toward the back where it didn't bleed noise. My attention noticing the sway of her hips a little too much before we sat down. I'd never been so glad to get my ass in a seat, my cock straining against the front of my jeans.

"So I have to ask, and this just isn't me being a superficial asshole, but just because I'm curious." I didn't waste time, one of the questions that had been burning through my mind shot out of my mouth. "Why the image overhaul? Just the job or personal choice?"

"Partly because of the job." She shrugged, lifting the coffee to her lips. Mmmm. Yum. And I wasn't talking about the coffee. "Teaching jobs in good schools are so competitive and showing up at an interview with a jet-black exaggerated bob wouldn't have won me any favors." She smiled, her hands wrapped tightly around her cup.

"But the other part was I just needed a change, I wasn't a little girl running around the Bronx anymore, I figured I should look the part. It took a while to get used to, but I don't miss the stained tub every time I dyed my hair. It's really different huh?"

Different? Try out-fucking-standing. But then again, she could shave her head and wear a burlap sack and she'd still be prettier than any other girl on the planet.

"Yeah, but I like it." I went with a scaled down response. The I-want-to-bury-my-face-in-it-when-you-wake-up-beside-me not having a snowball's chance in hell of being repeated. "I guess we've both made some changes."

"Yes, we have." She grinned at my chest, the fact she was into it making me sit up a little straighter. "Whatever you're doing obviously agrees with you."

Not even going to pretend that her liking what she saw didn't give me more fucking pleasure than it should. The shit-eating grin not hiding even if I'd wanted, my plan on playing it cool waving goodbye as it took the first exit.

"So no regrets? The move?" I figured since I'd already jumped off that cliff why not fully commit.

"No, it was for the best and I love my life here. No regrets."

Well wasn't that just a mind fuck of a fucking paradox. Was I happy for her because she was *loving her life* or pissed because none of that equation involved me? A good man would have been happy for her, I hadn't decided if I was a good man today.

Which brought up another conundrum. Did her new fucking awesome life include a boyfriend? What little evidence I had— she lived with a girl, at least she hadn't shacked up with anyone and that Ivy wouldn't maliciously try and break up a happy couple—suggested no. Sadly, if she said she was with a dude, I can't say my intentions would change. Guess that answers that question of what kind of man I am, and I am absolutely fucking fine with it. Especially if it means I get her.

"So . . . you dating anyone?" I threw it out there with no segue. I mean seriously, what did I have to lose? Her thinking I was an asshole? I'd take the risk thank you very much.

"Nothing serious." She shrugged, her nose scrunching with dissatisfaction. "You?"

"Yeah, hard to date when everything you do ends up online. So that would be a big negative."

And halleluiah for that. She was single and I was single, so one plus one equaled totally asking her out.

"Well that's super depressing." She tried to hide the smile behind her cup. "If you aren't having any luck what hope do the rest of us mortals have?"

"I don't know what I'm doing wrong." I rubbed the back of my neck, biting back the grin. "Maybe we can try and figure it out over dinner?" And look at me just sliding that in like a smooth bastard. "You can critique my technique."

Not even going to try and pretend that wasn't the worst pick-up line of all time. That was dick-in-a-box level bad. Did I give a fuck? Not if the answer was yes.

"I'm almost positive there is nothing wrong with your technique." She gave up on her coffee and nailed me with a look that made my balls ache.

"We'd want to be sure though, you can't be too careful." I leaned in closer; her lack of *no* meaning there was still a chance for a *yes*.

"Okay, I'll go out with you. Just to prove to you there is nothing wrong."

Call me conceited, but I didn't care what got us over the line. Pity? I'd take it, I'd work that shit in my favor too. The end result was the same. Her and I—together.

"Awesome, you have a place in mind?" The urge to fist pump almost too freaking great as I forced my ass to stay in my seat.

"Well considering it's your experiment, I think you should pick the place."

This kept getting better and better. The ball was in my court and I wasn't packing up and taking it home that's for damn sure.

"That I can do." Without breaking a sweat. "What do you say, Friday night? I can pick you up around seven."

While it was five days longer than I wanted to wait, I

figured I'd play it cool.

"Maybe it's better if I meet you there. Fridays are usually crazy for me and I'd hate to keep you waiting. Besides, Jules will probably grill you with twenty questions if you stop by the apartment."

"Jules can ask me anything she wants."

"Yeah, you say that now, but you don't know her. Trust me." She'd barely finished the sentence when her cheeks pinked, her eyes having a hard time staying on mine. Oh, this was fucking brilliant. Something had been said and judging by that reaction, I was dying to find out.

"Beth, was there something she asked you about me?"

"No, of course not." She scoffed, dismissing me with a wave like I hadn't seen the red-light-glow on her face. "I mean, she asked how we met and stuff like that. Nothing personal. I mean, not overly personal. And I didn't say anything that was personal." She alternated between nodding and shaking her head, like she couldn't decide which would have been the more appropriate reaction.

"You said *personal* three times."

"Just reinforcing the facts."

Could she be more adorable? Her bumbling response a tip off the words had most definitely been spoken, what they were about remained the mystery.

"You can tell your friends whatever you want about me, Beth. I trust my friends, and we're still friends, right?"

That was probably the most honest thing to come out of my mouth. No playing, no ulterior motive—no game. She knew shit about me that could give the folks at TMZ a real hard-on and I still wasn't worried. Not because I thought I was bullet-proof, but because of all the people in the world to go there, I was sure Beth wasn't one of them. And if I was wrong then I would happily go down in a ball of flames.

"Of course we are." Any humor from her voice MIA. "I think we'll always be friends."

"Good." There was no humor in mine either.

**I was way more nervous than I should be.**

It's not like it was a date. Or at least that's what I told myself. I'm almost positive that two people of the opposite sex can meet for a meal and it not be a date. It was friends just being *friendly* and catching up. And everyone had to eat, it's not like I could starve. In fact, it was actually really smart, the multitasking of mutually fueling our bodies with nutrients while we talked. Most definitely not a date.

"Beth," his one word greeting enough to liquefy my sides. *Not a date*, I reminded myself as I shuffled into the seat opposite him.

Max had picked a cute local restaurant in the neighborhood, *Christina's.* It hadn't hit the social pages yet so therefore didn't require a three month advanced booking, but the food was out-of-this-world delicious. It's exactly the place I would have chosen, if I'd been deciding the venue. Which I hadn't, because I stupidly pretended to not care. Playing it cool as it were, except I was most definitely not cool.

"Sorry I'm late." I inched my chair closer, his eyes remaining on me the entire time. Smooth. "I got held up." Translation, I tried on fifteen outfits before I decided on what to wear. But it's not a date, of course not. I tried not to sound frazzled as I shot him a smile before directing my attention to my menu. Freaking delicious, and I wasn't talking about the culinary offerings of Christina's.

"It's fine, I haven't been waiting that long." He didn't even bother with the menu instead taking a sip from the beer he'd already ordered.

And being that he was as attentive as he'd always been he also ordered me a pre-meal beverage, a glass of white wine sitting directly in front of me. I offered my silent thank you for his thoughtfulness as I welcomed the chilled goodness into my mouth. I was definitely going to need a few more of these. A lot more and if I didn't think it would convey the wrong idea, I would have reached across and kissed him.

"So, how's things?" Really that was the best I was able to offer? At this rate I wasn't going to be able to make it past appetizers before I dissolved into a white-hot mess. I lifted the glass, draining almost half of it.

"Things are pretty fucking awesome. But you knew that." His lips twitched into an amused smile. All that smooth, sexy yum he so effortlessly had going on twisted my insides.

"Well, I guess that's one benefit of having your rise to fame documented in the press." My mouth babbled without proper consultation with my brain. "You don't have to waste time with filing in the blanks." Uh, why was I acting so lame?

"One of the benefits for sure. What about you?" His head nodded in my direction. "I haven't had the advantage of press coverage. How's *things*?" He asked with a finesse I clearly hadn't possessed.

"Great. Really, really great." I twisted the stem of my now

empty wine glass cursing the lack of alcohol in it. They should really make bigger glasses or at least pour these ones to the very top. Wasted space if you asked me. Crap, he was looking at me like I should be continuing, and I couldn't think of one single thing to say.

Thankfully I was saved—no exaggeration I was literally drowning in my own awkwardness—from having to elaborate as our server approached the table. The girl couldn't be more than twenty-one, her ponytail swishing as she moved with an eager ready-to-please attitude. And as my gateway to more wine, I immediately welcomed her interruption.

"Hi, I'm Natalie." She stared at Max her mouth opening and closing wordlessly obviously forgetting the script. The confidence she exuded two minutes ago evaporating as she took in the awesome that was Max Reynolds.

Honestly I felt bad for the girl, I'd been having a hard time getting my words out too and I didn't have to deal with the first time jitters the man in front of me seemed to invoke. "I-I'll be your waitress." She tried again, her hand nervously tugged at her apron. "Ca-Can I tell you about our specials?"

It wasn't new seeing women around him getting all hot and bothered. He'd always had that affect. His tall well-built frame, ridiculous good looks, paired off with an amazing smile—there's only so much a girl can take. That had been *before* he'd morphed into the super-hot version of what I was currently sitting across from. Add the fame factor and poor Natalie didn't stand a chance. I almost wanted to high five her just for getting through it.

"I'm fine, Beth? You want to know the specials?"

Max of course was oblivious; his *do-me* pheromone assaulting the female population as he sat there passively, completely unaffected.

"Umm. Sure." *Shit.* My mouth panicked, agreeing to hear the spiel of shit-I-wasn't-going-to-order. And other than buy me more time to get my shit together, it served no purpose other than to torture the poor girl. Call it a quirk, but if it wasn't on the regular menu—tried and tested—I don't want it.

Natalie seemed to share my momentary panic, her eyes widening in horror at having to continue. The flustered, unsteady words slowly making their way out of her mouth somehow coming together coherently. Just for that she deserved a decent tip.

By the time she'd finished I had no idea what she'd actually said. Sure I'd picked up a few key words—grain-feed *something* with a *something* jus—and nodded in all the right places. But none of it had been remotely helpful in ordering dinner, my open menu not providing any assistance either. I'd reread the thing at least ten times but had been unable to focus.

"Are you ready to order or would you like some more time?" She asked, the unspoken plea to put her out of her misery bubbling just below the surface.

"Ummm." Cue the deer in headlights panic that rose inside me. "More wine?" The only thing I was really sure I wanted— scratch that, *needed*—right now.

"The steak here is amazing." My eyes focused on his mouth as he championed the Porterhouse. Never had the word *steak* been so sexy. "Perhaps you could get that to go with the wine? Unless you've turned vegetarian."

At this point even if I had given up meat—which I hadn't—I would have agreed. Hell, I would have eaten fifty of them. It would have been worth a case of the meat sweats just to hear him say *amazing* one more time.

"Sure, sounds good." I nodded my head before refocusing on my still empty glass. "Can I also get another glass of white for now and then a red to go with the main?" Might as well be prepared, it would save me waving her over every fifteen minutes. Actually, could I just have a standing order for a refill whenever my glass was empty? Someone should really make that a thing.

"We'll have two steaks, medium rare and one of every side on the menu. We'll share." He handed back the menus as the waitress nodded hopefully committing our order to memory. The lack of pen and paper had me worried, not so much for the food per se, but for those drinks I desperately needed.

I watched as she ponytail-swooshed away from us, my eyes returning to Max whose attention hadn't moved from me the entire time. He wasn't even trying to hide the fact he was staring.

"Wow, every side, huh? You must be either hungry or carb loading." I giggled nervously before metaphorically shaking myself. *Seriously, get in the game, Beth. What the hell are you saying?*

"Well you can never be too sure what you're going to want until it's sitting in front of you. I've learned not to leave things like that to chance." Somehow I didn't think he was talking about the choice between baked potato and mac n cheese.

On cue, Natalie dutifully returned with my glass of white, placing it on the table before swooshing off again, Max's eyes remaining on me. Not in a way that was simply polite either.

While my stomach flipped somersaults at the attention—I couldn't be sure the flutter wasn't due to hunger—my brain was telling me to pull on the emergency brake. Been there, done that annnnnd had moved on. *This wasn't a date, remember.* I could be in a room and not have my heart hurt or want to rip out his and that had to count for something.

Besides, it didn't necessarily *mean* anything.

Max was a flirt. Always had been and always would be and his talent was to make you feel exactly like he was making me feel right now. Like everything else around me didn't exist. He'd done the same thing to Natalie unintentionally. So best all those expectations get pushed to the side right now. We were friends and that's where it ended.

"You know," I picked up my glass and took a sip. "This is really nice." A nice dinner, good company—it didn't have to be complicated.

"I think so too." His fingers curled around the neck of his beer as he brought it to his lips. "So tell me about your job."

I'm not sure if it was the second glass of wine or the easy conversation, but whatever nerves I had been feeling had eased by the time our dinner was served. We both laughed as Natalie struggled to fit the ridiculous amount of plates on our table. The calories about to be consumed enough to last me a whole week. Thank god I had found a new gym, one that didn't have micro penis as a member.

"I can't believe you got rid of your old car, you loved that thing." My hand unconsciously reached across the table and touched his. I blame the wine for the touchy-feel display. He didn't ask me to move it so I didn't.

"Nah, I only loved it because it was all I could afford. Besides, it was time for an upgrade."

Through the course of the meal we had done our mutual verbal spillage. Filling in the years that we hadn't seen each other, the distance seemed to melt away. We'd even found room for dessert, neither of us ready to call it a night. The food, the conversation—it was nice. *Really* nice.

Unfortunately the warm gooey feeling didn't last, the night destined to come to a crashing finale.

"Oh, fuck. Shit." I'd meant to only think it, but those words shot out of my mouth as I ducked my head. My peripheral vision caught sight of micro penis walking in. The quick second look confirmed that it was in fact him and not some weird coincidental doppelgänger talking to the host probably trying to get a table.

"What?" Max asked, turning around no doubt to see what had made me spew out obscenities for no apparent reason.

"No, don't turn around." I yanked on his arm trying to focus his attention away from the door. "If you look you'll attract attention."

The universe was surely conspiring against me. This had to be an elaborate prank. Or I was being punished for telling him I would call again when I had no intention of calling. Either way, the universe was an asshole.

"O-kay," Max refocused on me and kindly ignored the death grip I had on his arm. "You want to talk me through it if I can't turn around?"

"It's a guy." My mouth rapidly firing out an explanation. "I dated him once and it was a complete disaster. I said I would call, but I never did. I've been trying to avoid him."

I'm not sure if it was mention of my ex or my horrible *date* that made Max's jaw clench, his body straightening as he reached over and touched my hand.

"Did he hurt you?" His voice rumbled as his mood darkened, the casual laidback guy from five minutes ago replaced by *Captain Fierce.*

"No, no of course not. I just didn't think I'd see him again."

I mean what were the chances. I'd banished myself from the gym even though my recurring "discounted" monthly fee was going to be charged for the next six months. And there was no danger of me losing my damn mind and welcoming the clean-eating-holistic-taste-like-ass lifestyle he seemed to subscribe to. So our paths should have no reason to cross.

In fact, why the hell was he here? Christina's was literally swimming with bad food choices—ones loaded with butter and cheese—surely *those* would act, at the very least, as some kind of kryptonite? And if not why the hell didn't we eat here instead of that massacre of a meal where we did.

"I think he's seen us." I cursed softly under my breath, the full restaurant dictating he had to wait for a table to come available. "Pretend we're on a date."

"Ahhh, Beth, we *are* on date." He looked at me like I was insane.

"No, not like this." I whispered across the table, the insanity he'd suspected proving itself as I continued. "Like a proper one where you are really into me. Touch me and stuff. Like you can't keep your hands off me."

"So you want me to touch you, like I want you." An amused smile returned to his lips, his hand reaching across the table and tucking a lock of hair behind my ear. His thumb grazed my cheek as he stared into my eyes, his fingers curling underneath my chin. Oh, he was good. I even bought it.

"Wow, yeah. Keep doing that." I mumbled trying to discreetly glance in the direction I'd last seen micro penis. Torn between wanting him to be gone and wanting him to stay, his presence giving me a taste of Max even if it was just pretend.

"He's still watching." A quick survey found he was not only in the same spot, but now openly staring. "Here let me feed you some dessert."

"Beth, you can't, I—"

"I know it's corny, just please do it."

I was literally begging. Not sure why, I mean did I really care what the asshole thought? No, I didn't, but what I didn't want was some sort of confrontation in this nice establishment. Or anywhere because when it came to confrontation I sucked at it. Case in point, the boyfriend I hadn't really ever broken up with sitting across from me.

"Okay." A slow breath escaped his lips as he gave in, his eyes falling to the spoon I had dutifully loaded up with the strawberry shortcake I had barely touched.

He hesitated a beat before his mouth curled around the spoon, the strawberry coulis spilling onto his lips. The urge to lick it off was almost too great as I reminded myself where I was.

Damn he was good, his eyes closing as he savored the spoonful. I involuntarily moaned, not for anyone else's benefit—I doubted anyone could hear us—but because I just couldn't stop myself. His act completely fooled everyone; even I felt he was captivated by me.

"Beth." His fingers brushed my cheek again. "We should go."

Ordinarily I would have been onboard with this—my MO apparently getting out while the goings good—but leaving meant passing him. I mean, he was standing right near the door. Was I supposed to wave on my way out? Or pretend I'd developed blindness and couldn't see the almost seven-foot tall giant who was blocking the doorway? That confrontation I was so keen to avoid would be getting airtime.

"Not yet, we even haven't finished dessert." I gave him my best seductive smile and hoped I didn't look like a stroke victim.

"That must have been one hell of a bad date." Max smiled, either buying into my seduction routine or amused by the effort.

"Trust me, the worst." I loaded up my spoon again literally squirming at the thought of feeding him. I'll admit I was probably enjoying it too much but go hard or go home, right? "He's still looking."

"Well, then we should give him something to look at." Without warning Max was on his feet and beside my chair, his hand pulling me up to my feet. I had no time to even think about what was happening as his lips came down on mine.

His fingers trailed down my spine, coming to rest on my lower back as he pulled me in closer. His mouth devouring mine, possessively as I completely forgot what the hell we were doing.

It wasn't a sweet kiss—no—it was hot and deep, his lips owning mine as he pulled me closer. It was nothing like I remembered, about a thousand times more intense. It was bending the laws of public decency and I didn't care.

I took no notice if we were being watched—everything in the room fading into insignificance—as my body melded to his. And almost as suddenly as it started he pulled his mouth away. It was too soon, my lips still tingling from being pressed against his, my head slightly dizzy from the rush.

He didn't waste time or ask questions as he waved over our server while fishing out his wallet from his back pocket. The hand that was dangerously low on my back stayed in place as we watched Natalie scamper over like a dutiful puppy. Her face a little worried as to why we were standing, eating each other instead of the food we'd ordered.

"Hi, is everything okay?" She looked down to the half-eaten desserts and unfinished glass of wine, our dinner not able to come to a natural conclusion.

"We need to leave in a hurry." Max pulled out a couple of bills and handed them over. "This should cover it; dinner was great, thanks." And judging by Natalie's face, it included quite a sizeable tip.

She looked over the Presidents in her hand, reexamining them to make sure they were in fact Benjamins and not Jacksons. "Um . . . Do you want me to wrap anything for you?"

"Nope, thanks. You've been great." Max handed me my purse which had been sitting on the table beside us. "Beth, we need to leave now."

"Sure." I smiled a little too enthusiastically, and it had nothing to do with the audience as he guided my body away from the table.

In a maneuver that would have made Mikhail Baryshnikov jealous, he twirled me around and pulled me close into his side, waltzing toward the front door with his arms around me.

If anyone was still there and/or watching, I no longer cared. I wasn't even sure if he or I were acting anymore.

That kiss—the one I could still feel on my lips—had been amazing. It lit a fire inside of me that I could never have faked. And as bad an idea as I knew it was, I wanted another. My previous arguments on why we should remain just friends, no longer seeming valid.

We walked out, my eyes on Max the entire time. I legitimately didn't see nor care about anyone else in the room, my feet doing their best at keeping me upright and walking at the same time.

"My car isn't far." He didn't even ask if I was going home with him, he just rightfully assumed I was. I ignored the fact that we lived in the same apartment building, so *technically* he could just be offering me a ride. *Shut up logic, I'm way beyond you now.*

"Okay," I agreed, my feet moving faster than I thought they probably needed to.

Obviously I hadn't been the only one who needed another kiss, the desperation to get us to his car and alone evident in the pace we were keeping, at this point almost running down the street. Which considering I was wearing heels, took quite the effort.

"Um, Max, we should slow down." A sprained ankle would seriously put a damper on things. And while I was anxious to be alone—and have those lips on me again—we weren't racing against a clock. It was only nine-thirty tops, I was fairly sure neither of us were turning into pumpkins at midnight.

"Actually we can't. We need to get to a drug store, now."

We stopped in front of his classic black muscle car, which I'd assumed was either going to be the venue for more action or take us to somewhere that would be. The key going into the door confirmed it as he yanked open the door. "Please get in Beth, we need to go."

I hadn't thought past the kiss.

Normally, you could share a kiss after a date—even though it hadn't originally been a date—and there would be no expectations of more. There was a system, but when you had *already* slept with the person, there was a certain gray area as to what base we should be sliding into. Not saying I didn't want a homerun, I mean, maybe? Oh hell, I had no idea what I wanted, I was so confused.

"Max, we should slow down—I mean, we need to talk—"

"Beth, whatever you are thinking, it's not." He cut me off not allowing me to continue. "The dessert you were so insistent you shovel into my mouth had strawberries in it."

Well, yeah of course it did. It was a strawberry shortcake, it said right there in the title.

OH SHIT!

"You're allergic to strawberries," I almost screamed, my mind and body hitting the panic as his desperation made sense. "Oh. My. God." I struggled to not hyperventilate, was he going to die? "Why did you eat it?"

"I tried to say no; you made it very difficult."

"Am I going to kill you? Do you have epinephrine? I can inject you."

"Relax, I don't need a shot. The allergy isn't that bad, I'm not anaphylactic, but I'm already breaking out in hives, so we need to get to the drug store quick. Now, will you please get in the car?" He reached up and scratched his neck as his other hand helped open the door I had yet to climb through.

"Yes, Yes. Of course." I slipped into the passenger seat, waiting for him to get in on his side. My eyes glued to his chest in case there were breathing problems.

He slid into his seat and closed the car door behind him. The ignition roared to life before he'd even fastened his seatbelt.

"It's really going to be fine, don't look so scared."

I didn't just look scared, I was scared. Oh God, please don't let anything bad happen. I swear I'll never date again, just don't let him die.

**O**f all the stupid things I had done, I had never tried to kill someone before. Not that I had—Max was still breathing, thank you baby Jesus—but I don't think the jury would have bought my I'm-sorry-I-forgot when I shoveled potentially life threatening allergens into his mouth.

It didn't matter that Max had played it off as no big deal— the danger of death almost nonexistent—I was guilty and deserved to be punished.

I was a teacher, the severity of food allergies all but beaten into us. I knew the implications of it all and what damage they could do. While I'd been fortunate enough not have had to deal with one first hand, I'd heard the horror stories from colleagues and school parents. This was very much a big deal.

The drive to the drug store hadn't been far—another reason I was whispering heavenly thank yous—and with Max leaving the engine running while I sprinted inside and bought about ten packets of Benadryl and a bottle of water. Sure that didn't look shady at all. I was almost positive the pharmacist was suspicious, but last time I checked you couldn't make

Meth from antihistamines so he sold me the drugs with some serious side eye and a cloud of judgment. Like I didn't already have enough of that going on.

Then it was back in the car to get Max home and medicated.

I screamed. The car door behind me muffling my shirk of fear when I turned to see Max's face pinked and covered in red welts, his lips puffy from swelling. It wasn't as hideous as the scream had probably implied, I just hated the perfection of his face marred with the welts. Knowing I had caused it was even worse. His *it's okays* tried to reassure me even though it was *him* who needed help.

I couldn't even offer to drive him home. Not that I actually knew how to drive a stick shift, but I would have worked it out. Hopefully before leaving his transmission on the side of the road. But we didn't even get that far, my blood alcohol well above the legal limit courtesy of one or two too many refills on my wine.

Thank God—clearly I had found a renewed faith in religion—we were parked in the undercover garage soon after. The small mercy that Christina's and the drug store had been within blocks of our apartments.

The car stalled to a stop, with the ordeal hopefully coming to an end as well as I ran around to the driver's side and helped Max out of his seat.

"I'm fine." He'd tried to reassure me for the five millionth time while I clung to him with one hand and the paper bag with enough Benadryl to take down an elephant in the other. Max was a lot of things, *fine* was not one of them right now.

"No, I got you into this mess, I need to fix it." Or at least implement some damage control. I still wasn't convinced we shouldn't be heading to an emergency room, my fingers ready to hit 9-1-1 at any second. I was already hyperventilating at his refusal to take the meds before we got home, if I'd had my way I'd have shoved them down his throat earlier.

"It's not that bad, I'm not going to die. I promise." Max laughed.

He laughed.

Like I hadn't just tried to poison him under the guise of sweet creamy goodness. What's worse is it was for my own selfish reasons. There was sure to be a special place in hell for people like me.

Thankfully I didn't have to deal with any more judgment or evil stares, bypassing the lobby and heading directly to his penthouse. Once inside the elevator I let go of my grip on him as I tore into the paper bag, the bottle of water and boxes of drugs spilling onto the floor as we continued to climb.

"Shit!" I sunk to my knees snatching the packs and the bottle. His ever-present grin widening as I got back on my feet.

If this wasn't such a life and death—his assurances it wasn't hadn't convinced me—situation I'd assume that smile was less innocent, me on my knees in front of him. Although it was probably only my own sick perverted mind that would think something sexual at a time like this. I swear I'm not a bad person.

My fingers fumbled with the stupid child-resistant foil backing while I tried to pry the pills from the box's clutches. The elevator opening before I was able to complete my operation.

"You know the allergy hasn't made me incapacitated." He held out his hand's offering to lighten my load. No need, I had this. Or at least I hoped I had this. The paper bag that had given me so much trouble shoved under my arm so I could better deal with this ridiculous packaging.

"No, no, it's cool." I stepped out of the elevator, nodding my head repeatedly like an idiot, Max following close behind.

Success! Those pesky pills finally coming loose, popping into my hand as we walked to his door. And not a moment too soon, his hesitation to take them before we reached home because he had to drive and they made him drowsy.

"Take these." I shoved pills into his mouth without warning, his eyeballs opening wide at my hand against his mouth.

"Water." He choked, clutching at his throat.

Shit. I knew I'd forgotten something, the bottle of water I'd retrieved from the elevator floor returned to the bag where it stayed, not helping. My fingers quickly twisted the cap and pushed the lip of the bottle against his mouth, the water flowing quickly as he swallowed.

At this point I can safely say that I can rule out any career change into the medical profession. I sucked as a nurse. I mean realllllly sucked, the water I was trying to pour into his mouth spilling across his chin and down his chest. My effort to help, making him splutter.

"You really are trying to kill me." He coughed, sliding the bottle out of my hand and into his own. His shirt wet, as he used his other hand to wipe his chin. "You need to relax." His smiled returned, as he walked us to his apartment.

Relaxing was not something I could see happening right now. I don't know how he was blasé about it or how he couldn't hate me.

Anyone else would have probably looked like a scary mutant.

But not Max.

His lips had puffed, slightly swollen, but not so much that they were distorted, in fact most of the people I know would have paid big bucks for the same effect. Even the welts weren't that horrible. If it had been me, I'd have looked like I had some freaky skin necrosis. At the very least—okay, I was drawing at straws—I hadn't ruined his beautiful face.

He unlocked his front door, the process taking less than a second before we had walked into the dark open space. His hand reached for the light switch so the room flooded with brightness.

"I'm so sorry."

I wasn't sure how many times I'd said it, but it wouldn't be enough. Honestly, I felt terrible. What's worse is that I had always known about his intolerance to strawberries and in the panic I'd forgotten.

"How many times do I have to tell you, I'm going to be okay. It's really not that big a deal." Max moved closer, his hands moving down my arms, the paper bag still tight in my grip.

"Can't you just be angry at me?" I shook my head as he pulled the paper bag from my fingers and tossed it onto the coffee table, its existence meaning his new pad was now fully furnished. "I swear you being so cool with the situation is making me feel worse."

Not once had he blamed me, and if there was anyone at fault, it was me. Instead he wrapped me in his arms and pulled me close to his chest. I wasn't sure if it was the hug or the steady beating of his heart that gave me comfort.

"Do you remember that time you borrowed my car and hit a trashcan and scraped paint off the fender?" He laughed, his hand gently pulling back my hair.

"Oh God, how could I forget? I threw up three times before I worked up the courage to tell you."

It had been terrible. Not because I was worried about him being upset, but because I hated that I'd wrecked his beloved car.

"Did I yell? Or lose my shit?" He tilted his head to the side waiting for me to confirm what he already knew the answer to.

"Well . . . no." He hadn't even been upset. Just kissed me, asked if I was okay and told me accidents happened. He didn't even let me pay for the repair, saying it added character to the car and left it as it was. At the time I thought it had been incredibly sweet—the perfect boyfriend—now I know I should have insisted.

"What about the time you washed my white vintage Soundgarden T-shirt with a pair of red socks? Did I fly off the handle then?" Max smiled, his hands moving to my chin.

I had come home from college over summer. I had spent more time with him and Joey than my own family. He hadn't let me pay for groceries even though I was another mouth to feed and he was earning minimum wage so I did his laundry to try and thank him. I probably should have checked what was already in the machine before adding whites, his T-shirt coming out a lovely shade of pink when it was done with the spin cycle.

"Are you trying to remind me of everything I've done where I sucked? Clearly I was a terrible girlfriend."

If there had been a time Max had been upset at me then I hadn't been around to witness it. Not to say that he didn't have a temper, I'd seen him get his hulk out when it mattered but that fury had never been directed at anyone he cared about. Not even his moronic lazy pot-smoking brother.

"You were not a terrible girlfriend." His hands gently moved against the line of my jaw. "I'm trying to illustrate—probably badly because the drugs are starting to kick in—that I have a hard time being mad at you."

"Well that's dumb; those excuses alone would be very valid. No one would blame you."

It was hard to look at him. Not because I felt bad—fine, not the only reason—but because looking into those brown eyes of his time traveled us back to the Bronx. Being in the house he shared with Joey, both of us broke and yet to realize our dreams. How happy he'd made me, how safe I'd felt. It was like being home.

"I'm not interested in what anyone else thinks." He moved closer, his hands holding my face so I had nowhere to go as he pressed his lips to mine, softly, a tease. My mouth parted for him without waiting for my brain to give it permission, wanting more of what he was giving me.

"No one is watching this time," he whispered against my lips. "And the only person able to stop me, is you."

He didn't wait for my reply, his mouth owning mine as his arms brought me closer. His tongue desperate like it couldn't get enough. And it had my sympathies because I couldn't get enough either. I wasn't sure what the kiss meant or what was going through his mind, but at that moment, I didn't care.

My hands grabbed his ass and pulled him close, the evidence of his arousal hitting my stomach—I guess I knew one thing that was going through his mind—as my body flicked into autopilot.

A moan escaped my lips as his knee parted my thighs. His hands moved across my body and landed at the base of my dress, the hem finding its way to my hip as his leg pushed against my core. The heat in between my legs felt like I would combust if he didn't touch me more, his body reading my cues as his hands palmed my ass and he lifted me off the ground. The ridge of his rock hard cock stroked me through his jeans while my fingernails bit into his back.

If I thought I'd spent some time in the gym, it had nothing on what he had been doing. My constant tugging saw the shirt he'd been wearing very quickly removed. *Well done, hands*, I silently thanked them for their efficiency.

And if I'd been impressed before the removal of the shirt, then I had no hope dealing with reality. His firm body of chiseled perfection enough to make Chris Hemsworth jealous, my fingertips glided along the contours of his back while he yanked at my zipper.

Stopping would have been a good idea, or at the very least slowing it down. But I didn't want to stop, my body craving him more with every kiss and touch. He lowered me only for a second, just enough for my dress to pool at my feet, his battle with my zipper conquered as my skin goose pimpled under his hands.

We were both adults, I rationalized. It wasn't our first time and I had spent more time in a relationship with Max than out if it. He probably knew my body better than I did; this was totally not like a one night stand. Not that I assumed it would go on longer than tonight. So what if it was only for pleasure, no one was getting hurt. All valid. No reason at all to stop.

Except.

"Hey, are you okay?"

His mouth had stopped kissing, his lips opening and closing with no real rhythm. His motor skills were also off, his hands anchored at the base of my spine using my body more for stability, than for the erotic rendezvous I'd assumed we were moving toward.

"How many of those pills did you shove into my mouth?" His eyes had a hard time staying open as he swayed unsteadily on his feet.

"Ummm. A couple?"

It happened so fast I couldn't be sure. That stupid packageing had been the work of the Devil and I was trying to get them out quickly, I can't be positive of how many. Two, maybe three? Definitely not more than three. God, did I give him too much? No, no one was that stupid. There was no need to panic.

"Let me check."

I unwound myself from his body—risky considering he was having trouble with gravity—and thankfully his legs accepted his weight without my help. Small victories, but still too early to cheer— moving on. Next I grabbed the paper bag, and sifted for the box I had opened. Success. Another victory with the first one that tumbled out being our golden ticket. All I had to do was look at the vacant places where pills should be.

One.

Two.

Three.

Four.

Oh fuck!

"I need to lie down." Max groaned as his head fell forward on his chest, his fight with gravity entering the second round. Ding Ding.

If I thought this ordeal couldn't get worse, I was seriously mistaken. It could always get worse, which it was.

The fact I was standing in his living room in my underwear or that I had been dry humping his leg flew completely out the window as my attention returned once again to watching Max's vitals. The rise and fall of his chest had never been such a welcome freaking relief. I couldn't even appreciate its fine form any more, the only concern that the heart within it kept beating.

"I think you should try and stay conscious." My brain thankfully jumped online as I ran through my mental crisis checklist. "I need to call Poison Control."

"Beth, me staying awake is probably not going to happen right now." His eyes opened, before shutting again, his body fighting the good fight and keeping him upright.

"Oh fuck, please just hold on a little longer."

I grabbed my cell from my purse as I cursed every swear word I knew and even made up some, the number thankfully—probably because of idiots like me—printed on the back of the box.

"Bedroom, that way." Max started to limp toward the closed door down the hall, his hands on the wall to support his weight.

My fingers couldn't dial fast enough as I ran to Max, my body fitting underneath his shoulder as I helped him to his room, his feet getting more unsteady with each step.

Great, if he passed out, I'd have to add a head injury to my current list of misdemeanors. Once again I was mentally trying to make deals with whichever spiritual being was in control of this debacle.

Whatever I did, I needed to be fast, the call connecting just as we made it into his bedroom, a few feet away from his bed. He didn't wait for me, the last few steps taken under his own steam before he collapsed onto the mattress, thankfully not face first.

"Hello Poison Control . . ." I didn't hear the rest of the rattled off greeting, probably something I should have been paying attention to. Not that common sense had prevailed yet, I mean, really? Why start now?

"My friend took four Benadryl by accident; is he going to die?" I yelled into the receiver, my hand on Max's chest as it continued its up and down.

Of course that was a slight skewing of the truth, that I had forced fed them to him after I'd already tried to poison him glossed over in the need to get help. Oh, and these calls were monitored, so I would rather them call the police *after* I was sure he was going to see tomorrow.

"Ma'am, my name is Rhonda." Her voice was calm and level the polar opposite to my current freak out. "Do you need 9-1-1 assistance?"

"I have no idea, he's still breathing." You didn't need medical school to know that was a huge positive. And I needed as much positive as I could get.

"Well that's a good start. Is your friend a child, a pregnant woman or elderly?"

"No, he's not old or pregnant. He's thirty-one." I probably could have just said he was male and his age, but like always I was over complicating.

"So male, thirty-one. Is he responsive? Unconscious? Have any existing medical conditions?"

"Um, no he's healthy." I think, at this point it was a guess. "I don't know if he's conscious." How quickly can someone slip into a coma? Who gives someone four Benadryl?

"Ma'am I need you to calm down and check for me okay?" Easy for her to say, she hadn't drugged the bass player for Black Addiction. Calming down was a tall order. "Can I have your name so I know who I'm speaking with."

"It's Beth." I guess that's so they know who to address the warrant to.

"Max?" I sat down on the bed beside him and gently shook his shoulder. His lips parted as a breath pushed past. "Max I need you to stay awake for me."

"Beth, I'm awake. Tired. Need to sleep," he said without opening his eyes.

"He's awake but super drowsy." This time my words directed at Rhonda. "He responded though and his breathing looks normal."

"Okay Beth, that's great." I heard the clicks of her computer keyboard, hopefully the tapping producing a good verdict. "I would say that he is experiencing a side effect from the drugs. The typical dose is two tablets but if he is an adult male and healthy he should have no lasting effects. Are you able to observe him for the next six to eight hours?"

"Yes, I can stay here." The only way I was leaving was if someone dragged me out, even then I'd put up a fight.

"Wonderful, Beth. Just watch his breathing and try and get a response every hour. Other than that, he can follow up with his regular doctor."

"Are you sure he isn't going to die?" *Please tell me he won't die.*

"I can't give you guarantees but I'm almost positive no one has ever overdosed from four Benadryl," Rhonda laughed. "He'll be fine. Probably drowsy for a while though."

"Oh thank you, thank you so much."

"No problem, Beth. Now stay on the line while we get some information for our records."

It was such a relief I wasn't sure if I had to call 9-1-1 for myself, my heart beating way faster than it should be. And it was with absolute pleasure that I gave the heavenly being on the other end of the phone—or Rhonda if you want to get technical—Max's and my details. I guess so they knew who to charge if things didn't pan out so positively. Not that I was worried about that anymore. Jail time would be worth it if it meant Max was going to be okay.

"Beth." Hearing him say my name made me so relieved I almost cried. "I've never broken a promise to you; I promise I'm going to be fine."

He was right—in all the years we had known each other, he had never broken a promise. And if ever there were a time for him to be consistent, it would be now.

# Max

My head felt like a hundred pound weight was chilling on my forehead. That, and I was struggling to open my eyes. My lids able to crack open for a second before slamming shut. It was a game I was playing, my body wanting to stay asleep while my brain was telling me to wake up. Neither of them wining at this point as I floated in and out of some weird lucid state unsure of whether or not I was dreaming.

To test out the theory, I figured I'd try and move. The message from my cortex obviously got through as my arm lifted off the mattress and stretched out. I worked out that it wasn't my foggy state that had stopped me from moving, but instead the warm body lying on my chest. Beth.

The night's events hadn't escaped my memory. I recalled all of it, its hilarity rivaling the best comedy stand up I'd ever seen. What started as Beth's desperation to avoid some dude at dinner—I still needed more intel on the asshole— was quickly followed by a few bad decisions. It was like a series of unfortunate events, shit just started to unravel. And yet given a choice, I wouldn't have changed a damn thing.

If I had known that all it was going to take was some

strawberries and four Benadryl to get Beth in bed with me then I would have it done the day I'd knocked on her door. Sure I'd said all the bullshit about me being happy to just be friends with her, but I had been kidding myself. Given the opportunity for more, I would definitely take it.

Sadly despite the good fortune of last night—I refused to see it any way but positive—I hadn't been able to enjoy being in bed with one of the hottest women who walked the planet.

Things had started out promising, the kiss and my hands on her giving me a hard-on from hell, but before I could get to any of the good parts, the freaking drugs knocked me so hard on my ass I could barely think. Of course, she'd given me enough antihistamine to take down a fucking horse, so it was no wonder I went lights out, goodnight.

While I felt sluggish, I wasn't blind. Before I'd lost my ability to stay upright, I'd managed to get the dress off Beth and onto my living room floor. It was a much better place for it. Which meant my parting view had been of her knock-out body—seriously deserved a standing ovation—in her bra and panties. And thank fuck when she crawled into my bed she didn't only keep her threads where I'd left them, but also helped me lose the rest of mine. My T-shirt, the only thing I remember taking off.

Another win was my grid coming back online; the shit causing the Z's easing out of my system. And if any part of me was still sleeping, it sure as hell wasn't my cock. The bastard was still antsy about the hard-on that had been wasted last night. And given half a chance, I wasn't passing it up. No, sir. Not this guy.

"You're awake; how are you feeling?" She lifted her head off my chest, her eyes focusing on mine.

I wasn't sure if it had been my arm moving that woke her or

she'd been sitting vigil the whole time. Her beautiful smile, my reward for finally shaking the fatigue.

"I'd tell you I'm fine, but you didn't buy it the thirty times I told you last night." My hand ran down the length of her arm. "You stayed?"

I'd assumed she would have tucked me in and said goodbye. I couldn't imagine I would have been good company. Unless hanging out with a corpse is your idea of a good time. She hadn't only gotten me into bed and wiggled herself beside me, but also spent the night by my side. Couldn't have hidden my grin if I'd tried.

"Well of course I stayed." Her hands moved across my chest, the shiver traveling all the way to my dick. "I didn't want you to die alone. It was the least I could do." She shrugged, giving me a smile.

"Oh, I think you probably did enough." I laughed, pulling her into a hug. Mmm. I liked that. I liked it a lot.

"I swear to you, I am never putting anything into your mouth again." She hid her head in the crook of my neck; I felt her smile against my skin.

"Well that's a shitty promise to make." In fact I had a list of things I wanted her to put into my mouth, her embargo was not cool with me.

"I think it's for the best." She turned to the side treating me to the view of her beautiful brown eyes. "If last night is anything to go by, I can't be trusted."

"Last night was fucking fantastic." I wasn't even kidding, other than the case of narcolepsy, it had been stellar. Even the asshole we'd seen at the restaurant couldn't rain on my parade, his appearance working in my favor. Thank you, douchebag.

"Hey can you wait a minute." She lifted herself from my

chest, my arms stopping her from leaving. "I need to check something."

"What do you need to check?" I had no intention of letting her go, whatever it was, could wait.

"That one of the side effects isn't hallucinations or delusions." She rolled her eyes not buying my version of events.

"There's nothing wrong with my mind, sweetheart." My lips that up until now had been playing nice punctuated the point by kissing her forehead. "Or my body." My eyes shot down to the rod between my legs, the bastard begging for attention.

"Yeah, that's been there most of the night." She bit her lip, my hard-on not escaping her attention.

"I'm not surprised." Not like he had anywhere to hide, and I sure as shit wasn't embarrassed. "You were here and he knows what he likes, can't blame him for trying." I grinned like a smug asshole. Couldn't help myself, she was just too fucking adorable.

"Can you please be serious?" She elbowed me in the ribs, her little jab packing more of a punch than I'd anticipated.

"Fine, Beth." I rolled onto my side, our faces inches from each other. "I seriously want to kiss you right now. And you're going to let me because it's what you want too."

Maybe I was arrogant or didn't want to give her the chance to change her mind, but I didn't wait for a response. I wanted to very much pick up where we'd left off last night. My lips on hers. Which is exactly where I put them, my mouth hungry for hers as my tongue teased her lips apart. I should have been sweet, but I wasn't, tilting her chin so I could get even deeper. The only time I stopped was to give her a chance to breathe, my mouth pulling away and landing on her throat.

"We shouldn't." Each breath deep and desperate as her hand moved against my bicep. "We got caught up in the moment last night." Breath. "I'd had too much wine and . . . we shouldn't." Breath.

"Let me be clear about something, if all you want this to be is a kiss that's fine, I'll stop right there." Ain't no way we were doing anything if she didn't want it too. And even though her body was saying yes, if her mouth said no that is exactly how far it would go. "But the only good reason why we shouldn't is because you don't want to, everything else is bullshit."

Her fingers trailed along the grooves of my chest, each sweep driving me further into insanity.

"Beth?" This wasn't the time for mixed signals and I needed the words.

"I said we shouldn't, I didn't say I don't want to."

"Well good, because unlike last night I don't have a truck load of drugs making me stop."

"So don't stop."

I wasn't sure if it was the residual Benadryl hangover, or the fact I'd been hard for who knows how long. But hearing her say those words was enough to launch my back off that mattress and on top of her before it seemed humanly possible. I wanted her under me with her lips on mine, and I wasn't waiting a second longer.

She parted her mouth the minute mine hit hers, the access granted juicing me up even further as my tongue decided to take the guided tour. And so my hand wouldn't feel left out, it also joined in on the action, its own expedition happening as it moved up her leg and across her stomach.

"Max, I want to touch you." She moaned into my ear, her hands doing their best to move, given I had almost pinned her underneath.

"I told you I have a hard time saying no to you."

I'd barely tilted to the side when her hands went straight

for my cock, wrestling it free from the boxers it had been trying to jailbreak from since dinner. If my hands hadn't been so busy undoing the clasp of her bra I probably would have helped, but there was very little that could have pulled me away. And with a flick, the piece of lace did a *David Copperfield* and disappeared.

Boom. Better than Vegas.

"Fuck." The curse fell out of my mouth as her fingers moved along the length of my cock, her tight grip half way between pleasure and pain.

New plan.

I lifted my ass off the mattress and yanked down my boxers, cursing the SOBs for not magically disappearing by themselves. And with those taken care of, it was time to get Beth to the same level, i.e. she was losing her panties ASAP.

She arched her back pressing her tits against me as my hands got busy, my fingers hitting her wet core before I could get the lace off.

"Oh, Beth."

Her panties didn't stand a chance, what was left of them after I'd torn them from her body were tossed aside as I forced myself to slow the fuck down.

The hand job she was giving me wasn't helping me ease on the brakes, with the up and down along the length of my dick feeling so good I might completely give up jerking off. Clearly I had no idea what I had been doing when hands on cock could feel like that.

"Max, oh God, yes." She bowed off the bed as I plunged a finger into her. Her slickness coated me instantly as my thumb circled her pussy.

"I missed this," I added another finger as she loosened her grip on my cock, her ability to multitask severely hindered by my hand action. "You wet for me turns me on so damn much."

"I don't think your cock could get any harder." Her fingers moved to the base of my shaft and cupped my balls. "And I missed this too." The gentle pull on my nuts making me want to come before I'd even had the chance to enter her.

Yeah, that wasn't happening.

I had barely started fingering her and I was already moving to the second act, my body shifted off the mattress and repositioning between her thighs. Her look of surprise fucking priceless as my tongue got up close and personal with her sensitive flesh.

"Oh God," she screamed as my mouth moved over her core and sucked hard on her clit, her hands threading through my hair as I continued to suck.

"So good." Her body shook as my tongue dove deep, leaving no part of her unclaimed. "Please don't stop."

If I could have torn my mouth away—wasn't happening—I'd have reassured her that there was no danger of that. I would lick and suck her beautiful pussy until I developed lockjaw if it made her happy. No problem there. But it didn't take nearly as long as I would have liked. Her body convulsed as I added a finger, her pussy gripping me tight as I continued to play.

"Yes, yes." Her head thrashed against the pillow, my eyes alternating between watching her come and my perfect view between her legs. The struggle was real and thankfully I didn't have to choose.

"Max," she moaned, the orgasm I'd given her not enough for me stop. "I want you in me." Her hand yanked hard against my hair, my mouth losing suction.

"Well maybe I wasn't done yet." My tongue lapped against her thigh teasing her, even though my dick was cursing the torture.

"Okay then." Her back jacked off the mattress with her full body weight behind her, the momentum pitching us both off balance.

"What the fuck?" Her body landed heavily against me as her palms slapped against my pecs, trying to right herself. The warm sting against my skin sent a shiver right down to my cock.

"I'm stronger than I used to be." She laughed, her legs positioning either side of my hips as she straddled me. "And I told you what I wanted."

"You want this?" I swiveled my hips, the ridge of my hard-on sliding against her wet core, the sensation so fucking amazing I wanted to close my eyes and just absorb it for a moment.

"Yes, that's what I want." She joined me with the hip action as I reached up and palmed both her tits. Had to admit this position had some major advantages. The access to her body was one, the view another.

"Yeah, I like that too." My eyes shot down to watch as the head of my dick slid in and out of view as she rocked against me.

The wet friction between us wasn't just getting me close; I could feel the desperation in her as well. I had started this game of tease and I was fucking ready to end it, my dick needing to be inside her as of five minutes ago.

Her body lifted, my hands trailed down from her hips touching every inch of skin until they reached between her legs. The soft skin drenched as it grinded against my hand. And as much as I would have liked to get her off again, this time with my fingers, the decision had already been made that the next time she came was with me inside her.

I didn't think, my mind completely off the chain as I palmed the base of my dick and slid it inside. The shock of the invasion took her by surprise, her body slamming down onto me as she took my length in one thrust, neither of us able to move.

"You okay?" I asked, her pussy gripping me tighter than a fist.

"Yeah, I just need a minute." She winced, trying to readjust.

It was fucking tight, and I hadn't been gentle nor had I given her a heads up—the fucking irony—either.

"Do you want me to pull out?" My dick throbbed hoping like hell she didn't say yes.

"No." She slowly moved her hips, their glide up and down my cock getting easier with each pass. "Don't you dare pull out."

"Good because I need to fuck you hard, Beth."

The gloves were off and I grabbed her waist and plunged into her as she rode me hard. Both of us frenzied as we moved against each other, her hands gripping my shoulders as she tried to get more traction.

There was no more talking, unless you counted the "oh God," "yes," "more," or our names as dialogue. And there didn't need to be, everything that needed to be said transmitted loud and clear by the fucking moans we both were making.

Had it ever been this good? The sex with us had always been five star, but I couldn't be sure it had ever felt like this. The fit of me inside her so fucking perfect I was almost positive we'd been made for each other.

"Beth." I wrapped my arms around her pulling her down onto my chest. "I need to come, sweetheart."

Thinking was a tough ask—her tits pressed up against me while my dick was inside her ready to explode—it was a wonder I could talk at all. But as the need in me to come rose into levels of *Danger! Will Robinson* it occurred to me that one of the reasons it felt so good was because we'd forgone the condom. Not that there had been any discussion, both of us too interested in the fucking part to be responsible.

"It's okay, I'm on the pill." She panted against my neck. "I'm going to come too."

It was all I needed to hear, her pussy tightening around my dick stopping any hope of holding back.

"Max," she screamed her body shaking as I continued to move, my dick exploding into her as she rode out the rest of her orgasm.

"Beth, oh fuck."

I couldn't stop.

My back rose off the mattress as I pistoned into her, the pulsing of her pussy milking my cock as we both breathed out of control.

We didn't move, our legs knotted together as she lay on me. The weight of her body made me want to pull a *Leonardo*—this was king of the world type shit if ever there was—but I didn't move, not wanting to lose the connection.

"Hey," my hand swept the base of her neck, pushing her hair out of the way. "You still with me?"

Her sweat soaked body had yet to move and other than the steady beat of her heart, I couldn't be sure she hadn't passed out.

"Are you sure that Benadryl wasn't cut with Viagra?" She laughed against my neck, the gentle vibrations motherfucking bliss against my skin.

I barked out a laugh, loving her body on mine. "Well, we'll just have to do it again just to be sure."

"Purely for research purposes, of course." She moved her mouth against my throat, her lips kissing softly against my skin.

"Of course."

**I**t was a compulsion.

Whenever Max and I were in the same zip code we inevitably ended up in bed. It had been our MO for so many years, I had assumed that once I moved and put some distance between us the cycle would stop. Surely we could be next to each other and not dissolve into a pair of sex-starved teenagers.

But nooooooooooooooo, it seemed we couldn't.

We'd lasted exactly one week.

A week.

Not even a *full* week if you take into account hours.

Problem was, I didn't even know who or what to blame.

Was it my libido? The lack of decent sex and rather underwhelming dick I'd been exposed to? It would make sense since Max was a bonafide guarantee of toe curling pleasure. He was able to tease out an orgasm within minutes while the last guy I'd dated played *Battleship* with my vagina and I still had to fake it.

Maybe it was just habit? An unconscious compulsion like eating a cookie even though you aren't hungry, purely because there is a plate of freshly baked chocolate chips sitting in front of you.

Or maybe—going out on a limb here—it's because he looked freaking hot beyond measure and could make me cream my pants with just a smile.

Ha. Yeah, that was definitely *not* the reason. Didn't even notice his washboard abs or his impeccable ass.

Of course there was the obvious answer here—the one I had been dancing around because I didn't want to admit that I'd be that shallow—his penis.

Ahhhhhhh.

Yeah.

That.

It really was worthy of the hero worship it received online. Its pink perfect glory was not only sizeable—there was no false advertising with that man—but he knew what to do with it too. A well-trained beast he could either call to heel or let off the chain—each with their own set of rewards.

Great. Now I was a pervert too.

On top of all of that—because clearly that wasn't enough drama—I'd had sex with him without a condom. Repeatedly. Excuse me while I beat my head against a brick wall because that would have been a hell of lot smarter than protection-less sex. He even stopped, giving me the option for his happy ending not to be inside of me and what did I say?

*It's all good, all fine. Go ahead and inject me with your love juice I'm on the pill.* Okay, maybe that's not what I said, but it may as well have been. Hypnotized by the orgasmic glow or stupid pills, I wasn't sure which. Like an unwanted pregnancy was my biggest problem. God, please don't strike me down with some unpronounceable genital funk.

It was an honest mistake. We had been together so often

and so long we *sometimes* forwent the latex. I'd been on the pill since I was sixteen and I trusted that those times we had been with other people, both of us had been safe. Probably a little trusting, but there was no reason to not be.

But that had been in the past. And while I knew there were no mutating cells crawling around my private parts—Max was the only unprotected partner I'd ever had and I had regular rigorous health screenings—I had no idea what had been *crawling up* on him.

"You look like you've seen a ghost," Max laughed, his chest still glistening from his shower. The towel around his waist further fed my stupidity as I rationalized whatever the damage was it had already been done, so what trouble could one more time be.

"I should probably get going." Well there was an under-statement. Probably? How about *definitely*.

"Wait a second." Max stood in my path, the few steps I'd taken towards the door not enough. "What's wrong?" He lifted my chin so that he could see in my eyes, all traces of allergens completely gone from his beautiful face.

"Nothing." I shrugged, not willing to share the freak out currently happening in my head.

"You really expect me to believe that?" The raised eyebrow was a hint he wasn't buying it. "You're forgetting I *know* you. So, I will ask you again, what's wrong?"

Ah fuck it. He was right. He did know me, so I might as well get the *conversation* over with. That sexy dialogue of, is-there-a-chance-of-syphilis. *Way to go, dumbass.*

"We had sex without a condom." My eyes stayed glued to his. "I know it's a little late now." Once again, another under-statement. "And I said I was on the pill but—"

"I'm clean." He didn't give me a chance to finish. "And I

would never put you at risk if there was even the slightest chance."

"What about me? Aren't you worried?" I shook my head wondering why I was the only one of us with the concern. He had no idea what I'd been doing in the years since he saw me. I could have thrown caution to the wind, screwing with reckless abandon.

"Nope, not even a little." There was zero hesitation in his voice as he smiled, in his eyes unwavering confidence that clearly I didn't possess. "Is there anything else?"

"No, that's it."

Well most of it. My own stupidity wasn't up for debate. I was having too much fun with that on my own. The whole *can we just be friends without fucking,* still very much the question of the morning.

"Good. What are you doing tonight?" He wrapped his arms around me ignoring the fact he was essentially naked and I had a bad track record of not sleeping with him. "The band is doing a gig tonight, and I know they'd love to see you."

"A gig? I've seen nothing in the press. In New York?"

Black Addiction had come a long way in the last few years. Their last album had gone quadruple platinum, with record-breaking sales in the UK and Europe. They weren't a bar band anymore with almost every concert selling out no matter how big the venue. So, maybe I stayed up to date with their rise to success, sue me.

"That's because it's not listed." Max's face animated with mischief. "Not as us anyway. Stadiums are awesome, but we miss the clubs, the intimate contact. We figured we'd do a couple of shows under different names so no one knows who it is until we show up."

"Really, well that's kind of cool. What's the band called?"

Talk of the band a welcome diversion. My freak out wasn't going anywhere, so delaying it a minute or two wasn't a problem.

"Cloak and Dagger. It's so fucking cheesy, I love it." He pulled me closer, his lips landing on my neck. "So you'll come right?"

"Sure." My mouth agreed before my brain had properly weighed the argument. *Not smart*, my brain warned while my mouth gave us all the finger. Awesome. I'm developing multiple personality disorder, how nice for me.

"Great." Max's arms squeezed tighter, ignoring he was still in a towel and his man bits were trying to give me a hug of their own.

*"Pick me,"* whispered my vagina thankfully quiet enough so my mouth couldn't hear.

"Show starts at ten, we're heading there to set up earlier though, but I can circle back and pick you up around nine."

"No, that's silly. It makes no sense for you to come all the way back." *Really*, my self-conscious glared at the irony of *me* identifying stupidity. Middle fingers and *fuck yous* internally being thrown at random. "I'll catch an Uber or cab, just tell me the address."

"It will be just like old times, huh?" Max's hands wandered down my back seeming to not notice his renegade cock was tapping Morse code against the towel.

"Yeah, it will be great." The big freak show smile on my face indicating I had now hit delirium. "I should let you go. Get ready. Get in the zone." *Get into some clothes,* the last option remaining unspoken as I unraveled myself from his hold.

"You don't want to stay a little longer?" The effort I'd made to create distance negated as he pulled me back. "Have breakfast?" The smirk on his face hinted that he wasn't talking about bacon and eggs.

"I need to get back." I tried again to escape, this time unhinging his hands from my ass so that I was able to step out of his grasp. "Jules has probably already called the police to issue a BOLO when I didn't come home last night."

"Fine, I'll see you tonight then." He watched with amusement as I walked backward toward his bedroom door.

"Yes, yes of course. Wouldn't miss it."

While it would have been perfectly acceptable to let me find the front door and continue on my journey solo he instead insisted on being a gentleman and walking me out.

In his towel.

So trying to keep my eyes above his chin—anything lower could mean some renegade body parts of my own—I said goodbye and finally made my escape.

Phew.

Now I could go and berate myself in private and work out how the hell I got out of the date I had accidentally agreed to. Because surely I couldn't go. No. That would be inviting trouble.

I had barely stepped inside the doorway when my progress was stopped, my body slamming into a very amused Jules.

"The allure of the twelve-inch cock was too great, well done, you." Her arms folded across her chest with a smile of I-know-what-you-were-doing beaming on her face.

"It's not twelve inches." I closed the door behind me and immediately jumped on the defensive. "And me spending the night with Max is not what you think."

"Oh, so you didn't sleep with him?" Her brow rose in a challenge to prove her wrong. "Him and his eleven-inch slong."

"I-I." My mouth opened and closed unable to finish the sentence. Or lie as the case was. I had definitely slept with him.

"It's not eleven inches either."

"You totally slept with him." Jules gave me a case of wiggle-finger-I-told-you-so. "Rode his ten-inch rod all night."

"No, stop." My hands waved erratically in front of me, an effort to stop what my mouth wasn't capable of. "I'm not telling you how big it is."

"You don't have to say a thing, just nod when I get it right." She nodded her head like it would assure my compliance. "Nine-inch nail?"

"I slept with him," I blurted out, the pressure too great. I knew I wasn't going to be able to hold out. Damn it, I sucked at discretion.

"Nine inches. Go, Beth." Jules raised her hand awaiting mine to join it for a high-five.

"Stop focusing on his penis." I scrubbed my face with my hands in frustration.

"Um, probably should have taken your own advice."

"Jules."

"I'm sorry, I'll be serious." She bit down on her lip trying not to laugh. "Tell me all about it."

The details of the night spewed out of me. From the wonderful meal, my bottomless wine glass and the guest appearance of micro penis at the restaurant, to my downward spiral where I tried to poison him. Twice.

"Who has to worry about Rohypnol when you can do all of that with dessert and some antihistamines." She'd stopped trying to hold back the laughter, her arms wrapping around her sides as she enjoyed the retelling at my expense.

I wanted to be mad, I mean it shouldn't be funny but laid out in front of us in its calamity it was hard to not crack a smile. I'd become my own punch line.

"It's not funny." The giggle unable to be suppressed as I

shoved her shoulder.

"Oh I disagree, it's freaking hilarious."

"Alright, Alright, Alright." My invisible white flag of surrender waved while I conceded there was mostly likely going to be laughter. "You have to help me think of an excuse not to go out tonight."

The sex with the ex had been done. Even if I wanted to—and I didn't—we couldn't go back in time and un-copulate so the more pressing issue was the date. The one I had agreed to. The one that I was sure would lead to more of *that*. The *that* not needing to be clarified.

"Why don't you want to go out with him?" Her confusion justified given I wasn't usually a one-night stand kind of girl, micro penis had been the exception. "Did his huge pole knock the sense out of you?"

"It's not that simple. The band will be there and it will be . . ." Just like old times as Max had put it. "Awkward, they'll assume we're back together. I don't want to send the wrong signals."

Don't get me wrong. I loved the band. Joey, Rusty and Angie were all amazing in their own individual way and over time, we'd all become tight. They'd never made me feel like the "girlfriend" and happily welcomed me into their circle. Even Angie who had the best resting bitch face ever.

But.

When I'd waved goodbye to my old life they had also been part of the separation. Clean break being what it was it didn't make sense to continue to see them. Even though I had separate and meaningful relationships with each of them independent of Max. So the not seeing them was partly guilt—fine, a LOT—related.

The sending the wrong signal thing was valid too. Of course

they would assume we were back together. Why wouldn't they? We'd only been down this road five thousand times.

"So let me go over this just to be sure I've got it." Jules tried to reason with my logic. "Your ex-boyfriend is not only hot but turned out to be a huge rock star."

"Yes." I had no idea where this was going, but I was willing to humor her.

"And he wasn't a dick who broke your heart." Fingers were lifted for visual cues in case I couldn't keep up.

"Yes." So *maybe* I knew where she was going with this.

"And he wasn't even pissed when you tried to kill him." More fingers were added. "Not only once, but twice."

"Uh-huh."

"And he has a huge—"

"Can we move to the point already."

"But even with all of that." She waved her hands around like a lunatic. "You don't want to date him. Do you see how insane this all sounds?"

Well yeah, when she put it like that. "We had a good thing, I don't want to ruin it."

"Girl, I'm telling you, none of this makes any sense." Jules refused to buy my—fine, probably convoluted—argument that Max and I shouldn't get back together.

Except.

No, the sex didn't mean we were back together. We were definitely not back together.

"Well sense or not, I need to think of a good reason not to go tonight and you are going to help me."

# Ten

# Max

**"Y**ou moved in with Beth?"

Angie let me get an entire three steps into the bar, the usual *hello* apparently obsolete, as she went into mother hen mode. The douchebag who was most likely responsible for the misconception tipped his chin hello.

"I didn't move in with Beth. I moved into her building." The conversation I planned on having with my band happening a little sooner than expected.

"Dude, I'm sleep deprived." Joey rolled his eyes like I was the asshole, and having a few hours less shuteye was a good enough excuse to spill my biz. "I can't be held responsible for what comes out of my mouth."

"So are you guys getting back together?" Angie was front and center on the mission: acquiring information, the to-and-fro between Joe and I not registering on her radar.

"If I have anything to say about it, yeah we are." It was the condensed version and one no doubt Angie was after. She was a long-story-short kind of girl and I admired the quality.

"Who's doing what?" Rusty breezed in pulling a Top Gun, gold-framed aviators chilling on his face despite it being already dark out and the smooth motherfucker was indoors. "You're supposed to wait till I get here before you get to all the gossip." The asshole flashed his Hollywood grin as he nodded to Angie and Joey. Fucking lead guitarists, cocky sons-of-bitches.

"Max and Beth are getting back together." Joey didn't bother letting me do the fill-in, his big-ass mouth talking shit out of turn.

"Dude, seriously?" The shut-the-fuck-up I was directing his way hopefully coming in loud and clear.

"I can't help it." Again Joey went with shifting blame. "At least I didn't say you guys were living together this time." The bastard grinned knowing full well he was stirring the pot.

Wonder how long it would take to get a replacement drummer for the night. We were going to need it, because I was going to kill this one.

"Well then the day just got a whole lot more interesting." Rusty rubbed his hands together with motherfucking glee, the shades coming off as he settled in. "I'm gonna need some details."

Better to get it over with. It was either do the show-and-tell myself, or have my moron of a best friend sham-wow us with his fairytale adaptation of events. Not wanting to leave my little niece fatherless, the only reason why the bastard was still breathing.

"The apartment I recently moved into happens to be a few floors up from Beth. Something I didn't know when I bought it." There was no need for the extended dance version of how it came to be, the core facts being more than sufficient.

"Max, I'm kinda crushed, dude." Blond Maverick, AKA Rusty Crawford clutched at his chest laying the dramatics on real thick. "You've been living there over a week and I'm just now hearing about it. Dead to me, asshole."

"I swear this was a lot more fun when it was directed at someone else." I shook my head knowing karma had a big black rubber stamp with my name on it. The amount of shit I had dished out to the other three of my band members had me primed for a serious amount of payback.

So cliff-noting our initial welcome-to-the-neighborhood through to the last twenty-four hours, I got the band up to speed on how I was now sharing an almost identical address with the chick I dated for more than a decade.

"She's coming to the show tonight and I want everyone on their best behavior." I eyed them all equally, being sure there was no one who could claim the oh-sorry-I-didn't-hear. "No fucking third degree, especially you Angie." Our front woman notorious for going full metal jacket.

"What could I possibly say?" Her freaking grin proved how right I was to be suspicious. Seriously, the lot of them were a bunch of loose cannons, and I wasn't sure who was the weakest link.

Usually the band didn't get involved in my relationships, but Beth had been a little different. She'd been more than just a girl I'd dated; she'd been friends with each of them in her own special way. Not that anyone had any grounds to harbor bad feelings. Sure, she'd blown out of town with no goodbye but we'd all—especially yours truly—had time to find her if we'd wanted. And if I had no problem with the way shit had played out, then the band didn't have grounds for issues either. And if they wanted to get technical, we hadn't even been together when I left town, so there was no way I'd let them give her a hard time for it.

"Whatever. Play nice."

# Stand

•••

Waiting to go on was giving me the scratch. We had been hiding out backstage like a bunch of shady SOBs looking to rob the joint. Of course mingling with the general population would ruin the *ta-dah* moment when we jumped out of the shadows and blew the doors off the place. Which is why I had absolutely no idea if Beth was one of the faceless bodies on the dance floor or if she'd pulled a no-show and the back of my neck was sweating for no good reason.

"You want Ali to look for her, dude?" Rusty's heavy hand landed hard on my shoulder as we both looked out into the abyss. "She can scan the room and report back."

"She doesn't know what she looks like." Sadly, the only thing that stopped me from agreeing.

"Digital age, my friend. We grab her picture from her Facebook profile, and text it to Alison. It's at most a five minute operation." The smug bastard pulled out his iPhone from his back pocket ready to go.

"Sure, that isn't creepy." Because getting eyestrain from staring into the dark was soooooooo much better. "I'm sure she's out there, she said she would be."

I'd checked my phone a few times, the lack of *sorry-I'm-washing-my-hair* text giving me hope she was right where she should be. Pity there was a gnarling feeling in my gut that hinted that she might not. I guess I'd find out soon enough.

"You ready to Cloak and Dagger the shit out of this place?" Rusty bounced around doing his usual pre-show routine, shadow punching and dancing on his feet De La Hoya pretty.

"So ready!" A Red Bull loaded Joey Shaw was pumped having shaken off the earlier fatigue. After shot gunning four of them, that come down was going to be a bitch.

"This is going to be so fucking cool." Angie tucked away her phone, her pre-show routine of saying good night to her kid and husband over. The killed call signaled it was show time.

"Well then, let's go."

The four of us stepped onto the blackened stage, the house light just enough to keep people from running into each other and spilling drinks. The bar manager knew the minute our cover was blown there was going to be a text/social media frenzy that would rival any flash mob. Extra security was in place so shit didn't get too out of control. And the excitement of getting up close and personal with the crowd had pushed aside other thoughts of whether a certain brunette was going to be among them.

Joey tapped his sticks, counting us in as Rusty and Angie hit matching opening cords. The lights that hung on the truss above swayed as the cans came to life, the speakers blasting the marriage of noise as we opened with one of our older tunes.

It hit the audience like a crash-cart, their feet stilled as their brains tried to register the what-the-fuck. But it only took a second with the resurrection of the noise loud enough to rival what was coming out of the amps.

Rusty was working his end of the stage, his fingers all over the fretboard while he oozed that rock god charm. The girls in the front row paying no mind to the fact Rus was happily off the market.

Angie was another matter. In front of the mic stand with none of the theatrics of our lead guitarist, slaying the audience with the pitch perfect tone while playing rhythm.

And Joey, well, you've all seen Animal from the Muppets right? It was like that, but in time.

My fingers moved along the nickel-wound strings of my

bass, muscle memory doing its job as I scanned the crowd. A hundred or more brunettes, and not one of them the one that I wanted.

Well.

Fuck.

That really sucked.

I gave myself a second or two of licking my boo-boos before sacking up. The audience wasn't here for love songs and dedications, and I was going to give them exactly what they had come to expect from Black Addiction. Pure rock with no BS.

I don't think I could have performed any better if she'd been in front of me, the energy blasting out of me as I played the fuck out of my bass. The four of us moved through the set list, old songs and new getting equal time as the crowd spilled out onto the street.

And with the last song wrapped we took a group bow at the front of the stage and said goodnight to the over excited audience.

"Man, I could play another thirty songs." Red Bull Joey was still riding high off the buzz. "It's not better than sex, but a very close second." He matched me stride for stride as we headed to the band room.

"I'm glad you revised your choice, asshole." I punched him in the arm as Rus came up behind us, his hands giving us both a bro tap as he squeezed in between.

"Dump your shit and let's get to the bar. I want drinks with our people, Angie is even staying for a few so there is no pussying out." He gave us both a pointed look before bypassing the band room all together and heading straight to the public area. His interest in us and the conversation, obviously over.

"Yeah, that's what I'm talking about." He raised his hands

like a moron, his enthusiasm wasted seeing as it was only the two of us in the area. "We need to write material faster so we can tour again. I want to be doing this every fucking night."

I neglected to point out that his feelings of euphoria were going to fade pretty fucking quick when his daughter wanted her daddy at six in the morning. The silent knowledge making me happier than I probably should be.

"Well we have another six of these local shows, so that should keep you satisfied for a while." Keep us both happy, and feed the creativity as well.

Following Rusty's directive, we *dumped our shit* and headed to the bar. The well-lubricated crowd hadn't thinned, instead milling around sharing footage they'd captured on their phones while drinking. The welcoming hollers we received were almost as loud as when we'd been on stage, the slaps on the backs and *well dones* thrown at us from every direction.

"Beer." I leaned over the bar, the dude with the 90's No Fear shirt on behind it shaking his head when I handed over the cash. The drinks for the night were a gift from the management.

"I'd assume you'd be doing shots of Jäger?" A voice called from behind me, the owner of it the person I'd been dying to see all night. "Or are you slowing down in your old age?"

Seeing her standing there was a one-two punch straight to the jaw. She was flawless in a pair of fitted blue jeans, her tight black top doing jack shit to hide what was underneath despite not showing any naked flesh.

"I'm driving." I ignored the other part of her statement because we both knew I was far from old. "But I have a bottle at home if you're interested." The grin widened all by itself as I moved closer to where she was standing, my interest in the beer forgotten.

"Oh he's fucking smooth." Her roommate who, up till now I hadn't noticed, gave me a smile and a wink. "Good playing up there by the way, she barely looked at your ass."

"Jules." Beth cursed under her breath, shaking her head gently as the smile crept across her lips.

"Okay, okay it was me who was looking at your ass." Jules rolled her eyes before giving me a nod of approval. "Two thumbs up."

"Appreciated." The head returned the nod, my eyes not moving from Beth. "You want to come say hi to the rest of the band?"

"Sure." Beth's eyes flicked to the left and the right, the rest of Black Addiction chilling over on the other side of the bar.

The addition of her friend wasn't going to be a problem for me, and I was going to give her my greeting exactly how I'd wanted to.

"You look great." My hands wrapped around her waist without waiting for the invitation. "I didn't see you out there, I thought you decided not to come."

"I was here the whole time, just at the back." Beth stepped back out of my hold. "Right, Jules?"

"Yep, here the whole time," Jules added, the need for a wingman obvious.

I wasn't sure if it was the PDA or something else, but she was sending a blast of don't-touch-me I didn't understand. Especially when ten hours ago I was doing a lot more to her than giving her a hug.

Not wanting to make an issue of it here—but trust me, it was going to be discussed—I dropped my hands like a good boy and led them through the crowd to meet the band. The chill hopefully going to be warmed by hi-how-are-yas that looked to follow.

Joe was up against the bar, his hands raised in animation as he talked to the crowd in front of him, each of them enthralled in whatever it was he was saying.

"Hey, stranger." His head moved to Beth who was standing back waiting for a lull in the conversation. "You just going to stand there or give me a proper hello, considering it's been freaking years." His mouth shooting her a grin.

"Hey." She laughed back, her arms giving the bastard the hug she hadn't given me. It was the first time ever I'd been jealous of the bastard, but at that moment I would have given my left nut to trade places.

"Wow, Manhattan looks good on you, good work." The asshole continued, my fists white-knuckling by my side as he spun her around making her fucking giggle. "Hopefully it will have the same effect on Max and he can finally get some style." The SOB had the nerve to smirk in my direction.

The irritation I was feeling was not because I was worried Joey was making a play for my girl—well technically she wasn't mine, but whatever. That dude and I had been through thick and thin, and even if his dick wasn't owned by his beautiful, talented and mouthy wife Kenzie, he would never get involved with Beth. Sure he'd had a tendency to sleep with girls either Rus or I had been with in the past, but now it was about as possible as a eunuch getting an erection.

So what ate at me was not the asshole's charm, but that he was doing the shit I wanted to do. Making her laugh and wrapping her in a hug.

I wasn't given too much time to ponder with Alison and Rus making their way toward us.

"Beth." Rusty held up his beer, his other arm wrapped tightly around his girl. "So you got a new neighbor I hear, my sympathies."

Great another smooth bastard I needed to contend with.

And wait for it.

Yep, there was the laugh.

Beth did the intro of Jules to the boys. Not that she needed to, her roommate was holding her own. Rusty did what he always did whenever Ali was with him, keeping his hands on her while making sure everyone heard how awesome she was. I had to hand it to the guy, he'd become a one-woman guy the minute those two even got a sniff of being serious and he hadn't so much as glanced at another chick. Earned him lots of respect, especially on account the chick he was dating was my kin.

"I still can't believe your Phil's daughter." Beth's face reared back in a mixture of shock and surprise. Yeah, I'd told her the story, but it didn't get any easier seeing the evidence in front of you. Clearly the only thing my oxygen thief of a brother had done right, even if every single time I thought about the situation I wanted to beat the living shit out of him.

"I don't really know him," Ali sipped her drink, the subject of daddy dearest not being her favorite. "I met him a couple of times but—"

"But he's an asshole and she's better off without him in her life." I added, aware that I had been sitting on the periphery of the conversation for too long. "We're all better off without him."

"Surely we have something better to talk about other than Phil." Angie joined our happy little gang, pulling Beth into a hug. "It's been forever."

There was another person I would be happy to pull a Freaky Friday with, instead I was pouting like a fucking three-year-old doing the why-don't-I-get-one.

"Yeah, a long while." Beth smiled back, whatever tension

she had earlier being shelved as she chilled with the band. "Last time I saw everyone was at Rusty's before you guys went on the Power Station tour."

"Ahhh, the night legends were made." Rusty wiped a fake tear from his cheek. "And we lost our front woman to another band."

"You didn't lose me, moron, I'm still here." Angie popped Rus in the arm. "But since you brought it up . . ." She whipped out her phone with its thirty thousand pictures of her big-shot husband and her seriously cute kid. Can't say I blamed her, and it was sort of heartwarming to see.

"Jase is home with Zack." Her finger flicked along the glass showing photos of her kid's second birthday. "It's hard to get sitters." Hiring a nanny not an option for our ballsy front woman.

"I could watch him if ever you guys wanted a night out? I love kids, it's one of the reasons why I went into teaching."

Cue the sound of screeching fucking tires as Beth's words settled in, almost every single one of us developing muteness with eyeballs turning directly to Angie.

"Or not." Beth added, the silence being pretty fucking obvious that as gracious as the offer was, Angie probably wasn't feeling it. "It was just an idea."

"It is a great idea. Maybe Zack can meet you and we can see how it goes? I'd still have to talk to Jase as well, but I'd definitely think about it." Angie didn't shoot down the idea like we'd all assumed, the rest of the band still reeling from the shock.

"Of course, the offer is there." Beth smiled, giving Angie's hand a squeeze.

"I'm glad you're back." Angie continued the loving feeling and gave Beth another hug. "Don't go disappearing again."

"Wow. That's some neat party trick you just pulled, Angie hardly lets anyone watch her son," Rusty added, the risk of an Angie stare-down not enough to keep him from opening his mouth.

"Yeah, yeah. I'm protective. I don't care what you idiots thinks." She ignored the shade she was catching. "Now I'm going to have my one beer before heading home to my hot husband." She moved to the bar and ordered her drink.

"So, are we drinking or standing around?" Jules looked around, her hands firmly on her hips. "Because it's a Saturday night and I'm in a bar, I came here with the understanding there'd be booze."

"Let me get you a drink, Jules." I smiled, immediately liking the girl even if at present she was standing between me and the girl I wanted to put my hands on. "Beth? You joining your friend?"

"Sure, that would be good." She gave me a nod, her chill thawing a little toward me. "Thank you."

Awesome. At least she was planning to stay a little longer and I was using that shit to my advantage. And I was totally going to be finding out as to why it was perfectly acceptable for everyone else to lay hands on her, but not me.

Oh, and I am almost positive her wingman had been given special instructions to run interference as well. I might not have seen it right away, but the way Jules had subtly stepped between us was a huge red flag. As was the fact Beth was more comfortable giving Joey a hug than me.

Not happy.

And like it or not, we were having a discussion and she was going to shed some light on why the sudden one-eighty.

Tonight.

We were having that fucking chat tonight. Probably on the

way home when I drove her and her crazy friend back to our apartment building. I have to tell you, I was really starting to like this new address of mine.

**J**ules and her bright ideas.

Instead of coming up with a good, valid and non-offensive reason for not turning up at Max's gig, she instead convinced me to go but bring reinforcements—her. Because I couldn't possibly get into trouble if she was standing beside me. Chances were that any trouble we got into would be engineered by her, and she was supposed to be on my side.

We'd arrived late, the should-we-shouldn't-we taking up valuable time, stepping into the club just in time to see the start of their first song. The crowd that would be reasonable for any Saturday night, soon swelled as talk that Cloak and Dagger was Black Addiction incognito spread.

People packed into the room, our great position toward the back center of the club was forfeited as assholes squeezed in front of us. And all of them seemed to suffer from giant disease, which meant I'd occasionally need to elbow people just to be able to see. It really did suck that even with the added heel ratio, we were relegated to peeking through gaps between people's heads.

But it didn't matter. We'd heard the whole thing. The prized glances we'd been able to steal through the crowd an amazing visual—each one of them awesome. I was so glad I had listened to my instinct—and Jules—and come to see the show.

They had always been good.

It had always been Max's intention to turn pro, the seedy bars and clubs just a stepping-stone until they did. But seeing the morph from then to now was truly mesmerizing. They were . . . amazing. And they sure as hell deserved their success, the roaring response they got, proving it.

And just like every time I'd watch Max play, my heart squeezed with pride. Not because I felt I'd had a hand in it, but just because he'd made it, like he said he always would. In our own way, we both had.

Which was why even though I'd given myself a pep talk I was having a hard time keeping to the plan. The one where I told him that despite our sexy-time last night—or this morning if you wanted to get technical—we were going to keep it more above the covers for the future. It was better that way, less complications. Besides I didn't want a no-strings sex-only relationship with Max and I was fairly sure that was all that was on the table. I wanted to be his friend, one that didn't sleep with him every time she got within sniffing distance. The idea was losing its appeal the longer I looked at him and when he touched me it took every ounce of willpower I had not to jump into his arms and make out with him. In front of all these people. Like I would have five years ago.

Thank God for the band. My mouth kept busy keeping my attention safely in their direction, the old connections rekindling with very little effort. It was like I'd almost never been gone, the ease of each conversation making it easier to forget the man I wanted to lick from head to toe was standing not more than two feet away. All was going well too, with affectionate hugs exchanged. All until I mentioned babysitting Angie's little boy.

Not that the offer wasn't genuine, but I'll admit that the loved up feeling in the room had me lose control of my mouth. The spur of the moment decision not really thought out.

"Ladies, your drinks." Max returned from hunting and gathering, a handful of longneck beers, his bounty. Jules' request for beverages had bought me more time to get my mouth back under control.

"Thanks." I took one without making eye contact while trying to keep my libido in check.

Not that I believed that *not looking* at him actually guaranteed anything, chances were that given half a chance I was still going to end up naked in his bed. Which is why I brought in reinforcements. Jules—my secret weapon—who was doing a wonderful job at slipping in between Max and me whenever he got within touching distance. And it wasn't his hands I was worried about.

The conversation continued without me as the cold crisp pilsner slid down my throat, my eyes happening to stray while I tried to focus on what was actually being said. Not that I had planned where they might end up, the silly things having a mind of their own as they roamed without purpose. There was no need to guess where they landed.

They had started at his heavy, thick-soled boots doing the slow tilt as they traveled up his body. His denim clad legs the next part to get my attention, my trip pausing when it got to his strong thighs. *Oh, Yes.* I tried not to lick my lips as I continued further north. The fly of his jeans was doing a freaking magnificent job fighting to keep all of *that* contained. And had it not been completely inappropriate I would have searched the label so I knew best where to direct my admiration and respect.

But it wasn't just the jeans that got all the praise; the cotton of his T-shirt stretching out, wrapping around his chest like it was hanging on for dear life. The hard lines of his chest and abs begged to be unwrapped. Which I would have happily done, it would be the compassionate thing to do.

And all of this would have been fine—the silent appreciation of his fine form—if I had stopped there.

Which I hadn't.

Oh shit.

Busted.

His eyes locked on mine, the raised eyebrow and smile hinting they had been watching the entire time.

And because the universe seriously hated me or had an extremely warped sense of humor, Jules picked that exact moment to excuse herself to go to the bathroom. Leaving me there to deal all by myself.

If she'd only had the call of nature a second or two earlier, it could have been my out, but noooooooooooo she had to wait. Her announcement missed as Max's and my eyes tangoed in a heat.

"Something on your mind, Beth?" Max's head tilted to the side. *Go on, tell me you weren't just undressing me while everyone else was oblivious.* The taunt not needed to be said.

"Nope, nothing on my mind at all." I tried to wipe all thoughts from my mind in case he had some freaky mind reading abilities. "Completely blank." I shoved the beer to my lips so they'd stop moving.

The others—thank you, baby Jesus—hadn't noticed. Each of them too involved with fans and their own conversations to worry about what I had been doing. All except Max, who had given me his full attention.

"Why don't you take a walk with me?" He pulled the half-consumed beer from my hand and placed it on the bar.

I'd been paying so much attention to clearing my thoughts I hadn't noticed his hand was now resting on the small of my back. Damn Jules and her need to pee. This was exactly why I had needed a buffer; I couldn't be trusted to multitask.

"I probably shouldn't, Jules might come back and not know where I've gone." Could I have given a lamer excuse? Probably not which is why I had said this one.

"I think she'll work it out. It's not like you would leave without her." Max's hand hadn't moved, nor had his intention. "Besides, we'll probably be back before she is."

*"Don't do it,"* my brain screamed, but neglected to give me one workable excuse.

"If we're not going to be long—"

"We won't."

My head nodded before my mouth could answer. Not that there was ever any doubt on what that answer would be. Which is why I was here in the first place, my inability to resist whenever Max was added to the equation.

"Just this way." His hand guided me through the sea of people and to a narrow closed door. The handle opened as soon as he turned it, his body stepping through the doorway first before mine obediently followed.

I expected it to be dark, a narrow corridor with dim lighting. And it was exactly how I'd imagined. A perfect venue for him to push me up against the wall and take my mouth like he had last night.

But he didn't, instead continuing to walk until we got to another door, this one just as compliant as the first and with a quick twist of his wrist flooding the corridor with exceptionally bright light, the overhead LEDs blinding me momentarily as we stepped inside.

"Ummm . . ." The dots from my vision had started to fade, the room obviously some sort of backstage area if the couch and the two tired chairs were anything to go by.

"I have a strong case of déjà vu." His hand moved to my arms and held me still, even though I had nowhere to go. With the door directly behind him, I'd have to tackle him to leave and I wasn't that strong. "Oh, I know why. We had a very similar conversation earlier today."

"I'm confused." I didn't even bother trying to lie. I mean, what was the point? I was terrible at it. "I'm attracted to you, obviously." *Really obviously.* "And I don't regret last night, but I think it meant something different to you than it probably did to me."

Not that I had fully fleshed out what it had meant to me. But the common theme was that while it had been mind-blowing—exactly what my body needed—it wasn't going to work for the other part of me. My brain.

"That would mean you knew what I thought." He circled his hands around my waist. "And seeing as you haven't asked, I doubt you do."

"Maybe. So I'm guessing. But I know that continuing to do what we did would be a bad idea." *Well done, me. Stick with the script.* Sex equals bad, even if it felt good.

Max didn't seem to be getting the message nor was he removing his hands. Of course I hadn't asked him to, my body still torn I was making the right decision.

"And how did you come to this wonderful conclusion?" I was surprised the heat from his eyes alone hadn't burned the clothes right off my body. And while I hadn't asked him what he wanted, he was making it very clear.

"It's so hard to think when you look at me that way." I swallowed, the effort making it hard to breathe.

"Then maybe you shouldn't think."

"No, no." My hands flew up between us like that would be a sufficient reliable barrier. "I want to really try something new, Max. I want us to do this without the sex this time. I want us not to end up back in a relationship."

It was the first time ever we had talked about breaking up or getting back together.

First time *ever*.

Which was huge considering the amount of times those things happened. But this was important. Adults talk things out, we were more than two wandering bags of hormones.

"We both know we're not going to avoid each other." Nor did I want to. "Clearly I suck at all of this considering I am probably sending mixed messages." Sleeping with him then pulling away. Yeah, it wasn't the right thing to do.

"But this time it has to be as friends. Only friends. Ones that don't kiss and don't end up in bed together."

I was glad when I'd finally said the words. Glad that I hadn't punked out like the last few times and glad that it was finally my brain running the show.

"I want you." And judging by the way he was looking at me he most definitely meant it. "I'm not going to pretend I don't so it's easier for you to hear. I want all of you. Unrestricted."

"That's not on offer, Max. I'm sorry." I had to look away.

The scrambled thoughts in my head jostled for position as I continued to fight an internal war. Max and I weren't meant to be. Not romantically. If we were supposed to have worked out, it would have happened already.

"Give me a good reason." His hands moved to my jaw and brought my attention back to him. "And not some crazy thought process where you assumed you knew what I thought."

"Because seeing you again made me realize how much I missed you." The words were so hard for me to say. "How much I still care about you and if we do this again, I just know it's going to end badly. We had a good run. If we do it and then—then it finishes, I know it will be forever. I'm not ready for that."

"You can't know the future, Beth." His voice was soothing as he swept of his thumb along my jaw. "You can't know what is going to happen."

"It's because I *don't* know what's going to happen that it has to be like this. I was worried about coming here tonight. Worried about seeing you because I knew I'd want to kiss you and I don't want to feel like that. I want us to be able to see each other. To be friends."

"Oh please tell me you aren't giving me the let's be friends speech." The chuckle bubbled in his throat. "We've always been friends. And it always ends up as more."

"Just not *this* time."

"I'm not sure I can go there with you." He shook his head, confused why I had decided now was the time to flip the switch on our merry-go-round.

"You can, and it will be better than what we had before, I promise."

"Then why do I want to kiss you right now? And not in a friendly way." He moved his head closer, his nose skating across mine.

"And right now, I would probably let you. But it would go nowhere." Not long term, not in a way that would matter.

"Then let's find out."

Before I could answer he did what he had threatened to do.

Because of all the things Max was, a liar wasn't one of them.

His mouth crushed mine, my rebuttal not even fully formed in my head when his tongue slipped through my opened lips and sought refuge in mine. It wasn't just our mouths that were misbehaving, our bodies had disregarded everything I'd said and were clawing at each other too. Mine just as badly as his. And as much as I wanted to keep kissing him, I hated what we'd become.

"We need to stop, please stop." I finally found the courage to whisper.

His head snapped up no less violent than if I'd grabbed his hair and yanked it back myself, his body completely disengaging as he took a step back.

"You have never asked me to stop before."

"I'm asking you now."

He raked his hands through his hair, before his eyes settled back on me, on his face was an emotion I couldn't read.

Just as he had, I also took a step back. The distance necessary because I wasn't sure my body wasn't going to pull him back in again.

"No, don't do that." He raised his hand, the shake of his head following soon after. "You don't want to be with me in that way, all right. But don't move away from me. You know I would never hurt you."

"I know. I didn't think that." He would be the last person who'd hurt me, it hadn't been him that I'd been worried about.

"Then what were you thinking?"

It hadn't occurred to me that that one step away might be seen as something other than what it was. Distance. But he was right; I had no idea what was going on in his head, which meant he had no idea what was going on in mine. Being afraid wasn't it.

"That this is my fault. I'm leading you on." My actions had certainly pointed to it. The hot and then cold. It wasn't fair.

"That's something else I won't allow you to do, take responsibility for how I'm feeling and what I'm doing."

"Max—"

"Fuck, Beth." He blew out a curse. "I showed up on your doorstep and it was obvious that you had put distance between us for a reason. I might not have tracked you down, but I sure as hell pushed the issue."

"Do you think we can move past this? Just be friends?" God, I hoped so, because if he couldn't this would be the first time I would ever have to say goodbye. And that would hurt more than I could ever imagine.

"Yes, because losing you again isn't an option."

This time when he reached for me it wasn't with the intention of kissing me, but it was with no less intensity. My head nestled against his chest as his arms wrapped tightly around my body but he didn't try for more. The steady thump of his heart matched my own as we stood still. Just there. The two of us.

"We should go back, everyone is probably wondering where we are." I was the first one to speak, the words getting muffled by his chest.

"Yeah, are you and Jules sticking around for a little while? I'd offer you guys a ride but the 'Vette only has two seats." He slowly let his arms fall, this time the distance being initiated by him as he took a step back.

"No, it's fine. We'll grab a cab. And I don't have anywhere else to be." I tried so hard to force my lips into a grin. "A good friend of mine's band played tonight. I want to hang out with them. They are pretty awesome."

"Yeah?" Max laughed, "Maybe you should tell your friend

how awesome he is all the time. If he's in a band he probably has a huge ego and would love to hear it."

"Then I should probably get going. I think I saw Joey out near the bar." I laughed, glad the tone of the conversation had turned.

"Oh God, please no." He shook his head, pulling back in mock horror. "Not even as a joke, Beth. His head can barely fit through the doorway now, anymore and we're going to have serious problems."

"Okay, Okay." My body shook as I laughed. "As long as you buy me a new beer."

"Deal."

# Twelve
# Max

**I**f anyone had noticed we'd been missing, it hadn't show-ed when we came back.

Rusty had a larger than usual circle around him, girls vying for his attention even though his girlfriend was right there. Joey was talking the loudest; his hands moving constantly with whatever he was talking about always seeming to need visual cues. And Angie was sitting on a bar stool, chatting to Alison who seemed completely cool with her dude being the center of attention.

Even Jules didn't notice, the long line at the bathroom keeping her away longer than we'd been gone. Something we all heard about when she returned and expressed her displeasure of being inconvenienced because of her lack of dick. The comedic relief a welcome addition to what had been pretty intense a few minutes before.

Last call was announced and I walked the two girls out to the street, making sure they were safely in a cab before I went back inside the bar. Then I said my goodbyes, grabbed my shit and headed to the garage where I'd parked my car. One of the perks of the larger success was having roadies to take care of your rig, the guys already taking care of our instruments while we'd been shooting the breeze at the bar.

The drive home fucking sucked. Even the joy of driving my car didn't raise my mood with Beth's let's-be-friends speech rolling around in my head on constant repeat. Yeah, 'cause that shit was easy.

Oh, I'd agreed to it. Of course I fucking did. Not like there was an option. But while my mouth had been all yeah-let's-be-bffs the rest of me wasn't buying it. Which was a really shitty thing to do to say the least.

I wasn't in the business of BS and I had never fed any to her. But there was also a bigger chance of me putting down my bass and winning an Olympic gold medal for the US swim team than giving up on her. Not because I wanted to fuck her—because if that were all it was I'd go find someone else to fuck—but because I honestly believed she was wrong.

She had been accurate in presenting the facts. We'd gone around the same block a few times, but that didn't mean we were done. Not the way I saw it. In fact, I thought it proved the fucking opposite, that fate had seen what we'd not been smart enough to see ourselves. We belonged together and every time either of us tried to stop that and moved away, whatever force that was moving the chess pieces saw to it that we course corrected. Which was back to each other.

Now, I had never been a big believer in destiny other than the one you made for yourself. But I had seen some pretty strong evidence to suggest that some shit was in the cards whether you wanted it or not. Beth had always been in my cards and I sure as shit wasn't changing my deck now.

So where did that leave me? Apart from the obvious—I was a sad sack who wanted what apparently wasn't his anymore. But it also meant I was going to have to win her back.

This time for good.

My work was well and truly cut out for me. Flowers and candy weren't even an option, neither was almost anything else I had in my bag of tricks. She had seen it all before. So if I wanted to change the outcome, I needed a completely new game plan. One she'd not only hadn't seen from me, but from any of the assholes she'd dated over the years. Because my end game, was long term. As in there would be no other assholes. Just me. Asshole, number one.

Friends? Not an option, sorry. This was the only way it was going to be. That or I was going to end up the breaking news bulletin when I was arrested on stalking and harassment charges. Jail time would ruin the touring schedule so I guess we hope for the best.

It was something that kept me up most of the night, tossing and turning after I'd gone to bed alone. Not like I didn't have options to share the sheets with someone if I'd wanted, but there was zero chance of that happening. As in, if it wasn't Beth, I wasn't interested in any other women. I didn't even mourn the loss; happy to give my dick a time out while I figured out a way to convince her she was wrong.

So the next morning instead of sitting around in my empty bed and feeling like a jerk-off, I got up and started to put the pieces into place. I'd wasted enough time and if the band's success had taught me anything it was that if you wanted something, you went out and got it. Not sure why it had taken me so long to wake up. Possibly because I'd been a self-centered dick with his head up his ass, or maybe I'd been too focused on my career. But thankfully I'd woken the fuck up, and there was no mistaking what I wanted. Her. And not in the way she'd suggested.

First thing I had to put up with was the bullshit charade

where I didn't seem interested in more than just friends. Well, okay then, can do. Of course it was going to be close to impossible to hide the fucking hard-on she gave me with little more than a smile, but we'd just have to work with what we had. And short of cutting my dick off, that shit wasn't going to stop.

And being that I was such a good *friend,* I knocked on her door bright-eyed and bushy fucking tailed at eleven the next morning. Two obscenely large coffees I'd snagged a few minutes before, in my hands as I rapped on the wood.

"Hey." Beth pulled open the door, the messed up hair and eye rub hinting she hadn't been awake. "You brought coffee?" Her eyes moved from my face to the two cups of piping hot java I was balancing in my hands. The fucking smile it earned me better than I'd hoped.

Better yet, she opened the door and invited me inside, the view infinitely better of her in all her mussed up glory.

"Sure did." I tried to not notice the fact she was wearing sleep shorts and a tank top with no bra. That hard-on that threatened to be my undoing, looking for a way out of my jeans. "Figured you might need it. There's one here for Jules too."

"That's so sweet of you." She took one of the cups from my hand and gave me the best hug she could considering neither of us wanted to end up with third degree burns. "She's still sleeping."

*Yeah, sorry Jules but didn't really care you weren't awake.* "No sweat, I'll just leave it here then." The other cup I'd been holding was lowered on to their kitchen table. "She can have it later." I stepped back and watched as Beth's cup moved up to her lips, the way her eyes closed as she savored the mouthful.

Annnnnnnnnnd on that note. "Need to get going. Catching

up with Joey and Kenzie. Chat soon, okay?" I gave her a two finger wave and headed back toward the door.

"Oh, well thanks." She followed, her grip on her coffee maintained as she walked me to the door. "This is heaven."

"No probs." Seriously, the least I could do. "See ya."

I didn't look back.

Just turned my ass around and headed back to the elevator, unsure if she'd still been looking from the door.

The catch up with Joey and Kenzie was a real thing. He'd been too drunk to drive his sorry ass home and even though I'd offered, he instead caught a ride with Eric, his drum tech. The offer I'd extended had been partly for my own benefit, wanting to see his sorry ass stumble up the front of his stairs and try not to wake his six-month old while Kenzie shot him the evil eye. It was great because Joey wasn't quiet so the chances of his wife tearing him a new one were high if his kid so much as cracked an eyelid open.

Sadly while I was initially denied the pleasure, I was hoping some of it was still playing out this morning when I went to get Joey so we could pick up his truck.

"Hey Max," Kenzie threw her arms around me as she answered the door. "Come in, he's still in the shower." She stepped aside so I could walk past.

Just after Kenzie and Joe had tied the knot—before Layla had made her entrance—the two of them got serious. They did the grown up thing by buying property and dropped mega bucks on a sweet, newly renovated townhouse in Chelsea. The place was ridiculous, fully pimped out with a pool and everything and thankfully not turning either of them into douchebags. Not that I had been seriously concerned.

"There's my girl." I scooped up my goddaughter who had been too enthralled with some singing and dancing dinosaur on the television to notice I'd walked in.

Her cheeks puffed as her lips pulled into a grin, a squeal of delight being my reward as I twirled her around. Her giggles louder than what would seem reasonable given such a small package.

"She loves her uncle Max that's for sure." Kenzie watched amused as I planted kisses all over Layla's face.

"Yeah, well the feeling is mutual." Layla stopped squealing as I laid her against my chest. "And if anyone ever hurts her they better have their headstone picked out."

That wasn't idle talk either. The kid in my arms couldn't mean more than if she'd been my own and I'd throw down for her in a heartbeat.

"Ha, like there'd be anything left of them once I got done." Joey's hair was still wet as he strode into the living room, his face not looking morning fresh despite it being closer to the afternoon.

"You guys are both terrible." Kenzie held out her hands, her daughter mimicking the action. "God help any of her boy-friends." She laughed moving her daughter into her arms.

"No need to worry about that." Joey dismissed his wife, kissing his little girl's forehead. "She's never dating. Ever."

"Agreed." I nodded, willing to back up my best friend if any kid had the balls to ask her out.

"You're both delusional." Kenzie rolled her eyes, her smile mirrored by the sweet girl in her arms. "Now go get your truck, dumbass. Layla and I need a nap because I have a gig tonight." She shot me a wink before she left the room.

"So, how you feeling, Joe?" I popped the bastard right in the arm knowing full well his answer wasn't going to be "peachy, thanks."

"Why did you let me drink so much?" His fingers squeezed

the bridge of his nose. "I feel like an air bag exploded in my head."

"And ruin your great night?" I scoffed, the asshole big enough to make his own bad decisions. Especially ones that amused the hell out of me. "Not how I roll, brother."

"Yeah, well fuck you." Joey flipped me off. "Let's go get my fucking truck."

•••

Problem with karma was it went both ways. Joey had a motherfucking field day grilling me about what the score was with Beth. And despite being lit up, apparently noticed we didn't leave together nor seem to be together.

Which of course meant I had to come clean that while we weren't together I was planning on changing that. The heated stare he threw me from the passenger seat enough to tell me he didn't approve. Which was completely fine considering I didn't need his approval, my mind stuck on the one track.

"You better know what you're doing, Max." The evil looks hadn't been enough so he'd started verbal warnings as well. "This has epic fall out written all over it."

"Oh, because you would have just walked away from Kenzie if she'd said she wasn't interested. Yeah, I seem to remember how *okay* you were with it when she'd tried the let's-just-be-friends BS." He winced as I reminded him about his ass being sidelined over a massive misunderstanding. His girl had been willing to walk away except he hadn't been so keen.

"That was different." He swallowed, not having more of an argument.

"For you. Not for me."

And that was the end of that. He'd said his piece and I'd said mine, and we were happy to disagree. I'd delivered him to his truck and waved him on his way.

My morning charity efforts had left me hungry, so rather than heading back to my pad, I parked my ride in search of lunch.

The Raw Deal was bustling with activity. Every hipster, hippie or douchebag was itching to try their uncooked rabbit food which looked exactly as unappetizing as it sounded. But, right next door was a burger joint that made the best cheeseburger and chili fries I'd argue in Manhattan. And it gave me a warped sense of pleasure to walk past the vegan haunt and chow down on cooked meat. Yeah, I know that makes me an asshole but I didn't much care.

"Hey, I know you." I felt a tug at my arm.

Not for nothing but I got that a lot. Some days more than others, and usually after a photo or an autograph I was back on my way. No one mobbed us in New York, the residents spoiled for choice with the amount of celebrities living in its city limits. So I was all set to say hello and get on with the task at hand i.e. feeding my face, when I turned to see who it was getting my attention.

Funnily enough, I knew him too.

"Hey, dude. Don't think you do." The smug smile was unable to be suppressed. "Are you a fan?" I pulled off my shades so I could get a better look at him.

I was almost certain the dude wasn't a fan, and I knew exactly where he knew me from, but I wasn't giving him the satisfaction.

"I saw you the other night at Christina's." The asshole rounded out his shoulders, posturing like the fact he was almost seven-feet tall wasn't enough. And funnily enough, it didn't do shit because I couldn't give a rat's ass how big he was.

"Yeah, good food there. I go there a lot." The mention of Beth purposely avoided. If he wanted to ask me about her, he was going to have to man up and ask. I wasn't giving him a freebie.

"I wouldn't know, I've never eaten there. My sister is the host." And so continued our dance. I swear, conversation with Layla was more enthralling and the kid couldn't talk.

"Nice, well. It was great seeing you." I gave him a patronizing tap on the arm as I moved to the side. "Enjoy your tossed salad."

"I saw you there with Beth." The words barely coming out of the neanderthal's clenched grill. "She dating you now?"

It could have gone on longer, me curiously asking how he knew Beth or why he gave a fuck but I knew the answer and was already bored. Add to that hungry and couldn't understand what she'd ever seen in this guy, and you were somewhere in the neighborhood of my level of displeasure.

"Listen buddy, you seem like a nice guy but who Beth decides to date isn't really your concern is it?" And I was lying about him seeming like a nice guy, he *seemed* like a douchebag.

"It is when I assumed *we* were dating." The dumbass proved how much he didn't know as he continued. "That's fine, I'm not the possessive type. Just don't expect your little fling to last." It was his turn to be smug, except he sucked at it and didn't even come close to pulling it off.

No seriously.

Could this dickhead be more clueless?

Which is why I couldn't help but laugh. His big face contorted in confusion as I chuckled my ass off on the sidewalk. The bulge at the side of his neck only made it worse, my amusement kicked up a notch with his added fury.

"I'll be sure to let her know when I'm holding her tonight. And every night after."

So a few things.

It was a complete dick thing to say, but this asshole was trying my patience. And sure I could have gone another way without rubbing his nose in it but I think short of a note strapped to a brick aimed at the douchebag's head, he wasn't getting the hint. Which brought me to my last point, *saying* I was going to be holding Beth didn't make it true. Nor was it the gentlemanly thing to do, which I'm sure if she found out about it, she would be mega pissed. She'd be completely entitled to kick my ass or chew me out. All of which I would take willingly because I'd have deserved it. And yet I couldn't make myself take any of it back.

"See ya." I pushed past the asshole, his bulging neck and his bad attitude and proceeded to eat my burger, even though I'd lost part of my appetite.

It did highlight a pretty valid point.

If she assumed we were friends there was a chance she was probably going to date. Hopefully she'd recovered from the brain injury she'd suffered when she'd agreed to date that asshole and would raise her standards, but I'm sure there were more assholes to fill his spot.

Fucking great.

This was going to be soooooooooo much fun.

Dick.

Yep, I just called myself a dick.

Here we fucking go.

The coffee Max had hand delivered the morning after our *moment* hadn't been an isolated incident. And it wasn't just restricted to coffee. With Max proving what an amazing guy he was, even though he wasn't going to get lucky.

Monday morning had come and gone without incident with Jules and I reviewing our eventful weekend. Class was usual, with nothing remarkable happening through the day.

A runny nose here, a grazed knee there but all in all stock standard for a Monday. Except for late afternoon when instead of Jules meeting me at my classroom door to head home, Patricia, our assistant principal, appeared instead.

"Hi, Beth, just reminding you about the bowl-a-thon next Friday evening."

"I'm sorry, what?"

Every time I saw her, I had a hard time concentrating on what she was saying. Her well-coiffured hair was filled with so much Aqua Net, it hadn't moved since 1985. Which I could only guess tried to act as a distraction to the five pounds of foundation she was wearing, the thick matte finish getting caught in the deep crevasses of her face.

"The fundraiser for the art department," she announced slowly like I should know exactly what she was talking about. "We know it's not as much fun as a bake sale, but we really need for as many of our teachers to get behind it."

"Oh, yeah that." The mention sounded vaguely familiar, probably brought up at a staff meeting where I should have paid more attention.

"Yes, and lots of parents will be there too, it's a great opportunity to show your support for the school and their children. I've signed you up for the red team."

Which essentially was a courteous way of telling me my attendance was required unless I didn't value my job. Or I didn't support my kids, which would have been equally as bad. I guess my plans for next Friday night were set.

"Red team, are we having a pie eating contest?" Jules' face beamed at the doorway, her timing perfect.

"No, of course not." Patricia laughed obviously not aware at how serious Jules was. "It's a bowl-a-thon. I've signed you up too, Julie. You and Beth are partners."

It was only fair if I was roped into throwing a nine-pound ball and wearing someone else's shoes that she should get to share in that pleasure with me.

"Aww thanks, Patricia. I couldn't think of anyone better to be my partner." My grin widened as I glanced at Jules. No matter how much I was going to hate it, she was going to hate it more.

"Of course, it was the least I could do." She clapped her hands enthusiastically. "It's going to be so much fun, and the kids are so excited. We're even having pizza and soda."

"Wow, that *does* sound exciting." At least there was food there, beer would have been great too, but everyone was so PC these days. Alcohol at school functions was frowned upon, sadly.

"It sure is, and I have even managed to get a hamper donated from Bath and Body Works. Some lucky person is going to get a wonderful prize."

"Great. Can't wait." I nodded, thankful I had a couple of weeks to build some genuine excitement.

"Yeah, me too. How cool we get to do this together," Jules added, no one fooled by the fake smile she'd tried to muster up.

"Well, I'm just pleased you're both coming." Patricia straightened her strand of pearls, satisfied. "See you there."

We both watched as she left, the echo of her heels against the floor finally fading after she disappeared from view.

"This is our punishment for you being late, I hope you are happy." I laughed as I closed my classroom door, ready to get home and relax.

"Me? Please. She would have cornered you tomorrow or the day after, she had plenty of time to guilt us into going." Jules shoved off the blame as she kept up beside me.

"You're probably right. Ugh, you have no idea how much I hate bowling." My dislike was only superseded by camping, which I broke out in hives just at the thought.

"Don't even go there." Jules held her hand up, no doubt a story responsible for her strong reaction. Last time I bowled I slipped in the lane and landed on my ass. It didn't help that I was wearing a skirt at the time and flashed my panties. Worse still was my date didn't want to leave because he'd just bought a jug of beer."

"Who bowls in a skirt?" My head fell back as I laughed. "You were asking for trouble."

"Yeah, where were you then? Your advice means nothing

now." She mused sarcastically, our bowling night bound to be interesting.

It was when we eventually got home—having missed our original train—that my next surprise visit happened.

Having just changed out of my work clothes, a glass of wine in my hand when Ben the doorman knocked at our door, his shift having just ended.

"Hi Beth, Julie." He nodded politely at both of us. "I was told to give you this when you got home but was busy when you both came through the lobby. Here you go." He handed over a crisp white envelope that had my name handwritten on the front.

"What is it?" I turned over the envelope hoping that might gain me a clue, the back not presenting any further details.

"Ah, it's from Max Reynolds." He straightened on his heels as he eyed the envelope. "He mentioned you were old friends?"

"Yes, we are." I nodded, my heart racing a little faster than it should over stationery.

"He said sorry he wasn't able to deliver it himself but he was getting in late this evening. Have a good night, ladies." Ben delivered a curt bow before turning back down the hall.

"Ooooooo what is it?" Jules hovered over my shoulder as I peeled it open.

"I'm trying to find out." I pulled out a piece of thick card, Max's unmistakable handwriting all over it. My eyes scanned over the letters, my ability to read obviously missing.

"Well, don't keep me in suspense, what does the note say?" Jules tugged at my arm, her patience lasting less than a minute.

"He bought us dinner." I stared at the note confused, the information it contained making my head spin.

"Say what?" Jules stopped her tugging clearly as surprised as I was.

"Here read it yourself." I passed over the card partly for confirmation I hadn't either misunderstood or misread it. Yeah, because I had such a poor grasp on the English language that a few sentences would be too much.

"Beth, hope you had a great Monday." Jules' eyes glided over the note as she read out loud. "Stopped into Matteo's today, it's the Italian place down the street. His kid is a fan so I took some photos and signed some stuff. Figured you and Jules might want a night off from cooking. Call Matteo and he'll deliver whatever you ladies want. It's on me. PS. I ran into your "friend" from the restaurant yesterday, he was a *real* catch. I told him we were still dating. Don't be mad. Just remember what a nice guy I am—allowed you to poison me, and I am buying you and your roommate dinner. Smiley, winkey face."

Yep, she had read exactly what I had.

"Girl, I have to tell you." Jules handed me back the note that I stupidly reread. "Between this and the coffee, he is seriously winning some brownie points. He's not even sticking around for the adulation." She returned to tugging at my sleeve, her point of view not over. "And kudos on his work with micro penis. I wouldn't be mad; I'd be giving him a round of applause."

"Yeah, I know." Both gestures being incredibly sweet. "He has always been a great guy."

As Jules grabbed the phone—the allure of dinner cooked by someone else so exciting she couldn't wait another minute—I tucked the note away in my purse, not able to bear tossing it away. Our order placed a few minutes later.

The delivery came sooner than we expected. No doubt courtesy of a certain name that had organized the delivery in the first place. And the food had been absolutely beautiful. Jules and I even shared a bottle of wine, camping out on the living room floor as we watched television, the alcohol and full stomachs making us drowsy.

"I should call him." The thank you text I'd sent earlier not seeming thankful enough. "Should I call him?"

"You should call him." Jules nodded, fighting her own food coma. "And tell him I'm in love with him. Then tell him next time he needs to bring us dessert. I want banana cream pie, the nice kind from the place on 2nd."

Not that I needed Jules' endorsement—I was totally going to call—my fingers grabbed my phone and dialed, my breathing increasing while I waited for him to answer.

"Beth," Max answered, my name the only hello I needed. "You enjoy your dinner?"

"Yes, it was fantastic." I rolled onto my side, the last mouthful of pasta one bite too many. "Thank you so much."

"Tell him that I love him," Jules hollered from her place on the floor, not bothering to lift her head.

"Jules said she loves you," I repeated, almost positive he'd heard without my echo.

"Tell Jules, thanks." He laughed, the beautiful sound filling my ear.

"And that he should bring us pie, the nice one," Jules again called out, my foot managing to kick her but not before he'd heard.

"What about pie?" Max asked, clearly amused.

"She said next time you visit you should bring banana cream pie, from the bakery on 2nd."

I figured I might as well relay the message. Short of muzzling her, she was going to say whatever she wanted. I was surprised she hadn't already grabbed the phone.

"I'll do my best," he said, probably because he was too polite to tell Jules to take a hike. "But only if the two of you agree to come out and see us again Saturday night."

"Of course. What's your name this time?" That deal, an easy one to make.

"Dirty Secret." His voice rumbled through the phone causing us both to laugh.

"Okay, well send me the details through the week and I'll make sure we'll be there." *I wouldn't miss it for the world.*

"Awesome, will do. Goodnight, Beth."

"Goodnight."

"I'm gonna kill you." I tossed a pillow from the couch, my aim on target as it found its mark—her head. The blow not as hard as I would have liked but I was dealing with limited projectiles.

"What? He knows I was kidding. Lighten up." She tossed the pillow back and we continued to laugh.

It had been fun and games on Monday night—the good food, the wine, the safety of talking through a phone—but the conversation with Max had been great. No sexual undertones, no innuendo—just friends.

Tuesday brought its own surprise. Jules and I had noisily entered the foyer of our apartment building, still talking about work when Ben waved us over, calling our attention.

"Hey Ladies, hold up a minute. I've got something for you." Ben briefly disappeared into the office before emerging. A beautiful cardboard box placed on the counter in front of us.

"He didn't?" I looked at Jules as we both approached the box.

This time there had been no note, there didn't need to be. We all knew who it was from. My hand lifted the lid tentatively. Like there would be anything *other* than baked goods housed inside.

"The pie, of course." A perfectly-baked banana cream pie sat proudly at the bottom of the box, the freshly baked smell wafting up to my nose. "Thanks so much, Ben." I don't know why I was surprised. This was Max Reynolds, considerate, kind and a man of his word.

If I was honest with myself, it was probably more neighborly than needed, and even with our history he was going a little above and beyond the call of duty. But at that moment I didn't want to think about ulterior motives, the fact that I enjoyed it so much making me more than a little uncomfortable. I would happily bury my head in the sand a little while longer, I couldn't stop what I wouldn't acknowledge.

"No problem, ladies; enjoy the pie." Ben grinned, discreetly leaning over the counter to whisper. "He got me one too. It's from that nice bakery on 2nd."

"Okay, I said I loved him last night but now I *really* love him." Jules made ga-ga eyes at me, her hands clasped together like she was a Disney princess.

"You are not allowed to ask for anything else." I balanced the box while shoving her towards the elevator, happy to deflect my own feelings on Max's generosity and attention. "I swear, you're a menace."

"Hey no one is holding a gun to his head." She shrugged taking a healthy sniff of the sugar, cream and banana laden air.

The pie was delicious.

And of course I called to thank him for his incredibly thoughtful—and completely unnecessary—gift.

"Jules is considering replacing me with you as her best friend. Fair warning, not sure you're ready for that kind of crazy."

Max's chuckle played in my ear. "The pie was strategic. That transaction locks up our agreement. You don't come on Saturday night to my gig, I can sue you for breach of contract."

"I would have come anyway." I laughed, no intention of backing out having even entered my mind.

"Well you have to now, my new best friend will insist, I'm sure." I heard the smile in his voice, loving the easy conversation.

"Hey, I haven't been replaced just yet." I scoffed, barely able to contain my giggles. "Steady on."

"It's only Tuesday, sweetheart. You're history." He laughed before saying goodbye.

Wednesday came with no surprise coffee, dinner or pie and I hate to admit, but I was disappointed. Not because I wanted something—well other than to talk to him. So when I finally said goodnight and crawled into bed, I did so with an irrational sense of sadness. Which was pathetic.

Thursday morning came and so did my determination to not be a loser. He lived a few floors above me goddamn it, if I wanted to see or talk to him all I had to do was take an elevator. I also found it strange that in the past week I hadn't seen him around. What was even alarming was how much I desperately wanted to.

I checked my phone trying to rationalize if I had time before work—I could be quick, even if I woke him to say hello—when I saw there had been a text left through the night. The stupid thing had fallen under my bed and I hadn't heard the alert, my heart pounding as I opened the unread message.

*Hey Beth,*

*Working on new material so spending a lot of time at Angie's. Everyone says Hi. I'd hoped to stop by and see you tonight but it was super late when I got home. Figured I'd let you sleep. Maybe dinner*

*Friday? Well call it a take two, hopefully we won't run into anymore of your ex boyfriends, I don't think my body can take it. Tell my BFF I said hey. Talk soon. xx*

I smiled at the phone—because I was an idiot—just re reading the words over and over again. The warm feeling washed over me as I typed my response.

*Max,*

*Weds was ordinary. We had staff meeting so my brain was fried when I got home. Would have loved to have seen you, you should have woken me. Dinner sounds great, no more ex boyfriends and I'm never eating another strawberry again. I'm still trauma-tized. Are you sure you wouldn't prefer to go with your BFF? She's free Friday, just so you know.*

I ignored the judgmental digital display of my alarm clock telling me I needed to hurry up and get ready for work as I hit send. Being a few minutes late would be worth it.

Sadly my phone didn't ping back a reply—the telepathic wishing obviously failing—so I got my ass in gear and went to work, my mood infinitely better.

"Miss Hart," one on my students raised her hand.

"Yes, Monica?" I nodded my head waiting for her to go on.

English always got the most amount of questions. For a language that we speak every day there sure were a lot of exceptions, trying to explain it to kids—well, we'd get there eventually.

"Why is Miss Cornell at the door?" Monica pointed to the glass window of our classroom door, a very amused Jules waving from the outside.

"Um. Please excuse me, class." I rushed over to the door, expecting to hear someone had either died or she'd finally been busted for unauthorized playing with the instruments in the band room. It was probably the instruments.

"What's up," I whispered, my body hovering just outside the doorway. "Why aren't you in class?"

"They had gym, get out here." She pulled me out into the corridor, her face grinning so wide it might split apart.

My students leaned forward in their chairs trying to catch a word or two, the excitement of the interruption too much for many of them as they started to giggle.

"Everyone, sit down and read over what we were just learning." I spun around letting them know the show was over, and with their synchronized groans they went back to their books.

"Start talking." I nodded, knowing we probably had five minutes before the classroom descended into anarchy.

"Max sent flowers." She pointed to the colorful box on the floor at her feet, five stunning pink gerberas standing proudly from the box. "Aren't they beautiful?" She reached down and picked the box up bringing them to eye height.

"Why did he send them here?" I looked around for a card. "And why do you have them?"

"Because he sent them to me." She hugged the box proudly; the card I'd been searching for had been in her hand the whole time.

"What?" I tried to keep my voice lowered while trying to mentally calculate how long we'd been out in the hall. Three minutes? Four? And why did Jules get flowers and not me? Not that I was jealous. Okay, maybe just a little, which was crazy because there would never be anything between them. Okay so it's probably been five minutes. Crap.

"Hey, I'm just doing as instructed." She smiled smugly. "Apparently you need to check your phone. I can take your class."

I had no time to ask further questions, the rumbles from the class were starting to grow so we both walked and explained that Miss Cornell would be filling in for a few minutes while I took care of an emergency. And with my phone in my hand, I made my walk back out of my room and down the corridor pushing open the main doors. After all, the last thing I need was the faculty assuming I was sending a tweet or replying to a snap chat, I liked being gainfully employed thank you very much.

It was only once I was outside that I dared to look at my phone, the little envelope icon notifying me I had one unread message. Except I didn't get that far, my eyes catching on Max's Corvette parked across the street, the owner of the car relaxed as he leaned against the driver's side door, amused as he looked at me.

"Max," I didn't bother to read the message instead crossing to where he was parked, avoiding traffic so I didn't end up someone's hood ornament in the process. "What are you doing here?" I didn't hesitate and threw my arms around him in a hug.

"I wanted to give you these." He pulled out a colorful box similar to the one he'd sent Jules, except instead of flowers there were a dozen chocolate dipped strawberries sticking out with the tissue paper. "I was concerned about your trauma." He grinned.

"You have a death wish." I bumped his shoulder and accepted the box, my vow to never eat another strawberry in serious doubt. "And don't you think bringing them here is going to make it worse."

"Nope, I checked with a therapist." He pumped my shoulder back. "I have it on good authority that you can minimize the anxiety by . . ." He pulled out a piece of paper from his back pocket. "Presenting the stimuli in a relaxed setting with positive reinforcement."

"A therapist, huh?" I smiled; shaking my head he'd gone to this much trouble. "Thank you, they are beautiful."

"No problem. Just make sure you eat them before Friday." He winked, a beautiful smile lighting up his face.

"Consider it done. And Jules loved her flowers, I think she is probably wanting to marry you now." I couldn't help adding.

"Well as much as I like Jules, the flowers were strategic." He playfully bit his lip. "I knew you'd probably need someone to cover for you and she'd make sure you'd get out of class."

"And who would cover for her?" I asked. Unless he was either psychic or a stalker there is no way for him to have known she would have been available.

"I knew she'd work it out." He nodded, his assessment correct. She would have faked a fire drill if she were really under the pump. "See, I'm really *not* that nice a guy."

Oh nothing had ever been further from the truth.

"I should go." I looked between him, the box of strawberries and the school knowing I had run out of time. "I'll see you soon."

"Of course, see you Friday *and* Saturday." He didn't make a move to hug me goodbye, his body staying glued to his car. "Enjoy the rest of your day."

"Okay bye." I gave him a wave before crossing back over the road. My heart was beating a little faster and not from the quick jog across the asphalt in heels, that's for sure.

It was going to be a long couple of days.

# Fourteen
## Max

**H**oly. Mother. Of. God.

If I'd had a teacher like that I would have definitely stayed in school.

I'd never had the pleasure—and I am talking *pleasure*—of seeing her in her work clothes. And it really had been a crying fucking shame.

The white floral shirt she was wearing was made of some kind of flimsy material that, if I concentrated hard enough, I could see the outline of her bra.

Which would have been worth the aneurysm it may have caused.

But the show didn't end there; the do-you-see-me-don't-you-see me top was tucked neatly into a tight black skirt that went all the way to her knees, hugging her body like its life depended on it.

Well done.

The black patent-leather pumps were a nice touch too, adding not only a little height but also some rock and roll, which suited me just fine. And her beautiful long brown hair was pulled back off her face, the makeup kept minimal.

Hard not to imagine yanking up that skirt and putting my hands all over her ass. It's something I had lots of time to ponder as her hips Shakira-ed their way across the road as she headed back to class.

The week had been busy. And that was putting it mildly. The band had decided it was time to start writing and feeling out some new material, a new album not far in our future. And while I loved the process, being holed up for sometimes twelve to fifteen hours a day sometimes sucked donkey's balls.

And given I was seriously committed to showing her we could be friends without the horizontal hula, it was pissing me off I hadn't had time to see her. My work hours not syncing with hers forced me to get creative.

Which is what I did.

Her morning text gave me some extra inspiration.

And I was up to the challenge.

I didn't have to look too far.

Troy Harris.

While he boasted a successful career as the cymbal smasher for international rock band Power Station, he was also part owner of the label we were signed to. Add into the fact we'd known him and his buddies for a bunch of years, I was fairly comfortable calling him and asking to speak to his wife, Megs, who happened to be a psychologist. A few questions here and with her good sense of humor, I had all the information and technical terms I needed. It was either in poor taste or fucking hilarious, and I was happy to roll the dice on the chance it might make her smile.

Thankfully it had paid off and had given me an opportunity to see her, considering I was probably going to be working well into the night.

I was a good boy too, keeping my ass planted against my car

with my hands behaving themselves. But I wasn't fooling myself into thinking my epic restraint was going to last forever. Or that my actions were purely platonic.

Rearranging my dick in my pants—another reason my ass hadn't been in a hurry to move—I got back into my car and headed to my *office*. The place I'd been clock-punching the past few days—Angie's.

The session was solid. It was the usual back and forth with Rus being a smart-ass and Joey being tired. Angie was somewhere in between, tossing guitar picks at us whenever we got off track, which was a lot, my head not in the game.

"Hey, we're going to need to push back tomorrow/later today. Kenzie is recording all day, so I'll have Layla until six." Joey put down his sticks, the long ass day finally over. It had to be sometime after one in the morning, maybe two?

"Yeah, that's not going to work for me." I unplugged my bass from the amp and gave my hand a stretch. "I've got plans tomorrow."

Plans I had been waiting all week for in fact, and last thing I wanted to do was call Beth and cancel. Let's mark that under not going to happen.

"Later would suit me better too, actually." Angie rolled up the cord from her mic, siding with Joey's request. "Means I'll be able to spend some time with Zack before bedtime. Can you change your plans?"

"Nope, not really." I shook my head, wondering why the fuck we had to flip the script now. We'd been doing late nights all week, Friday was supposed to be our short day. Start at ten, wrap by five, which would give me time to get home shower, change and head out my door. Beth had even agreed to let me drive her, which gave me bonus time.

"Dude, what's so important." Rusty weighed in, not

understanding my hard-on for keeping to our original schedule. Not that I blamed him, I usually was happy to go with the flow. Not on this occasion.

"I'm having dinner with Beth." No point denying; they were going to find out anyway, and if there was going to be any mouthing off about I'd rather get it over with.

"Didn't you guys decide you weren't dating? Or did I miss something." Angie stopped rolling leads and gave me the look. Amazing how without any additional words she could say, "but seriously, asshole." It sure was a talent.

"We're not, it's just as friends." Ha ha fucking ha. Now I was a comedian as well.

"Oh, right. Keep telling yourself that, buddy." Rus walked over and clapped his hand around my neck and gave it shake. No one was fooled, my lack of conviction a big ole neon sign.

"Whatever, I don't think anyone in here has room to talk."

Each of these bastards had gone through their own shit-storm. Angie, well she had done the love/hate thing to death. Her and Jase went through hell and back with so much fucking baggage it was a wonder they'd made it through at all. Then Rusty and Alison had their own dramas. My asshole of a brother/Alison's deadbeat of a dad mixed with some ridiculously shitty circumstances meant the ride was far from smooth sailing for those two either. And don't get me started on Joey. The dumbass *accidently* knocked up one of our good friends—who was a fucking catch if ever there was—and he takes his sweet motherfucking time realizing he actually loves her. Far as I saw it, Beth and I were in the minor leagues.

"Well if you are just *friends*, what's the big deal in re-scheduling? Not like it's a date." Rus, aka the wiseass, decided I hadn't made myself clear enough before and wanted to needle me a little more.

"God, I hate you." I laughed. As much as I hated it, the bastard had a point.

"Once again, keep telling yourself that. I ain't buying any of it." Rus shrugged, freaking beaming that his point had been made.

Sure it wasn't a proper date, or any kind of date if you want to get technical, but I wasn't interested in postponing. Partly because I was desperate to spend more than ten minutes with her. With the other side of that coin being I didn't want her to think I was dicking her around. Dinner had been my suggestion. I didn't want to do the sorry-something's-come-up bullshit.

"Max, I know you have plans, but this is important." Angie shifted uncomfortably on her feet. It suddenly didn't feel like we were talking about whether a.m. or p.m. was a better option. "We get the hard work done now it means we get back in the studio soon. And I'm going to want to cut an album before the next baby's born."

What. The. Fuck.

Three sets of eyes got nailed to Angie, unsure if we'd just heard what we thought we just heard.

"Say what?" I'm pretty sure it came from my mouth although Joey was doing a whole lot of *huh?* as well.

"It's early, I'm only eight weeks, but yeah." She gave her non-existent bump a tap. "We're giving Zack a little brother or sister."

"That's awesome. Congrats." I closed the distance between us with a couple of steps and engulfed her in a hug; my head still reeling from the shock.

"Jason Irwin needs to keep his dick in his pants and stop knocking up our lead singer." Rusty gave Angie a pointed look even though no one actually believed he was pissed off, the freaking grin he was wearing a mile wide. "Fucking Power Station, don't they realize we haven't got time for domestication?"

"Shut the fuck up, not like you can talk." Angie flipped him and threw back a pointed look of her own.

Well then, I guess the newsflashes weren't done yet. And stop the fucking press, because I was still trying to get over the first one.

"Alison's pregnant?" Joey asked stealing the words right out of my mouth.

"Nooooooo." Rusty reared back, our guess obviously off the mark.

"Then what?" We were all too tired to play guessing games, so Rus either spilled really fucking soon or I was going to beat it out of him.

"I proposed." Rus leaned back on his heels, the bastard's chest puffing out like a freaking peacock. "Ali's been really gun-shy about the marriage thing so I've been waiting but I finally popped the question last night and she said yes. We're doing something small; a big wedding will probably freak her out."

"Congrats, man." I pulled him into a hug and slapped him on the back. It was high time they both put a ring on it and I for one couldn't be happier for them.

"What about you?" I turned to Joe wondering if we were going for a hat trick. "You got any life-altering announcements?"

"Layla ate oatmeal for the first time, other than that I got nothing." Joey shrugged, nothing further to add.

And thank fuck for that, the extra cargo and a wedding announcement more than exceeding the limit for excitement for one day.

"I'll change my plans," I heard myself saying even before I'd finished thinking it. Of course I would, not like I could refuse.

It really wasn't time to be an asshole, especially when it was just a dinner. Not that it made me feel any better about canceling. Oh no, I still felt like a complete cock but it was the right thing to do. For the greater good and all that.

Well.

Shit.

Tomorrow was going to really suck.

• • •

I had intended to wake up before Beth went to work to either knock on her door and tell her face-to-face or call her. Yeah, great fucking plan except some fucking dumbass forgot to set the alarm. By the time I'd managed to pull my eyes open, the morning was toast; the afternoon sun giving me the big middle finger as I got out of bed.

Fucking perfect.

There was no way in hell I was doing this via text and with my options drying up I was starting to get antsy. Pissed at myself and pissed at the situation. Oh, and I was also in a shitty mood, as well.

So, I could pout some more and feel sorry for myself, or I could try and salvage some of the situation. Without giving it any more thought I threw myself into the shower, into some clothes and was in my car ready to roll. The 'Vette's disgruntled roar matched my own vibe as I punched the gas to get where I was going.

By the time I'd made it to Beth's school, the grounds were almost deserted. The SUVs and Sedans that you'd expect to line the street had long gone.

Damn it.

My fist punched my steering wheel, the horn protesting under my hand. And because it had been real fucking helpful, I gave it a bitch slap too. If I was going to be sitting in my car acting crazy, might as well go all the way, right?

"Max?" Beth leaned into the open car window, her beautiful eyes clouded in confusion. She was either wondering what I was doing in front of her school or why I was abusing the dash of my car.

"Beth?" I wasn't sure if in my heavyweight bout with the interior I hadn't knocked myself out and was now seeing things.

"Ummm, you said seven, right?" Which was a nice way of saying, *what the fuck.*

"Yeah, I did but I'm not going to be able to make it." I cursed out a breath. "I'm sorry, Beth. I was really looking forward to it, but I can't." Not unless I could work out how to be in two places at the same time. That would be a handy trick right about now.

"So, you came here?" She was no less confused than before. Can't say I blamed her, I wasn't exactly making a lot of sense.

Rather than continue the conversation through the window of my car door, I got my ass off the seat and ejected. Her eyes followed me the entire time as I walked to where she stood, her hot-for-teacher outfit making my jeans tight where my junk was.

"I didn't want to leave you some bullshit message; that would be a shitty thing to do." Not to mention a total fucking cop out. "And I had every intention of catching you before you left this morning . . . look, it doesn't matter because it didn't happen. I just wanted you to know I'm sorry that I have to postpone tonight."

If I had any game at all it was truly MIA, my mouth doing its best to make me sound like a moron. Or a pussy. Maybe because I was and couldn't fess up that the reason I was so fucking desperate to see her had nothing to do with us being *friends*. Yeah, there was always that.

"Is everything okay? Nothing's wrong is there?" Her beautiful eyes nailed my ass, my attempt at it's-all-good failing miserably.

Not like I could tell her the truth. *It's been exactly one week since you called time out and I can't fucking do it.* Like that wouldn't get her power walking in the opposite direction.

"No, but I need to work." Not like it wasn't the truth. "If there was any way around it, I'd change it in a heartbeat."

"I know you would, and thanks for stopping by and telling me." She gave me a beautiful smile, and I reminded myself that kissing her would not be a good idea.

"Where's Jules?" The distraction needed if I was going to keep my hands to myself. "You going home by yourself?"

Her usual sidekick was nowhere to be seen. Odd considering they both taught at the same place and lived at the same place. You would think they'd share the commute.

"She got the stomach flu, it's not pretty so had to take a sick day. Needless to say I'll probably be coming solo tomorrow."

Well, that answered that. And I liked Jules, but wasn't I just too fucking pleased that her bestie wasn't going to be joining us tomorrow. Beth without the entourage equaled damn awesome by anyone's definition.

"I'm glad you're still coming."

She had a couple of valid excuses to cancel—the sick BFF the most obvious—so that she was still planning on showing up made me want to fist pump.

"Of course I am, we made a pie deal. I can't back out on

that."

I didn't care what deal it was, I was thankful. And I'd take my chances where I got them. Including the one that had unexpectedly presented itself. Girl needed a ride home, dude with a car standing right there. It was a beautiful thing. And as fucking *awesome* as it was standing on the sidewalk outside the upscale school that she taught at, I'd rather have her inside my ride. It would give me more time with her too. Desperate much? Yep, pretty sure I already fessed to that so no point hiding it now.

"Can I give you a ride home at least? Unless you were going somewhere else?" In which case I'd slap on my chauffeur hat and take her wherever she wanted. No problem at all. I had a full tank of gas and no issue being late. Considering I had reworked my plans for the band, they could deal.

"Nope, home is good. And I'd love that." She smiled as I opened the car door and watched her slide in.

Great.

The long way home it was.

**J**ules was still sick.

Whatever demon had possessed her wasn't letting her go just yet. It was like the exorcist, but with better hair. The last twenty-four hours far from pretty as she spent some quality time camped out on the bathroom floor connecting with Jesus.

"Are you sure you don't want anything before I go?" I cracked open the bathroom door just enough to toss her a Gatorade and bottle of Clorox. I really hoped she didn't get the two confused; one call to the Poison Information Line was enough for one lifetime.

"No, no get out of here before I infect you with the plague." She waved me off, her arms flapped wildly in front of her as she opened the Gatorade. Good, she got the right one. "Go live your life, be happy. See hot men on stage." She laid her head on her arm dramatically. "There's no hope for me, but you still have a chance."

She really had missed her calling. My head shook as I watched the theatrics on my bathroom floor, resisting the urge to tip her.

"Call me if you need anything." I gave her a wave from the doorway, short of sitting down in the hall and watching, there wasn't anything more I could do for her. And besides, I really wanted to go.

My nerves jangled wildly as I hopped into a cab, the ride not taking as long as I'd thought it would. The traffic gods had smiled on us, the cab pulling up to the destination just as they were letting people in the door.

Ordinarily, I hated to be among the first few people in the club, especially if I was alone. The awkward standing around while waiting for a band to go on sucked. But I wasn't making the same mistake as last time, crawling in at the last possible minute and getting stuck towards the back. Nope, not this time. I wanted a prime view and a spot right up front, which is why I sashayed my butt to Max's side of the stage and planned on waiting it out.

I knew he wouldn't be out in the bar till later; the under-cover band idea only worked if the band remained *undercover* until they hit the stage. But just knowing he was somewhere close gave me a cool shiver down my spine. I was excited to see him play.

"Can I buy you drink?" A voice startled me from my staring competition with Max's mic stand. Like if I had looked hard enough, he might appear on stage sooner.

"Ah, no thank you." I blinked trying to smile politely. "I'm meeting someone."

"My loss then." He gave a broad smile; his blue eyes twinkling like they'd been retouched with Photoshop. He walked away, probably to go find a more willing participant.

Drink guy hadn't been ugly. His well-maintained body was dressed in classic, neat casual clothes that probably cost more than my rent. Armani? Tom Ford? He looked good and he knew it. And a few weeks ago I would have been interested in that *drink*, but I wasn't anymore.

He did highlight a valid point. That I was standing in a bar with no drink. Actually, it might be a good idea if I avoided the alcohol all together. And it wasn't because I was worried about some creeper coming on to me. No, the real reason was I didn't want anything to dull my senses, I wanted to enjoy every second without the warm haze of alcohol around me. Besides Jules wasn't riding shotgun to make sure I didn't make a fool of myself, so it was better I didn't take a chance.

It seemed like forever. My toe tapped nervously on the floor as the overhead lights dimmed. The crowd didn't stop talking. Their loud voices tangled in the air as they waited to welcome an unknown bar band, *Dirty Secret,* they'd never heard of before. I smiled in the secret knowledge that they would soon find out that their low expectations couldn't be further from the truth.

Rusty's guitar rang out in the dark; a single strum before the wall of lights above them ignited and flooded the stage. Their little *secret* revealed.

The crowd erupted, realization sinking in that instead of some dime store rejects, they were getting an intimate show with Black Addiction. And it didn't take long before the crowd doubled, social networks spreading the word #TheyDidItAgain.

Seeing Max on stage never got old. It got better and better each time, his charisma winning over the audience as much as his playing. He oozed sex. The subtle nuances in the way he moved to the stroke of the strings on his bass—completely flawless. I'd felt firsthand how powerful those fingers could be, the sweet music he was teasing out of his bass not even close to what he'd been able to tease out of me.

Girls pushed against me as they tried to get closer, reaching out their hands with illicit intentions. The band laughed as they continued to play. Each song fed into another, and yet still the crowd demanded more.

And then it was finally over.

The house lights fired up again, as did the DJ music, and the crowd finally gave up the one-more-song they'd been chanting. And while the non-alcohol ban was still in place, if I didn't get a drink of something soon I was going to pass out. I was lightheaded, either from the heat or from the Max vortex of awesome—it could go either way.

"What are you having?" The bartender leaned across to try and hear me over the noise.

*Stick to the plan, stick to the plan.*

"I'll just have a Coke." Thankfully my mouth didn't let me down.

My heart beat wildly in my chest as Max and the band approached the bar. Their journey slowed by the crowd wanting a photo or an autograph, smartphones working overtime in order to capture the magic.

I hung back and waited, allowing Max to do his thing. My smile widened as he caught sight of me, a matching one of his own shot back in my direction.

He apparently didn't have the same idea about waiting, pulling me into a hug as soon as he was close enough. "I got to see you this time. I liked you looking at me."

"Do you realize how creepy that sounds?" I laughed as my arms wrapped around him, resisting the urge to bury my head in his chest. Me and my stupid ideas about keeping it non sexual. For a smart girl, I could sure act dumb.

"Nah, it's more conceited than creepy." He laughed back. "But if you want creepy, I'm sure I could think of something."

"Beth." Rusty pulled me from Max's arms and into his own. "How many times do I have to tell you? Bass players are just guitarists that didn't make it. You're better off just watching me." Rus was riding solo tonight, his girlfriend nowhere to be seen.

"Your ego sure hasn't gotten smaller." I returned the hug before giving him a playful shove. "I'm surprised it hasn't got its own zip code."

"Hey, Beth." Another hug, this time from Joey. "Don't listen to either of these jerk offs. Everyone knows the drummer is where it's at. We can be hidden behind the kit and *still* get more attention."

"Not a virtue, Joey." I shook my head, not realizing how much I'd missed this, missed all of them. "Where's Angie?" One Black Addiction member not accounted for.

"She had to sneak off early. Plans with the husband." Max winked as he moved closer, his lips at my ear so I could hear him. "You should call her; I know she'd love to see you again."

And now that he was no longer touching me, I really wanted it. To lay my head against his chest while he spoke, his arm slung around my waist like old times. It felt like it was the easiest thing to do, but he wasn't mine anymore. A choice I'd made. But tonight I didn't care. I was all about the prerogative to change my mind, and I didn't care what people thought. Or if I had the right to do so.

"You were really great tonight." My arms wrapped around his waist with no intention of leaving, a smile creeping on his lips. Good. He didn't look like he was going to remind me we weren't doing the touching thing anymore.

"Thank you." He took his cue from me and let an arm move across to my hip, inching me in closer. "I'm glad you enjoyed it."

Not as much as I was enjoying it now.

"How's Jules? Still sick?" he asked, my mind wander interrupted by important things. Like the health of my friend who I'd yet to think about.

"Deathly so. She'll probably have perished by the time I get back." I threw caution to the wind, silliness prevailing.

"That bad huh?" He grinned.

"Probably worse." I giggled like an idiot. No shit, I'm pretty sure I threw my head back and everything.

"You're not drinking tonight." His eyes dipped down to my hands that were noticeably without a glass. The half-sipped Coke I'd been drinking abandoned earlier at the bar. "Anything I can get you?"

"Not at this bar, but if you take me home I can give you a list," I whispered only half-joking.

"Sorry?" He lowered his head in an effort to hear me better. Or maybe he had heard, his *what-did-you-say?* more out of surprise than lack of volume.

"Nothing, it's been a long week, so I thought I'd give the drinking a pass." I completely chickened out and substituted for a more appropriate answer.

"Oh, well if you want to go, we can leave." He looked around the crowded bar and then back to me. And he seemed serious too. Ready to throw in the towel all because I had agreed to let him drive me home and I was *tired*.

God, could he be any more thoughtful?

"We can stay awhile; I don't mind." I was so torn. Ready for the two of us to say our goodbyes and be alone, but knowing he should probably stay. It's not like I was really tired, the bed I was looking to get in not my own.

Crap. Was I really considering it? Sex with Max again?

Did I break my own rules?

Would it just confuse us both?

Sadly, common sense wasn't running the show tonight as I threw it all out the window. The old Beth pushed through the cracks, and the old Beth wanted Max.

Unfortunately, *stay awhile* was a very broad directive. Max was sucked from one conversation into the next, chatting amicably with fans. And why the hell shouldn't he? After all, *I'd* said I didn't mind; it's not like he could mind read.

Finally, he either got the subliminal messages I'd been trying to send or exhausted people to talk to, and we said our goodbyes. My heart pounded so hard in my chest as he took my hand, I was worried he'd be able to hear it rattling around in my chest cavity. Or feel my hammering pulse that was racing out of control. All of which I was trying to hide as we walked out to a side street where he'd parked his car. *Nothing to see here, move right along,* fooling no one as he kept looking at me strangely. Probably wondering if I was going to suddenly go into cardiac arrest on the short walk.

And thank god the car wasn't far, his prized Corvette shining under a streetlight. Of course, the danger now was that I would throw him down on the hood so we could make out. The no back seat was a problem too. My smile tightened as he unlocked the car and held open the door.

*Just get in and stop thinking crazy,* my subconscious rationalized; the rest of me convinced it wasn't going to uphold their side of the bargain.

"You good?" He turned to look at me before starting the ignition. My crazy eyes as my internal debate wore on, not helping.

"Yep, all good here." My head nodded, crazy smile joining crazy eyes in the worst display of *all good* I'd ever seen. Awesome, he was probably going to have me committed by the end of the ride, any seduction I was trying for failing miserably.

My eyes stayed glued to the window as the miles passed. My mouth stayed shut too, because I didn't trust it. Not with words and certainly not if it got anywhere close to Max's. It would be a mutiny—tongue and lips flying at him in reckless abandon. Oh, please lord, just let this ride end quickly.

When we finally arrived at our parking garage, I breathed a sigh of relief. My knuckles had gone white from gripping the upholstery so tight; I was sure I'd left nail marks in the leather. Shame considering I'd rather be leaving them in his back. *Just get out of the car, get out of the car.* My hand fumbled with the handle as I threw myself from the car before he'd even shut off the ignition.

He was probably thinking I was either A: acting like a basket case because I had completely lost my mind, or B: was acting like a basket case because I had completely lost my mind. In which case, he was probably going to kiss me goodnight and go on his merry way. So, this was totally going to be my move.

Which I was fine about.

Girl power and all that.

I waited patiently as we entered into the elevator; his hand instinctively went to press the button for my floor.

Well, that wouldn't do.

Not at all.

Girl power, remember?

I was sooooo getting laid.

Before his finger had a chance to make contact with the console, I pulled his hand away; his brow scrunched in confusion as I pressed the button for his floor.

It wasn't subtle either. The big round illuminated number

shining like a beacon. Not the place where I'd find my own bed, which meant . . .

It took him a second.

Just one.

His body stalked closer, forcing me back against the mirrored wall of the elevator. His breath tickled my neck as he closed whatever distance there had been. While I may have started it, he was taking control, no further encouragement needed.

"I've waited a really long time for this." He moved his hands up to my jaw and pressed his mouth against mine. My lips parting for him as he explored me with his tongue.

My body felt like it was going to combust as I struggled to get closer; the ridge of his cock teasing me through his jeans threatening to drive me crazy. Those claw marks I'd left in his leather were *nothing* compared to what I had planned.

"I thought you were fine being friends?" My fingers twisted in his hair as his lips moved to my neck. "But in case you haven't worked it out, I've changed my mind." You know, in case he missed the memo or that my hands were probably going to have to be surgically removed from his body.

"I was never okay with it." He sucked hard against my throat, the warm sting spreading across my skin. "I told you I wasn't going to be good with that plan." And boy did he mean it, his hands palming my breast as he worked his length against me.

There was no more talking, our mouths finding better things to do. Which was a good thing, because I wasn't sure I could have formulated words. They were highly overrated anyway.

"God, I want you right here." Max's lips traveled down my neck again as he clawed at my clothes. And like the god he'd been praying to him heard, the elevator pinged as we reached our destination.

He didn't hesitate, pulling me through the separated metal doors as I kissed him back hard.

Thankfully no one on the fiftieth floor had a burning desire to step outside their door. The hallway remained empty as we continued with our elicit display, his neighbors missing one hell of a show.

Not that I would have stopped at this point. Not a chance. I was hungry for him, my body bowing against him having been deprived too long.

It was by some miracle that we didn't drop to the floor right there on his doorstep. Close enough, right? Who needed something as silly as a bedroom? But with some wicked coordination, all our legs and arms managed to make it inside Max's apartment. His hands deserved the most credit, performing the almost impossible task of unlocking the door while continuing to touch me.

Seriously, I still don't know how we did it.

Tom Cruise in *Mission Impossible* had nothing on us.

"I hope you don't have plans for tomorrow, because I'm not going let you leave my bed." He walked me backwards in the dark toward his bedroom, his mouth only off me long enough to talk.

"That's a big call considering I'm not even in there now," I teased back, completely aware that if I did have any plans they would be canceled.

"I'm a *big call* kind of guy."

Well, that didn't really need to be said.

Oh, he was talking about the *call*.

Uh-hmm.

It wasn't slow, and that was more than fine with me, our

bodies hitting the mattress as we continued to grind against each other. The bed beneath us a much better venue for what was about to go down, not that its lack would have stopped me. That talk of combusting wasn't just talk, the friction from our clothes alone enough to start a fire. That's exactly what it felt like too, like the fabric was burning against my skin.

"Off," he demanded, his fingers sliding down my zipper of my dress so fast I wasn't sure he hadn't broken it. Not that I cared; I had no use for it any more. The offending object up over my head before he needed to ask again.

It wasn't just *my* clothes that were offensive, his jeans and shirt also on that list. My hands worked overtime in a combined effort with his—all of his clothes disappearing from his body.

"Wow." I ran my hands along his beautiful, toned abdomen, my hands fully appreciating what my eyes were straining to see.

"I'm naked and you're not." He grinned, taking care of my bra with a flick of his fingers. My panties were the next victim; their fate sealed as I shoved them down my hips and reunited them with the rest of our clothes.

"Max." I moaned, unable to stay upright as his fingers moved up my legs, his body kneeling between them exposing me completely.

It was dark, but not completely black; a stream of light from the partially-opened drapes filling the room with a soft golden aura. Just enough for me to see exactly what was coming for me.

His hands moved down my thighs, his lips twisting into a grin before he lowered his head, his tongue lapping at my core as he pushed in a finger.

"Yes." I struggled to keep my eyes open, wanting to get lost in the sensation, his lips curling around my clit as he sucked hard.

His mouth had always been talented, add those fingers to the mix and it wasn't going to take long, my nipples hardening as my fingers moved across my breasts. His eyes darkened as he watched me twist my tight pink peaks.

"I like you watching me." I threw back the same line he'd given me earlier, my mouth curling into a smile. "I want you to watch me suck your dick."

"You can have whatever you want after I make you come." He tossed back a grin of his own as his fingers pumped inside of me. His thumb also got in on the action, sweeping over my clit, sending shivers down my body.

"You want my cock, sweetheart?" he teased, his fingers thrusting into me as he watched my hips buck against them.

"Yes," I begged as I fell apart, my body splintering around his hand as it shook.

"God, I love watching you come." His fingers slowed down while they continued to move, my core convulsing against him, my body unable to stop.

The wave was still moving through my body as my back snapped off the bed and pushed him down on the mattress. "We had an agreement; now I'm going to take what I want."

I didn't ask for permission, lifting myself off the bed as I knelt in front of him. My hands gripped him tight, slowly moving up and down, twisting when I reached the head. His face inches from mine as I jerked him off, getting harder as I lowered my head.

My lips stretched around his hard cock as my eyes flicked up to meet his. His body jerking as I got a long and hard suck, my mouth sealed tight around him.

"Fuck, Beth." His fingers threaded into my hair as he

cradled the back of my neck, my fingers gripping him while I continued to suck.

My eyes stayed on his as I watched his lids lower, the rock of his hips trying to fight the urge to go faster as I licked and sucked the length of his dick.

I loved having him in my mouth, watching his body tense as my lips and tongue played with him. Over and over again. First fast, then slow—getting him to the brink before pulling back. The power was completely in my hands—and my mouth.

My lips popped, the suction broken as he pulled his cock free from my mouth. "Condom on or off, Beth? Because I need to be inside of you, now." His hand gently stroked his shaft as he waited for me to answer.

"Off." My mouth answered before my brain had a chance to weigh in. The need in me just as desperate as it was in him.

The green light was all he needed.

Pushing me back down to the mattress, he wasted no time. The head of his cock circled my entrance as I struggled to stay still.

"I want you so bad." The words barely audible as his eyes moved across my body.

The cords of muscle along his neck flexed as he braced both his fists on the bed and thrust into me. His cock slid in, my body tensing at the invasion.

"Relax, sweetheart," he whispered into my ear as he gently slid out and then back in again, my core stretching to accommodate him.

I couldn't think; every inch of me tingling as he filled me. His face inches away from mine as he grabbed my hips and pushed into me, my pussy accepting his entire length.

"Yes," I screamed, my fingers clawing at his back as I pulled him closer wanting every inch he had to give me. "Yes, harder."

"Fuck, yes." He cursed out a breath, his fingers gripping my skin so tight I was sure it was going to bruise.

Tilting my hips so he could get in deeper, he drove in so hard my back lifted off the bed, his hands on my hips the only thing keeping us connected. Over and over again he pistoned into me, his body dominating mine while I struggled to keep up.

"I'm going to come," I screamed as I felt the nerves in my body go haywire, my limbs feeling like jelly as the momentum built.

"Look at me, Beth." His jaw tensed as he continued, his own body coiled so tight I was sure he must be close too. "Right here, I want to see you."

Without any thought—my ability to think completely obliterated—I gave him what he wanted. My eyes on him as my entire body shuddered, giving way underneath him as everything exploded inside.

"Beth," he moaned, his body tensing as he found his own release pumping his hot load into me. "Yes." He continued to move, teasing my body until I couldn't stop shaking.

He collapsed beside me, rolling my body to the side with his arm as he panted heavily. My own breathing out of control as I laid there boneless; my arms and legs refusing to move.

It wasn't just my limbs that were failing to cooperate, everything else offline as I tried to form a sentence. Say something—anything—that would make sense.

Max's lips pressed against the back of my neck, his hand moving to my breast as he pulled me closer. "No take backs this time. This is exactly where we need to be."

I didn't argue. Mostly because I couldn't. My brain misfired on random thoughts. None of them involved me staying away.

"Okay," I mumbled, forcing my mouth to operate so he

knew I was still awake.

I had no idea what I was actually agreeing to. But I was too tired and too blissed out to care. All I knew was that I wanted to be in Max's arms, and in his bed, and that's where I was. And I was going to enjoy every second of it.

# Sixteen

# Max

**I had been prepared to wait a little longer.** Give her space, while keeping my hand in the game. And short of her telling me to fuck off, I wasn't going anywhere.

Seeing her tonight while I was on stage was like a kick right to the nuts, and it took everything I had not to go with my gut and kiss her the minute I got close enough. Of course the black dress wasn't helping, wrapping that tight little body of hers while hinting at what was underneath was torture. Not that I could have looked away if I'd tried.

Nope, I kept my eyes on her the entire night and she did the same, staying front and center instead of hiding out in the back like last time. And it was a total douchebag move but it made my chest puff out a little wider knowing that she was down there looking at me.

Getting her into bed tonight hadn't been the plan. Kiss goodnight—probably. Letting my hands linger longer than I should—most definitely, but sex . . . well, let's chalk that up to didn't think it was going to happen. So, imagine my pure fucking delight that something had changed her mind. No shit, I was laying beside her feeling like a fucking superhero.

My need to touch her didn't end after the sex. No fucking way. Even though we'd basically fucked each other to exhaustion, my hands stayed on her as I tucked her up close.

My fingers traced circles on her back while she slept, the tips ghosting her skin, barely making contact. Like I needed the reminder she was real, the how-the-hell-did-that-just-happen still tossing around in my mind as I refused to close my eyes.

Of course, I had no idea what was going to happen when she eventually woke up. If we were going to go through the same bullshit we-should-be-friends crap we'd gone through the first time. Not that it mattered; this time around I was winning that debate.

She was so fucking adorable, mumbling as she turned in her sleep. Even better, now her face was inches away and I had to talk myself out of Sleeping Beauty-ing her. Those pouty lips begged for mine as her lashes gently bounced off her cheeks. Yep, no way I was letting her call time out a second time.

"Max." Her hands reached for me in her drowsy haze, her eyes still shut leading me to believe she was still asleep.

"I'm here, baby." My hand moved to her hip as she settled back into dreamland.

Never in my life had my name sounded as good as it did at that moment on her lips. Completely unprompted, unaware and wanting me. Gave me a head swell a mile fucking wide with a grin to match.

Not sure how long I watched her, but I kept my eyes on her until my lids started to fall, and eventually when I couldn't stay awake a minute longer, I fell asleep.

●●●

If you ever asked a guy what's the ultimate way he'd like to be woken up, almost every single one would reply—blowjob. No hesitation just boom, answer. And the ones that don't are flat-out lying. Oh, they might tell you just having their girl beside them is enough, but I guarantee you once you wore him down he would eventually come clean. There is something so fucking sexy about opening your eyes and seeing your cock between the lips of a beautiful woman.

Blowjob.

Every. Single. Time.

Which is why, when I cracked my eyes opened and saw Beth between my legs with my dick in her mouth, I almost blew my load right there. No shit, ultimate fucking turn-on, and I had to blink a few times just to make sure I wasn't dreaming.

She took me deep, her lips stretching around me as she sucked hard. Her hand, tight around the base, glided up and down as her tongue swirled around the head, her technique so fucking perfect I was sure no other blowjob would ever measure up.

"Jesus, Beth." My hands bunched up the sheets either side of me, my balls so tight I was positive they were going to explode. "You're going to make me come if you keep doing that."

She tried to smile, her effort coming up short on account that her mouth was full—no seriously, did it get any better than this—and ignored me while she continued what she was doing.

"Fuck." I bit hard on my bottom lip wanting to stave off the inevitable. My body was at war with itself, unable to decide if it wanted her to keep going or to fucking end it all now.

In the end the choice was made for me, her fingers curling around my balls and sucking me so hard it was either come or lose function of my dick altogether. The tidal wave rolled through me hard as my curses echoed off the walls, every single part of me tingling like I'd been zapped by an electric fence. And she swallowed every last drop.

"Okay, you're going to need to give me a minute, or five, so I can regain some feeling in my legs." My dick twitched as she pulled it out of her mouth. "Then I want to play."

"Maybe later." She licked her lips and tossing her hair off her shoulder. "I should probably go for a run." She made a move to get off the bed. "I need to go to my apartment and—"

"Waaaaaaiiiiiitttt a sec, Missy." She didn't get a chance to finish, my hand catching her arm and pulling her back down. "Do you not remember what I said last night? Pretty sure I was really fucking clear."

"Come on, Max. We can't stay in bed all day." She laughed, wiggling around as I strengthened my hold. She could do the shimmy all she wanted; she wasn't going anywhere, anytime fast.

"Like hell we can't, and you already agreed, so don't pretend this is news." I nipped at her shoulder, my cock pressing up against the seam of her ass. And would you look at that, looks like the bastard was already warming up for round two.

"I haven't been to the gym in so long I'm sure my ass has started to jiggle." She laughed, not fully grasping I was not freaking joking.

"Beth, trust me when I say I have looked at every square inch of your ass and it's fucking perfect. You're not going anywhere."

And that was the god's honest truth. Her ass was a work of fucking art—it didn't get any better—so, whatever *jiggle* she was seeing was clearly a fucking illusion of some sort. Maybe she needed better mirrors.

"So, what are we going to do all day?"

"Well first I'm going to go down on you." My hand moved across her stomach and then dipped into the cleft of her pussy. Mmm and what do you know, sucking my cock didn't just turn *me* on. "And then we're going to go from there." My fingers moved across her clit in slow steady circles. "Or maybe we do something else. I'm more of a fly-by-the-seat-of-my-pants kind of guy. No need to plan everything out."

"I-I think I like fly-by-the-seat-of-your-pants." She moaned as my fingers moved a little faster, her hand reaching down and resting on top of mine.

"You want to touch yourself, sweetheart?" My finger slid inside of her as she rocked against me. My dick completely hard considering she'd been stroking it with her ass while I played with her pussy.

"Yes." She arched back against me, pushing my dick further against her ass, my other hand pinching the nipple of one of her tits.

"I think I would like to see you play, baby. But only if I get to play too."

While the current position was fucking stellar—my hand finger-fucking her while she grinded against my dick with her ass—it wasn't the easiest position to see. And if she was going to be reaching down and touching herself then I sure as hell wanted to be able to eyeball that.

Not a problem. Just a little maneuvering and we were back to business. The kind where she comes with my cock buried inside her while she fingers herself. I almost couldn't think about it, the thought alone juicing me up so bad it was making my balls ache.

"Move to the edge of the bed, baby." Both my dick and my hand protested as I shuffled to the end of the mattress. "I need you over here." I watched as she moved, her hand sweeping down between her legs as she relocated to where I was. Fucking perfect.

"Legs down." I planted my feet on the floor and stood up. My hands on her thighs guided her legs to hang off the edge, parting her wide so I could see her slick and ready pussy.

Now I wasn't so sure that the blowjob was the best way to wake up. I'd say it would be a coin toss as whether that *or* having a beautiful, wet pussy in front of you would be the better way to go. And wasn't I just the lucky son of a bitch who was getting both.

"That's it, sweetheart." I watched as her fingers moved a little faster, my dick jerking as my hand made contact. "Wow, baby, you're so wet."

Automatically, I sunk to my knees, my mouth on her as she continued to play. My tongue fucked her, getting coated in all she had to offer as it moved in and out of her.

She moaned, her ass lifting off the bed as her fingers moved faster, her hips bucking against my face while I kept up my assault. She tasted amazing, thick and sweet like honey and I couldn't get enough, pushing my tongue deeper into her.

"M-a-x." My name broken down into three syllables, arching her back as she moaned, my dick begging to get in the game.

I could have stayed down there and been a very happy man. Have her come on my face while she rubbed that beautiful pussy of hers, but my cock wasn't down with that plan. He had been bouncing all around doing the pick-me-coach-pick-me since we started this game, and I wasn't able to hold him off any longer.

My feet gripped the floor as I moved up the bed, my hard-on in my hand as I rubbed it against her. Her fingers alternated between touching me and touching herself, all slick and sticky with each delicious pass.

"You ready for me?" Because I needed inside of her in the worst possible way.

"Yes." She guided me to where she wanted me to be, the directions not necessary as I pushed in deep, the contact making her come hard against my dick.

"Oh yeah." I pumped, her tight pussy gripping me hard as I thrust in and out of her feeling every single pulse traveling along the length of my dick. "That feels so fucking good."

So. Good.

"Come for me." Her hips got in time with mine as I continued to pump, my balls drawing up tight as I got close. "I want you to come all over my breasts."

Correction.

That was pretty much all I needed and I was going to come.

I pulled out just in time, my dick jerking in my hand as my jizz spilled onto her beautiful tits, her hands spreading it across her skin.

Fuck the blowjob.

That was a thousand times better.

It was with a sick sense of satisfaction that I looked at her, her hands sticky both from me and from her, and I don't think I'd ever seen anything sexier. Fuck *PornHub*, I had all the spank bank material I needed for the rest of my life.

"You like that?" I climbed onto the bed, watching her shuffle back up the mattress, her hands still on her tits.

"I loved that." She couldn't even hide the grin. I liked seeing her happy, and knowing I had something to do with it. Oh, and PS. we were both going to need a shower.

"See, aren't you glad you didn't go for your *run*?" Like there had been any danger of that, my plans for her not even close to being done.

"Fine, I'll admit your idea was better." She rolled her eyes. "I guess I'm still technically getting a work out."

"You bet your non-jiggly ass you are."

•••

So, no surprise, there was shower sex.

Yep, who didn't see that happening?

Not that it had started that way but you put the two of us into a small, wet confined space with some soap and it was bound to happen. It was actually efficient of us if you really think about it. Getting clean *while* getting busy. It was a how-to in time saving. Not to mention it made the washing up infinitely more interesting.

When we finally got out of the shower, I bent a little on the staying in bed rule. She wanted to make sure her roommate hadn't actually died through the night like she threatened, and wanted a fresh set of clothes to change into. So, she headed to her apartment while I got dressed, deciding we were going to need breakfast. Or possibly lunch, considering I wasn't sure what time it was. In any case, both of us were starving. The ten million calories we burned might have had something to do with it, or maybe it was that we both hadn't eaten since yesterday, but refueling was critical.

I hadn't done much food shopping since moving in, so eating in wasn't an option. Which sucked because being out in public meant I had to keep my hands to myself. Not because I was worried about some asshole snapping our picture—couldn't give a fuck who saw us together—it was more about me not wanting to risk a public indecency charge. Now that I was allowed to touch her, I was having a hard time not to.

While my redress took only a few minutes, it took a lot longer for Beth. No doubt she'd been slowed by the twenty questions from Jules, so factoring all of that in, I assumed it would be at least thirty minutes before she was back. Longer if Jules was still dying.

So rather than sit on my hands or burn a hole through the floor pacing like a loser, I grabbed my cell and checked my messages. It was exactly where I'd left it last night, in the pocket of my jeans on my bedroom floor. No message, call or email close to being important enough for me to have given a shit before now.

As predicted, there were a few messages. A couple were of the female variety, those girls soon to get the thanks-but-no-thanks, see ya, bye. I wasn't the kind of guy to jerk anyone around, but I was no longer interested in anyone whose name didn't start with B and end with eth. Very specific and that's the way I wanted to keep it.

Two were from Joey at varying stages of delirium. The first asking if sleep deprivation could increase penis size, because he was positive his dick looked bigger, and the second was to let me know he bought a timpani while online shopping at three a.m. Apparently, he needed one, so I'm sure it was a relief to everyone that he found one. I shook my head and hoped to God he didn't follow Jason's lead and knock up his wife again. At least not until the poor bastard had some sleep.

Thankfully Jules had survived, Beth arriving back at my pad dressed in jeans and a T-shirt not too long after.

It fucking floored me how stunning she looked every single time I saw her. There wasn't a girl in the world that could even get close to that kind of beautiful. It didn't matter if she was wearing sweats with no makeup or a tight dress ready to go out, she owned it and knocked me on my ass.

"So, we're going out for breakfast?" She sat on the edge of the bed while I pulled on a shirt.

"I figured if I'm going to have sex with you all day, I should at least feed you. It would be the responsible thing to do." I smirked, thinking maybe we should just order in. Surely there was some deli or something that delivered?

"Smart. You are so clever." She pressed her hands against my lower abs; the need for food no longer seeing important. "I'm starving."

It wasn't supposed to be sexy.

The word wasn't loaded with suggestion or elongated for flirt factor. She was just hungry. For Food. And yet, watching her lips move around the letters made me instantly hard. Like a fucking deviant. And what was worse was I didn't actually care.

Nope.

Not even the slightest.

Instead I expedited the process, hauling her ass out of my apartment so quick her feet barely touched the ground.

Food and then sex.

Lots of it.

If she had a problem with it, she sure as hell didn't show it. Whatever objection she'd had with us getting together had been shelved. And I wasn't giving her the opportunity to change her mind.

When I moved from the Bronx to Manhattan, it wasn't just my area code that changed. I figured it was time for me to grow up and ditch my more-relaxed lifestyle. Plans, schedules—weren't super important to me before, but now it's how I mostly ran my life. That didn't mean I became anal type-A with no sense of spontaneity, it just meant that having a plan wasn't the worst thing in the world.

But, if the situation called for it, I would totally get retro and loosen the reins. And the current situation was one I was going to have to play on the fly.

I had had no intention of ever getting back together with Max. Happy for him to have been part of my yesterday while I looked to tomorrow.

But things change.

I'd tried to stay away.

Really, I tried.

And I sucked at it.

Predictably, I ended up where I always had, with Max and in his bed. Really, not sure why I bothered to fight it, I had such a bad track record. So, rather than beat myself up about it or tell myself I should walk away, I gave in.

*What's the worst that can happen?*

Yeah, I know, I was tempting fate.

The weekend had been awesome. I didn't even pretend like I hadn't enjoyed every second of being around Max. It was just like old times except, better. We laughed, we talked and we had a lot of sex.

A. Lot. Of. Sex.

Sleeping, not so much.

Which is why Monday morning when I crawled backed to my apartment to get ready for work, I had needed a coffee with a Red Bull chaser and an ice pack for my vagina. Probably a couple of Motrin as well.

"You know I'm pissed at you, right?" Jules handed me my second cup of coffee as I slipped on my shoes. "The guy is basically the Energizer Bunny with a huge dick; this was supposed to be my fairytale."

"Oh, I'm sorry." I pouted not even trying to pretend I was sorry. "I'll try not to enjoy it, and it's not that great." I lied, trying not to laugh. "Those little blue birds that fly around us when we have sex like they do in *Snow White* are really distracting."

"Oh, that's sick." Jules screwed her face up in mock disgust. "High five." She raised her hand waiting for me to reciprocate.

"We are not high fiving over sex, Jules." Her palm left un-slapped as I gulped the rest of my coffee and put the cup in the sink. "We didn't turn into frat boys last time I checked."

She rolled her eyes completely unimpressed. "Won't talk about his dick, won't high five over sex . . . remind me again why we are friends?"

"Because no one else in this town will have us." I laughed,

grabbing my purse and pointing toward the door. "And we need to leave now or we're going to be late."

Mondays were always difficult. It was hard enough for an adult to sit still and pay attention after two days running free, for a child—well it was a wonder why teachers didn't have a hip flask and a healthy whiskey addiction by lunchtime. Okay, so maybe some did. Not looking at anyone—*cough*, Mrs. Chapman, *cough*.

So after getting through the first half of the day with no tears from either me or the children, I was glad to get to the teacher's lounge and get something to eat. The Red Bull and coffee might have been a good idea this morning, but by ten I was regretting not following up with at least a bagel.

"Ladies." Rita Moson, one of the first grade teachers sat down beside me. Her perfect blonde hair, her perfect face and perfect body all coordinated like she'd just stepped out of the pages of Vanity Fair. "Did you have a good weekend?" Her brows lifted a little too enthusiastically.

"Yeah, it was great." I smiled politely and took a bite of my chicken salad, trying to wonder why the sudden interest. "How was yours?"

I figured it was the courteous thing to do considering she'd asked about mine. Even though I really didn't care. We had never been close friends, her tastes being a little too *pink angora cardigan* for my liking.

"You do anything *special?*" Another raised eyebrow, this time accompanied by a smile.

Jules and I looked at each other puzzled, unsure if this was some secret code we were supposed to know. A staff memo we'd missed? Maybe a new initiative?

"Well, I was sick—" Jules hadn't even finished her sentence when Rita cut her off.

"Not you, Julie. I mean Beth." She laughed, her exaggerated fake eyelashes winking like a spider was having a seizure on her face. "Or should I say, *someone* special."

Oh. Wow.

There was a conversation I hadn't expected.

How the hell did she know, and how the hell did I answer that? *So yeah, we spent the entire weekend screwing each other's brains out, but he's not my boyfriend or anything.* She'd have that shit on the internal circulation quicker than you could say hello, office gossip. Yeah, would really prefer not to deal with that. It was only freaking Monday; surely I had until Wednesday before I had to deal with crazy.

"Come on, Beth." Rita batted my arm softly before lowering her voice. "No need to be coy; it's all over the internet about you going home with Max Reynolds. You know, the hot bass player from Black Addiction."

"Oh, Max. Yeah, he lives in our building. Just moved there." I waved her off pretending to be bored, hoping my disinterest would throw her off the scent. Not likely given the look on her face.

"You looked rather cozy in the photos. Rather affectionate for a neighbor, wouldn't you say?"

Oh she was good. The sweetness balanced with the sarcasm to form the perfect mix of I-don't-believe-you.

"We're friends, I've known him for a long time." All true, something she could have probably found out herself if she'd widened her Google search.

"Yes, I saw that. You guys dated before he was famous."

So, she *had* Googled. Could've saved us all a lot of time if she'd led with that.

"Yep, all true." I smiled, hoping this would be the end of the conversation but knowing it probably wasn't. Today hadn't been a good day for food, my chicken salad in front of me remaining uneaten.

"He's awesome," Jules chimed in, her addition to the conversation welcomed. She was right there so helping to deflect attention would be much appreciated.

"Oh, I bet he is." Rita fanned herself, her pretty pink nails waving in front of her face. "So, you two aren't dating?"

"Max and I?" My head shook as I couldn't help but giggle. Not because it was funny, but because well, I didn't really know. We'd slept together but that wasn't what she'd asked and there was distinct difference between *are you having sex with Max* verses *are you dating Max.* "No, we're not dating."

"So, can you introduce me?" Her eyes flew open with excitement, her lashes threatening to fly off her face. "You know, I have a little thing for him. All girls want to have at least one time with a *bad boy.*"

Oh, please, no. She couldn't be serious? She wanted to meet Max and hopefully fill her bad boy quota? I didn't know whether to laugh or be disgusted.

"Well, I'm not really sure if he's interested in dating at the moment." Completely true, not like I'd asked and I hadn't seen him with any other girls. "He is really busy. The band takes up a lot of his time."

"One meeting. Come on, Beth," she pleaded, her hands wrapping around my arm in a show of desperation. "Just invite him out to drinks or something, you don't even have to stick around."

Because that made it so much better. Here, hook me up with *your* friend to earn *me* cool points but don't hang around or anything. Did the bleach she used to dye her hair—spoiler alert, she wasn't a natural blonde—seep into her brain? Let's file that under, not going to happen.

"Look, Rita." I was really trying to be cordial, the lounge filled with our colleagues not to mention the principal. "I'll mention it, but I can't make any promises. Chances are he'll probably say no." *As in hell no, over my dead body.*

It didn't matter whether or not he wasn't dating *me*, he could not date her.

As in ever.

Not even as a joke.

At all.

No.

"Okay, well do the best you can, huh?" She fluffed up her golden mane of greatness and gave me a smile. "I'd *really* like to meet him."

No shit. And still the answer was going to be an n-oh!

"Sure, will do." I gave her a finger wave as she returned to her posse of pink angora cardigan wearers. No doubt with news that I wasn't dating Max Reynolds and with any luck, she would be. Which totally had the same probability of an asteroid smashing through the window and killing us all in the next thirty seconds.

Oh, look. We're all still alive. Guess it sucks to be her then.

"Can you believe that?" I tried to replay it back in my head slower to see if it made more sense the second time around. Nope, still lame.

Jules laughed, not even trying to be discreet. "I was totally going to jump in there, but you seemed to be handling it."

"I stopped short of telling her Hell hadn't frozen over yet; I think that deserves a cookie." I eyed the vending machine, my salad no longer appealing.

"You totally do, me too because I had to listen to it." Jules pulled out a few crumpled dollar bills, the cookies obviously her treat. "But, I think you should totally set them up, but only if we get to go on the date."

She didn't give me a chance to answer, stalking to the vending machine and gathering cookies. The plastic wrapping crinkled in her hand as she handed over my reward.

"Are you insane?" I pulled open the wrapper, the fresh cookie smell making my mouth water. "Even *if* I hated Max, I wouldn't set him up with her, and I don't hate him." A piece of chocolate chip was tossed in my mouth. Yum. Almost got rid of the Rita after taste. Almost.

"No, you loooooooove him." Jules shot me googly eyes as she took a bite out of her treat.

"Are you twelve? I don't looooooove him." I countered with some googly eyes of my own to illustrate how ridiculous she was being. "We're friends."

"Who had sex," she pointed out, in case anyone had forgotten.

"Who care for each other," I corrected. It hadn't been sex without emotion, I'd always cared about him. Probably would until the day I died, but love? I just . . . didn't know.

"So, put yourself out of your misery already and date him."

"Maybe."

It wasn't that I didn't want to date Max; I mean I really, *really* liked dating him. He was an awesome boyfriend, an amazing lover and a great friend. But like always, we hadn't really *defined* what we were doing. I hadn't asked him if this was just a friends with benefit thing—something we'd done. Or if it was a relationship thing—something we'd also done. Orrrrr, if it was a casual sex thing that happened from time to time—something we'd also done. So, there really was no precedent, which really was an occupational hazard with us.

As much as I found him irresistible, there had been a reason I'd tried to stay away. My heart wanted more, and I was almost positive his wouldn't. He cared for me, sure, but more than that? It was a question I was too worried to ask. If he said no, it would hurt this time and I had walked away to avoid that kind of hurt.

We should probably stop it.

Like *after* this time.

The day progressed as normal. I wasn't hijacked in the hall by some other breathy debutant wanting a hook up so that was a plus. And other than an email from Rita reminding me to *try*, there was no further discussion of the sexy Black Addiction bassist. Another win. Not that my mind strayed far from him, our weekend together dominating my mind. The two text messages—one sweet and one dirty—he'd sent me, also made it hard to forget.

Classes ended with Jules and I heading back to the apartment. It was good to get home, waving to Ben on our way to the elevator, the doors opening when we'd reached our floor.

Of course getting home introduced a whole new set of problems.

Did I call him? Was I going to see him tonight? When was the next time we were going to have sex again? See, we really did have issues, me taking out my phone and scrolling through to his number no less than five times.

Gah.

I should probably not call.

My eyes were still locked on the screen when it started ringing in my hand. The name of the caller displayed on the screen. Max.

"Hey." I tried to sound cool, vowing to not bring up the should-I-call debate with him. "How are you?"

Oohhhhhh because *that* sounded cool; my saving grace was

he didn't see my face palm.

"I'm good, tired." He yawned followed by a laugh. "*Someone* kept me up most of the night and I've been at Angie's all day. Just getting into the car now actually; thought I'd call and see if you wanted to do dinner."

Whatever concerns I'd had eased when I spoke to him. He had a way of pushing back any lingering doubts and questions and for everything just to *be* with us. It was a calm that I couldn't explain, a stillness that I craved. Like he was able to center me just with words.

"Dinner sounds nice, but Jules and I were about to make something here." I cringed wanting to spend another evening with Max but being aware I'd been MIA all weekend. "I kind of don't want to ditch her." Especially as I had already offered to cook to make up for being gone while she was sick.

"That's cool, have you got enough for one more?" Max asked without any hesitation.

"You want to eat dinner with us?"

"Sure, I'm game. I mean what's the worst thing that could happen." He laughed, not needing to remind me what was the worst that could happen.

"I'm never going to live that down, am I?" My head fell in my palm, still horrified about my own stupidity.

"Nope, are you cool with a house guest, or am I forced to fend for myself?" The amusement playing in his voice as he spoke. "I would like to point out that I will happily pick up any ice cream of your choice for dessert."

"Ice cream, huh?" Not that he needed to sweeten the deal, but who could ever say no to a good-looking man with ice cream. That was a no brainer.

"Deal." Who was I kidding, even if he showed up empty handed, I was going to want to see him. He'd just made it a whole lot easier. He was great like that.

"See you soon, text me what flavor you want." The ignition started, the roar of his engine making it harder to hear.

"Sure, will do. See you soon." I ended the call; the grin I was wearing threatening to split my face apart.

"Jules, we're having company," I called out, the night taking an unexpected up turn. And I couldn't wait to see him.

# Eighteen

# Max

**I**'d made the decision when I kissed her goodbye on Monday morning that I'd be seeing her as much as possible. Why? Because I wanted to, and it felt like she'd wanted that too. And as far as I could see there was no reason to hold back.

I didn't care if inviting myself to dinner made me seem desperate. My life wasn't a fucking national survey, and I'd do what I wanted. Completely no fucks given on what anyone else thought, unless it was her. So, as long as she had no problem with having an extra mouth to feed—which she didn't—I was party crashing.

Dinner had been really nice. Nothing fancy, just some Hamburger Helper, crusty bread and a salad but it tasted amazing. Sitting in her kitchen, just the three of us, talking felt good. sort of like old times when she used to crash with me and Joey. Except this time it had been reversed and it was me who was crashing. Which was completely cool with me. And it was fucking awesome having a home cooked meal instead of take out.

The conversation had been easy too.

"How's the song writing going?" Beth asked in between

mouthfuls, the question lacking the usual obligation it normally attracted when asked. It was like she genuinely wanted to know and not fishing for when the album would be done or needing a conversation filler.

"It's going well. Lots of material. I'm writing this particular song about a girl who drugs this guy." I couldn't help but grin watching her face morph from the smile she'd been wearing into horror. "I think it would sell well."

"You wouldn't dare." Her eyes narrowed, my laugh spelling out I had been joking. "And it's still not funny."

"I disagree, I think it's hilarious." Jules weighed in, her head nodding in agreement. "Go ahead, Max. Number-one hit for sure."

Jules having an opinion was nothing new and I loved how both of them seemed real when they were around me. In a sea of people trying to please me, it was a welcome change.

"So, what about you ladies? How's school?" And I genuinely wanted to know, finding out what had happened during Beth's day pretty high on my priority list.

"It was fine." Beth gave me a tight smile, part of the conversation obviously missing. The sideways glance at Jules a hint, I was probably right.

"Really? Just fine?" I probed, curious as to what the story was. And when Beth was cagey, there was always a story.

"Yeah, everything was great," she added, the smile and the words not convincing.

"I'm going to go, and . . ." Jules rose to her feet and looked at us both. "Yeah, something needs doing surely." And if that wasn't a big freaking sign there was something that needed discussing then I didn't know shit.

"Something you're not telling me?" I didn't bother continuing the charade. More than just a little curious as to why she was being evasive.

"Some pictures of us are online." She hesitated before adding, "Together."

Pictures of me and who I was with often turned up online. It was par for the course. I didn't even notice the cameras anymore so it wasn't even on my radar. I didn't even think to give Beth a head's up that it might happen.

"Does that bother you?" I'd never cared on whether a girl gave a shit about it or not, but with Beth it was different.

"No, I mean. It's just weird because it's just me." She shrugged, not offering more of an explanation. "I guess it's a slow news day."

I was fairly sure there was more to it than one picture but I didn't push, figuring I had all kinds of time to get more info. I wasn't in a hurry; nope I want to savor every second I had with her. So, while she seemed to be done with that, we moved on to random every-day shit. Everything and nothing, at no time did it seem awkward.

And when it was time for bed, rather than kiss her goodbye and head out the door, I extended my invitation.

"I'm thinking I should stay." My lips traveled up her neck, our feet moving towards her bedroom. "I have something important I need to do."

"Oh really?" She didn't fight me, pulling off my shirt as we made our way to her bed. "And what's that?"

"Making you come." I licked my lips, wanting to taste her more than anything. "Don't get me wrong, dinner and the conversation was awesome, but I promised to bring dessert and I'm a man of my word."

"We ate the ice cream." She whimpered as my hand lowered to in between her thighs, my fingers desperate to get to skin.

"Then consider this the cherry on top."

Leaving her wasn't an option, and if I was honest, it wasn't just about sex. I didn't give jack about whether it was her mattress or mine that got the pleasure; feeling her beside me when I fell asleep, the only criteria I needed.

I could have gone home sometime in the early morning. Got a couple of hours more sleep, her alarm sounding way earlier than mine. But I would trade a few less Z's for more hours with her any day of the week and twice on Sundays.

Even woke up a little before we needed to be so I could give her a wake up of my own.

Best. Start. Ever.

And I only agreed to let her shower by herself, because I knew if I got in there with her, it would end up taking three times as long. Her schedule not as flexible as mine.

"Hey, big guy." Jules punched me in the arm. "Sleep well?" The grin on her face told me she was more than aware that not a lot of sleeping had gone on.

"Great actually." I took a mouthful of coffee as I stood in the middle of their kitchen. It was how I liked to enjoy my morning cup. On my feet, the cold tile underneath—substituting kitchens didn't bother me. "Never better."

"Riiiiiigggggghhhhht." She nodded, probably having heard more than she should. And if I'd had any decency, I might have been embarrassed. Not that she seemed to be. Looked like it was a win/win all around.

"So, I was wondering if you have plans for Friday night?" She rocked back onto her feet, her work gear already sorted as she waited for Beth to get ready.

"You asking me out on a date?" I bit back a grin. Not that there'd been a chance, but it was fun to watch her squirm.

"Hahahahha. No." The exaggerated laugh proving she knew

I'd been kidding. "I need a tiny favor." She pinched together her fingers giving me the visual cue. "It's actually more for Beth than me."

Well, wasn't that just the magic word. *It's for Beth* would pretty much guarantee I'd do anything. Need a spare hand? Sure, let me cut off mine.

"This Friday?" I waited for her to nod. "Nope, nothing solid. What did you need?"

Jules took a deep breath, which meant she was either going to spill one hell of a story or she was nervous, and I wasn't sure which was better.

"We have this thing, sort of like a fundraiser—a bowl-a-thon." Her mouth raced without taking a break. "And we both volunteered to go; Beth's really excited about it. It's only a couple of hours, but I don't think I'm going to be able to make it which means she'll be without a partner. I know she'd be so disappointed if she didn't get to go, you know. So, I thought maybe I'd just find a replacement for me. There's a cute single dad at school; I could totally ask, but I figured I'd see if you were interested first." She took a big suck of air, almost passing out from her detailed rundown.

I chose to ignore that part about the *cute single dad*, because that shit just pissed me off. And it was too early in the morning for me to be throwing back some verbal gymnastics of my own, so I let that slide. Plus, I knew when I was being baited, and Jules had the line out, lured and hooked just waiting for a nibble.

Wasn't happening.

She also seemed to have a case of motherfucking amnesia, failing to remember I'd known Beth a long time. Bowling? Please, I'd have a better chance getting her excited about going to a car wash.

"Beth doesn't like bowling." My arms folded across my chest wondering where the fuck this was going. Like it or not, I was interested so dismissing it wasn't an option.

"Well, of course she doesn't," Jules threw back her hand with a complete lack of surprise. "No one really *likes* bowling, but it's a great opportunity for her. To show how invested she is in the school community, how dedicated she is to the kids." She continued to lay it on thick. "Like extra credit. And her work means a lot to her."

Well, that part went without saying.

"So you want me to take your place?" It didn't make any more sense saying it out loud, the request very much of the WTF variety. And I was still no closer to knowing what the subtext was, because *bowling* sure as fuck wasn't it.

"Yep, exactly. It will be fun." She paused between each word and nodded her head. "But you can't tell her." Her smile evaporating as she got serious. "She'll just tell you it's no big deal because she knows you're busy." Her hand waved in front of her trying to illustrate her point. "But think of how cool it will be to meet the people we work with?"

Jules threw out another line and I couldn't help but take a bite.

"Something about this feels really shady. Don't you think blindsiding her is a shitty thing to do?"

We'd already established I'd do pretty much whatever when it came to Beth. Spending time with her—a given, tell me where and when and it was a done deal. Meeting the people she worked with—sure, see above. I'd have done all of it willingly.

If she'd asked.

Which she hadn't.

Soooooooooo.

Let's go over this one more time shall we?

"Blindsiding her?" Jules laughed, her happy-happy not convincing me there wasn't something else going on. "All I'm asking you to do is take my place on the team. That's all, nothing at all shady."

"This has bad idea written all over it, and you know it." Fuck, everyone knew it. Not to mention that if this blew up in my face, it would be the most epic fall out of all time.

"Fine, I'll get the cute single dad. It's probably for the best anyway, and I know he won't mention it."

And there it was again. Wasn't getting ignored a second time, and I didn't give a shit on whether or not she was serious. Even the hypothetical of her pairing up with this dude was giving me a nervous twitch. Which meant that Jules had snagged herself a two-hundred-pound asshole—me. And all that she'd needed was a bigger net. Well done. God, I hope I didn't end up regretting it.

"Yeah, that isn't going to happen. Give me the details."

"Thanks, Max. You're such a big help." She gave me another pop in the biceps, pleased beyond measure that whatever her objective was, had been met. "Dress nice though, huh. Not Meta Gala nice, a couple of steps down from there."

"Yeah, no problem." Bullshit, something told me it was very much going to be a *problem*.

Not that I had time to explore what that might be, Beth coming out of the bathroom not a minute later. The conversation was iced as I took a good look at her, the fitted dark-blue dress she was wearing making my balls ache with need.

"I'll be seeing you tonight." I lifted her chin and kissed her lips, the fact we had an audience not deterring me. "Your place or mine, I'll let you decide."

"Fine." She smiled, her arms wrapping around my chest as

she nuzzled in close. "I'll call you later."

"All I needed to hear." I gave her another kiss, Jules developing a sudden need to clear her throat as my mouth gave Beth something to remember. The *see ya* coming sooner than I would have liked.

It was the first time in a long time I didn't want to head to the studio, the drive to Angie's harder than it usually was.

It was a good distraction though, being with the band an awesome way of filing in time while Beth worked. It beat the hell out of sitting around my apartment like a loser, and with Angie once again in the family way, the hours of productivity were going to be reducing soon. Morning sickness, fatigue, moodiness—it was a roll of the dice on what we were going to get. Which is why we were putting in the hours now.

The week was pretty intense.

Holed-up in Angie's studio while we worked through material. What sounded good, what blew, and getting a solid list together so we could narrow what would eventually make it to our next album.

It wasn't all work, Joey and Rusty filling the breaks with comedic relief. Their back and forth probably partly due to fatigue, with each day running into the next. It would have been easy to go crazy, the walls seeming to close in, but at the end of each day came my little slice of awesome, giving me exactly the recharge I needed.

"Hi," she mumbled, her voice still thick from sleep as she answered the door. "I was worried you might miss dinner, so I saved you some." Her eyes slowly blinked struggling to stay open.

"Thanks, I'll grab it later. Let's get you back to bed."

It was my usual routine, coming home after a session with my only interests being a shower, food and Beth. Not necessarily in that order. And lucky for me I was able to combine Beth with the other two—showering and eating were better when shared. And sure, sometimes there was actual food involved too.

Every night she'd opened her door, no questions asked or demands made. Her body slipped effortlessly into my arms. And I couldn't be happier if I'd tried.

Work, Beth, Sleep—repeat.

It was probably the only thing getting me through the days, knowing what my reward would be when I finally saw her. Half the time we didn't even talk, both of us having better things to do with our mouths. Which was why—probably against my better judgment—my surprise bowling date wasn't mentioned.

The day got closer, and I hadn't so much at hinted that I had a clue. Besides, part of me was curious on what the grand reveal was going to be. We all knew something was coming and it had nothing to do with ten pins and a fucking ball.

Thankfully, I didn't have to wait too long. The long days with the band and nights with Beth finally got us to the end of the week.

Friday was textbook ordinary.

Rus and Angie were going back and forth over whether a different key would add more value on the current song while Joey was insisting we needed to use the timpani he bought.

Usually it would have pissed me off, but I couldn't wipe the smile off my face. Especially knowing we got to call time out early because it was Friday and I had a surprise date with my girl; it just made all the craziness worthwhile.

Sure, tensions were screwed a little tighter than usual. Add into the mix that Angie announced we were going to start recording in two weeks and suddenly it wasn't playtime anymore.

"A few more undercover gigs and then we pull the pin." Rus unplugged his guitar. "And I say we try some of the new stuff on the next one."

"Agreed." Angie nodded, grabbing a couple of bottles of water out of the nearby fridge. "We've got twenty songs completed plus the two we're working on. Playing a couple live will help us narrow them down."

To which a bunch of *yeahs* were tossed around and we said our goodbyes. Wrapping up early had worked in my favor. I was able to get home, shower—by myself this time unfortunately—and change before heading out. Jules had already given me the details of where I had to be along with a thumbs up emoji for keeping my mouth shut. I guess that's what I got for giving her my phone number, the few messages I'd received were like modern day hieroglyphics.

I hadn't seen the inside of a bowling alley in years, the trip through the double glass doors taking me back in time. Just not *my* lifetime.

With a distinct 1950's feel, *Pins* was too new-penny-shiny to be authentic. My guess was the walls had seen more than just one coat of paint over the years, the checkerboard linoleum floor buffed to mirror-finish perfection. Even the soundtrack was keeping the theme, Buddy Holly singing about "Peggy Sue" as kids and adults were tossing balls down lanes, laughing and talking as they did it.

"Oh my God." I heard the gasp from behind, my plan to find Beth quietly probably not going to happen. "You're Max Reynolds."

It always amused me when someone told me who I was. Like the fact was surprising to me as well as them. I wasn't sure it was something I'd ever get used to, but I made sure I didn't come across as an asshole when I did the "yeah, I am."

"Hi." I turned around and gave the blonde a smile. "I prefer just Max, the whole name usually means I'm in some kind of trouble." My eyes did a quick left and right but came up empty. "I'm actually looking for a friend."

"Beth invited you?" Her eyes Christmas-lighted as she took a step closer. "I can't believe you are really here." Her hand reached out and retracted suddenly like she thought better of whatever it was she'd planned. "Wow, I mean just wow."

What made me do the double take wasn't that she was star struck, but that she'd mentioned the exact person I'd come to see. Coincidence? Not when Jules was involved. Yep, this had her name written all over it.

"You know Beth?"

"Well of course, we teach together." She giggled, the fact they work together hilarious. "Didn't she mention that when she spoke about me?"

This time it was my turn to look like a deer in headlights. I had no idea what this girl was talking about, but her eager smile told me I probably should.

"It's been a busy week; we haven't had a lot of time to talk." Well that was the truth, not a lot of actually talking had gone on and even less of it had been about her teacher buddies. Blondie, was on the list of things that weren't discussed.

"Oh, of course. Sorry. I'm Rita." She shoved out her hand, the adding of her name not helping my lack of clue. "So, are you sticking around or you just stopping by to say hi?" Her fingers wrapped tightly around mine, a little friendlier than I'd expected.

"I'm sticking around." I tried to unpeel her hand while still being polite. "I'll be here for as long as Beth needs me to be." I'd hoped the mention of her might remind Rita I was here for someone particular. And sadly that wasn't her.

"That's very considerate of you. She's lucky to have such a good friend." Her hand cocked on her hip as she pushed out her tits, the friendly smile hinting at something else.

Was she fucking flirting? I mean, it looked like she was, her pouty-lip-look-at-my-tits combo was a dead giveaway, but if she knew about me and Beth . . . maybe I was wrong.

"I'd say we're both lucky." *Not everyone wants to suck your dick, asshole.* "Is she around?"

"Sure, she's chatting to some of the parents," She moved a little close, her voice dropping to almost a whisper. "But she won't mind if we get to know each other a little better first. There's a little courtyard out back."

Correction, this woman most definitely wanted to suck my dick.

"Not sure that's such a good idea." Also, wasn't going to happen, but I didn't want to be a total asshole.

"She knows about my intentions, if that's what you're worried about." The hand that had been doing the should-I-shouldn't-I reached out and rubbed up and down my arm. "She's totally okay with it."

What the actual fuck? Call me crazy, but I highly doubt Beth would be cool with me sticking my cock in this woman.

"Well, I should go say hello, let her know I'm here." And I might not be Einstein but if she wasn't suggesting we have sex then I'd had no fucking idea. Short of her offering me a hand job, I was doubtful this conversation could get worse, her eyes flicking down to the fly of my jeans not leaving any doubt.

"Well, if that's what you want to do." Her disappointment spelled out by her pouty frown. "But don't be too long. I *really* want to get to know you better."

I'm fairly confident I knew which part too, and it wasn't my stellar personality.

"Okay, talk soon." I gave her a wave as my feet and I did a bail out. Me and her not happening. Not in this lifetime. I moved through the crowd of people as I looked for Beth.

One thing Rita had reinforced was I was no longer interested in other women. Sure, I hadn't so much as looked at another girl since our reconnection but it was more than that. Like I was legit not interested. A girl could strip naked, get on her knees in front of me and my dick would still have a case of the snooze.

Beth was it for me. I mean really *it*. And I sure as hell couldn't replace her. She was a once in a lifetime, and no amount of time or other women would tell me different.

It was while I was giving thanks to the universe that I finally saw her. In the mix with all the noise and she made time stand still. You just couldn't help but stare. Dressed casually in jeans and a T-shirt, she was beautiful, and I had to wait a minute just to take it in.

I loved times like this, watching her when she didn't know I was looking, just to see her like that in all her pure perfection.

Someone around her said something that made her laugh, her head tilting back as her face lit up as she giggled. The unrestrained happiness was intoxicating, could make me feel good even on my worst days and that smile of hers—the kind a man would go to war for.

It was hard not to march my ass right up to where she was and claim her mouth right there. Not because I gave a shit her boss was watching, or there were kids around—I wasn't altruistic enough to give a fuck. The reason I didn't was because I knew that once I started I wasn't going to be able to stop. One kiss with her would never be enough. Not tonight, not ever.

"Heard you might be short a partner." I snuck up behind her, my hands finding their home on her hips. "I'm here to lend my services."

I didn't need to say anymore, her body turning between my fingers so she turned to face me, my appearance unexpected if the look on her face was anything to go by.

"Jules." She smiled, my girl smart enough to put the pieces of the puzzle together really quickly. "I should have known when she called earlier and said she would probably be late."

"Yeah, take it from me. She isn't coming." And whether this had been her grand scheme or not, I didn't give a shit. The reasons for me being there were no longer relevant.

"So not a surprise." She grabbed my hand, ignoring the audience who either had no idea of who I was or why I was there. "I can't say I'm disappointed."

Well, at least that made two of us.

"Come out here for a second." Her smile wide as she led me to the courtyard. Interesting choice of venue considering it's what her friend had suggested earlier, but I guess there weren't a lot of options that didn't include a crowd. It seemed I was destined to end up there one way or another. Which brought up another interesting point.

"I have a question for you." I stopped the minute the air hit our skin. "Your friend Rita, is she interested in everyone's cock or just mine?"

# Nineteen
## Beth

"**O**h shit, you met Rita?"

News of Jules and her bogus excuses were sidelined by the latest development. The annoyingly bubbly blonde somehow secured her own meeting without my assistance, like a freaking ninja. Did she repel down the wall the minute he walked in? Although *how* was irrelevant right now, judging by his reaction she hadn't been subtle.

"Yep, we met." He smirked, the raised eyebrow hinting that there was more. "Although I don't think it was as memorable as she would have liked. Anything you want to tell me?"

Ummmmmmmm. Yeah. There was that.

I'd never expected their paths to cross so mentioning Rita and her quest to dirty up her dating history seemed un-necessary. There was also the fact that I didn't want to ever see them together, so I swept that under the rug for *a cold day in hell.* It wasn't even a possibility as far as I was concerned; no need to even mention it.

Of course, it wasn't so hypothetical now.

Fuuuuuuuuuuccccck.

Seriously, the chances were zero. I swear I was going to kill Jules when I saw her next. I didn't care whether or not it was actually her fault; I was totally laying responsibility at her feet.

"Rita *may* have asked me to introduce you to her." I winced, wondering how much I was going to have to admit.

"Seemed like there was a little more than that. Keep going." The smile got wider as he waved his hand urging me to continue.

"She has a thing for you, wanted you to be her bad boy," I blurted out, his eyes searing me. "I think she wanted to sleep with you." Please, God, don't let him consider it. Not her. I mean, I didn't want him with anyone, but especially not her.

"And considering I'm dating *you,* that makes sense how?" He tilted his head to the side and let his words settle.

Hold. The. Fucking. Phone.

What did he say?

No seriously, what the hell did he just say, because I think the floor wax from the lanes must have wafted up my nose and fried my brain.

"We're dating?" I said a little louder than I'd intended, my voice rising a couple of octaves in the confusion. It sounded just as bad coming out of my mouth as it had rattling around in my head, my hope not to sound like a moron well and truly dashed.

"Are you serious?" Max looked on amused, like it hadn't occurred to him that we'd been doing anything but, the laugh that followed hopefully meaning he wasn't pissed. "I assumed you got the vibe when we kept seeing each other. What did you think we were doing?"

"I don't know, I guess . . ."

Nope, no words.

Deep down I hadn't wanted to explore the possibilities,

because if we weren't then I was worried I'd be disappointed. If I was honest with myself, really honest with myself—I wanted to be with him. Not just for sex but to actually *be with him*. And I didn't want it to stop. Which is what would've had to happen if one of us felt more than the other.

Oh, shit. I still hadn't said anything. Max looked on with an amused grin while he waited for me to continue the sentence I had no hope of finishing.

"Well, for future reference, we're dating." He moved his hand to my jaw, his eyes meeting mine. "Exclusively. So, no more trying to set me up with your crazy-ass friends. Oh and by the way, even if I wasn't dating you—and I am—she is so not even my type."

"That is so the right thing to say right now." The words rushed out of my mouth so fast they almost hadn't made sense. It was what I wanted to hear but had been too scared to ask. "You need to kiss me too." My lips needed to feel him, to make this more real.

"I think it's adorable that you thought this was going any other way." He chuckled as he brought my head in closer, his mouth inches from mine. "You weren't getting a choice this time."

It felt as though the air was sucked right out of my body, his lips on mine as he wrapped his arms around me. His tongue explored every corner of my mouth as I gave up complete control. His hands on me made me feel like my skin was on fire, my body arching against him seeking more contact.

I wanted him.

I wanted to tear the clothes from his body and have him inside of me, and still it wouldn't have been close enough. My mind completely disengaged as my body pressed harder against his, my tongue delving deeper as my fingers gripped his shirt so tight I was surprised it didn't tear.

"I like you, like this." Max smiled against my mouth, pulling back slightly so he could look at me. "I don't remember you so possessive."

"I was inspired." I smiled back, my mind choosing that moment to remind me we were still in public. "I always had control issues with you."

"Beth. Is everything all right?" Patricia and her ozone layer threatening hairdo stepped out into the courtyard, my absence obviously missed. "You disappeared and—" She stopped midsentence, her eyes focusing on Max as her hand fluttered at her throat awkwardly. "Oh, you have company."

"Hi, I'm Beth's boyfriend, Max." He held out his hand politely like I hadn't been dry humping him two minutes ago. "Pleased to meet you."

"Hello." She blinked, her eyes widening as her mouth dropped open. "I-I see." She fumbled slightly as she accepted his handshake, her mouth opening and closing a couple of times unable to find words. Not that I blamed her, he was a lot to take in all at once, especially the first time.

It was hard not to be slightly awed. Max had the ability to render women speechless, almost as if he had a force field that once you got close you were no longer able to think straight. It's what had gotten me initially. And every single time after. No amount of time built up immunity to it, and if there was an antidote I wasn't sure I wanted it.

"I hope it's not a problem that I take Jules' place." He moved his arm lower to my hip and brought me in close to his side. "It meant a lot for Beth to be here and I didn't want her to be without a partner." The beaming smile blinding us both.

God, he was good.

Just oozing confidence like it was no big deal. I had no

doubt he could have probably convinced Patricia of anything, letting him bowl as my partner the least of it.

"No, no that's totally fine. We'd love to have you." She shamelessly giggled, the blush creeping up her face. "To have you bowl with us." She corrected quickly, her cheeks getting even pinker. Poor Patricia, that force field was a bitch.

"Great." Max grinned, unaware that he was reducing my vice principal to a puddle. "And it really is a pleasure to be able to meet the wonderful educators Beth works with. It's such an important job." The grin got wider.

"Beth, you didn't mention what a charming boyfriend you have." Patricia's hand flew to her mouth, her face about to spontaneously combust. "He's just wonderful."

"He really is." I nodded wondering if perhaps the *charming* boyfriend I'd recently acquired could bring it down a notch. It would be super cool if we could make it through the evening without every woman in a ten-mile radius wanting to bear his children. Pretty sure Patricia would be the first volunteer if her current display was anything to go by.

"We should get started," she said suddenly in a wave of lucidity. "Yes, please join us inside." Her hands waved erratically as she gestured to the door.

"After you." Max moved to the side and allowed me to go ahead, his hand glued to my side as he followed close behind. "She seems nice." The raised eyebrows a clue he knew exactly what he was doing.

"You are terrible." I laughed shaking my head as we reentered the crowded bowling alley. "You could have gone a little easier on her."

"Where's the fun in that?" He laughed, each step taking us closer to the rest of the teachers, students and parents.

"Well everyone, we have a last minute substitution."

Patricia announced, all eyes moving towards us. "Beth's boyfriend Max has very generously offered to take Julie's place, who unfortunately can't make it this evening." She turned around and beamed. "Thank you, Max."

"Boyfriend?" Rita's eyes widened as she looked between us; her plans for the evening obviously foiled as they locked onto his arm around my waist. "You said you weren't dating." The words fired out of her mouth with little regard to who was around to hear them.

"Beth was just trying to be considerate of my private life," Max answered Rita, not seeming to care that the next things out of his mouth would probably be tweeted and posted on the internet by the incidental other ears who were listening. "We are very much together."

And there was tomorrow's headline. Max Reynolds, Black Addiction's bassist officially off the market. The couple's happy announcement made at Pin's Bowling Alley where he celebrated his newfound status with watered-down soda and tattered rented shoes.

Seriously, it didn't get more glamorous.

"Wow, Miss Hart is dating a rock star?" Kyle, one of my students looked up at Max with awe. "You're super famous."

"Sweetheart, that's not polite." His mother, Brooke, tapped him on the shoulder, a whispered sorry directed at Max.

"Hey, little dude." Max smiled and sunk to his hunches, meeting Kyle at eye level. "We don't really call ourselves rock stars but you can call me whatever you like. You're a little young to be a fan."

"Nah, my mom loves you." Kyle shrugged ignoring the mortification on his mother's face. "We listen to you all the time in the car; she says Rusty is her favorite, though."

"Kyle!" Brooke shook her head, not sure what would be

coming out of her son's mouth next.

"Yeah, Rusty usually gets most of the attention." Max laughed before winking at Kyle's mom. "Guitarists are such sensitive souls."

And judging by the look on her face, she might have been evaluating who was her new favorite; another victim of the famous Reynolds' charm claimed.

"I'm going to be a guitarist when I grow up too and play in a band." Kyle continued oblivious to his mother's inability to tear her eyes away from Max's chest. Not that I blame her, it was pretty impressive, even with the shirt still on.

"That's awesome, but make sure you finish school first." Max gave Kyle a pointed look, no doubt raising him to Jesus-status as he held out his hand and waited for him to shake.

"Deal." Kyle slapped him a high five before curling his hand into a handshake and yanked his arm up and down a few times, thrilled beyond measure.

"I think you're really great too." Brooke shyly smiled, her eyes struggling to meet his gaze as her son ran off to choose his ball.

"Thanks, you've got a great kid." Max grinned, watching Kyle informing all the other kids of who *the tall guy* was. "And I applaud your taste in music."

"Thanks." Brooke bumbled again. "I should go get a ball too." She put her head down and almost sprinted to where her son was animatedly explaining how big a deal Max was.

"Okay, you can stop now." I playfully jabbed Max in the ribs, rolling my eyes.

"Stop what? I'm not doing a thing." He shrugged his shoulders acting like he had no idea what I was talking about.

"Don't pretend you don't know the effect you have on women; I'm surprised I haven't been deafened by the sound of exploding ovaries." I shook my head. The threat was real, my own struggling to stay whole.

"Is that what the noise was?" Max threw his head back and laughed, thoroughly amused. "Huh, learning something new every day, thanks Miss Hart."

And lord help me, I was going to have to change my name, the timber of his voice sending a shiver right through my core.

"You're killing me." I bit my lip, thankful no one could read my thoughts—all of them involving the two of us naked.

Max was gracious, saying hello and answering questions from both students and parents. Everything from "do you have your own private plane?" to "do you need assistance on your investment portfolio?" The latter asked by a father who was doing his best to ignore his wife's swooning by his side.

We also bowled eventually too. No surprises, I still sucked at it. Max however fared a lot better, knocking all the pins down a couple of times, the kids cheering on his efforts.

I'd assumed my two worlds colliding would have made more of a mess. My past and present melting into each other as the common denominator Max moved seamlessly through it.

Though I probably shouldn't have worried. While the school I taught at liked to radiate a super-conservative image, the parents were well equipped at dealing with celebrities. Some even had their own claims to fame, while others who happened to be single parents sometimes dabbled in the TMZ end of the pool.

Even the other staff seemed surprisingly okay with it, their attitude ranging from a polite indifference to an enthusiastic interest. Lots of closet Black Addiction fans as it turned out. Who knew?

And when he took me home, it was to his bed. The hours of

being so close and wanting him made the sweet release even more delicious. It didn't stop the craving though, my body seeking his out through the night. Not that he seemed to mind, his husky laugh filling my ears as he moved his hands over me.

It's where I fell asleep and where I woke up, the smile on my face threatening to split my face apart as his arms gripped me tighter.

He didn't need to worry though; I wasn't going anywhere.

• • •

It was funny really.

Not just ironic but laugh out loud funny, that while I had been busy keeping Max at arm's length I was starting to feel something more. Or maybe there was no starting about anything, and I felt that way the whole time. I'd been too caught up with my master plan of not being together that I couldn't see I was falling in love with him. That deep down, I'd always been in love with him and that was why I couldn't stay away.

It was silly. None of it really made sense, we were both so different from when we first met, and yet the core attraction couldn't be denied. And it wasn't just sex. As much as I knew that body of his would do wonderful things to mine, I wanted more than just the nights with him.

Could he actually be my forever?

This whole time right under my nose and now I'd finally woken up?

It was Saturday when it I finally hit me. It honestly felt like I'd been in a dream this whole time, and now I was suddenly seeing clearly.

The day had started normal. Shower sex—which was

normal when you woke up with Max Reynolds—and then I went back to my apartment to kill my roommate.

We'd had a good couple of years, so I was honestly going to be sad to see her go, but unfortunately vendettas must be exacted. What I hadn't counted on was my revenge was going to have to be chilled for a while, Jules having already left for the day.

Well, that sucked. And more so because I wasn't sure if I should kiss her for pushing me and Max closer, or watch her bleed slowly for forcing my hand. The emotions fluctuated wildly so I couldn't be sure which was the one we were ultimately going to go with. I guess we were both going to be surprised.

So, there was that. My murderous rampage—or tearful, heartfelt thanks, it really was a coin toss—was postponed. Which gave me the day to fill until Max's gig.

Sure, I could have gone upstairs again and been with him, but I wanted to wait. Why? Maybe it was because I was overwhelmed. Wondering if he felt what I had been feeling. Or if I was on the ledge on my own.

The day passed slowly, which was great—insert sarcasm. It gave me so much time to obsess.

Obsess and worry.

Also panic, there was that too.

So, by the time I finally made it to his gig, I was just a big ball of nerves. Which was stupid because of all the things I should be feeling, nervous shouldn't be one of them. Try explaining that to my amygdala. Emotion center my ass, mine was currently the *freaking the fuck out* center.

Jules was still AWOL, promising to meet me at the venue in an earlier text message but had yet to show. Which made it so much worse; yelling at her would at least take the edge off things. It was actually really inconsiderate to be honest, after all this was all about me.

Then the wait was finally over.

Having played two gigs under pseudonyms, people had started to catch on. Most had already guessed that *Sleight of Hand* was really Black Addiction. Worst kept secret in town. Not that it mattered, the crowd still went crazy the minute the first note blew out of the speakers.

It was while I was in the middle of the mayhem that I had my moment of clarity. Max *was* my forever.

As I looked at him on that stage, the years flashed by in memories. Every year, each hour, each minute—and I couldn't think of one single reason why he couldn't be.

Nothing.

We made sense.

He caught my eye and winked, completely unaware of my revelation, his mouth at the mike as he sang back up with Rus. I recognized the song; it was one of their older ones and I had been there when they first played it.

Angie sung the chorus. *"And if this should end tomorrow, it will be worth it all the same. Because I would rather have one night with you, than a lifetime without pain."*

And I suddenly couldn't breathe.

I'd heard those lyrics a hundred times before, and they'd never meant as much as they did at that moment.

I loved him.

I'd always loved him.

And even if it didn't last forever, there would never be a moment I'd regret it.

# Twenty

# Max

**I** **loved playing.**

I loved the feeling I got when I plugged in and let go—the music, the way it flowed through me—it was the greatest high. But knowing there was someone waiting for you when you got off that stage, amplified it all by a million.

"Hey, beautiful." My mouth was on her the minute it got close enough. "You enjoy the show?"

"Always." She snuggled up closer, my arms pulling her in tight.

Fans made their way to the bar, the band standing around shooting the breeze. No matter how many platinum albums lined our walls we'd never forget where we'd come from and kicking it at a grassroots level was where we were most comfortable.

Of course, just because I was conversing with others it didn't mean my hands left Beth. Nope, not a fucking chance, the weight of her body against mine made me feel invincible. There were some concessions I just wasn't willing to make; not touching her was at the top of that list.

It was a rare occasion when everyone had made it to the

show. Ali was there; Rusty's arms locked around her while they chilled at the bar. Both of them relaxed and happy as they chatted with Angie and Jason. Jas wasn't so relaxed, his focus completely on his woman as he contributed to the conversation. If Angie hadn't already told us she was in the family way, the dude's protective vibe would have been a huge tip off.

And not to be outdone with the PDAs was my BFF and his wife, Joey and Kenzie were lip locked oblivious to who was watching. The rare night away from baby duties being put to good use as they *enjoyed* each other's company.

"How long do you want to stick around?" I whispered into Beth's ear, my quota for chit-chat met about twenty minutes ago.

"You got a date?" She laughed, her hands reaching up to where my arms had wrapped around her chest. "Somewhere you need to be?"

"Yeah, actually." I kept my voice low, the conversation tight between us. "In you."

Well that got her attention, her body stiffening against me. And that wasn't the only thing getting hard. My dick was ready to make good on that promise.

"There somewhere we can go to make that happen?" Her eyes lit up as she bit her lip seductively.

Yep, now it was *her* who had *my* attention.

"You feeling nostalgic?" Big-ass grin spread across my face as I considered the possibilities.

It had been a while since I'd had backstage sex. A long while. Firstly, because it was completely cliché; I preferred to get a girl home and take my time with it. And secondly, because I wasn't particularly interested in having a photo of my junk on the internet, the chance of some asshole with a camera phone capturing *the moment* almost guaranteed.

But in the early days I had most definitely partaken in the rite of passage, Beth more than just a willing participant.

"Some things haven't changed." Her hand wandered down to my ass. Well, I guess some things hadn't.

"Follow me." I grabbed Beth's hand, ready to ditch the crowd.

One thing was for sure, it had been a whole lot easier to sneak away the last time I'd done this. Every two steps we took, someone wanted to stop and have a conversation. No one even seemed to notice the bulge in my pants, advertising the hard-on that was begging for attention, each passing minute stretching my ability to be polite.

"Through here." My hand pushed open the door that led to the backstage area, thankfully spitting us out into a deserted hall.

The other differentiating factor from my last foray into club sex was that this particular establishment didn't really have a band room. It hadn't been a big deal with us, happy to chill in the hallway until we went on stage but it was a big fucking deal now. The lack of privacy threatening to derail our plans.

"This is the best I can do." The area that stored the road cases, only partially exposed. As long as no one decided to get curious, it would do fine. The alternative of waiting, no longer an option as she slung her arms around my neck.

"I want you, Max." Her lips moved to my throat. "Not just for tonight." Her mouth getting busy while her hands fisted the bottom of my shirt. "I want you. I want all of you this time."

"You've had all of me *every* time." My mouth moved to hers. "This time, I'm not letting go."

I meant it too, my hands on her desperate as I lifted her on a case, my feet staying planted on the ground.

"Touch me," she begged, the words struggling to get out of

our fused mouths as my fingers moved under her dress. And she didn't have to tell me twice.

I hadn't fully appreciated the outfit she was wearing until now; the loose fitting dress, falling off her shoulders was cinched in at the waist, the fabric underneath giving me easy access.

And while I got busy exploring, she did the same, her fingers undoing my belt and pulling down the zip of my jeans as my thumb played at the edge of her panties.

"These need to go." The panties were off her body and shoved into my pocket just before she wrenched down my jeans. My boxers not far behind, shoved down below my hips as my fingers plunged in deep.

"Yes." She arched her back, moving against my hand as my thumb circled. My fingers were coated in her honey as she gripped my dick hard.

The long slow slide of her fingers pumped my length, my balls drawing up tight with every pass. It kept me on a knife-edge, wanting to blow my load but refusing to let it end.

Every single part of me wanted her—my mouth, my hand and my cock—her pussy gripping my fingers so tight, my dick was getting jealous.

I should have made her come.

Let her ride my hand or my mouth until she screamed out my name, but I wasn't feeling either patient or polite as my fingers unpeeled hers from my cock and I pushed inside of her. No warning. Just a hard thrust of my hips giving her all I had as her heels bit into my ass.

"That's it, sweetheart." I felt her contract around me, my mouth kissing her neck while my hands kept us steady. Her tits heaved up and down as the top of her dress gave a little, the lace of her bra peeking out from under.

I didn't stop, pistoning into her with firm, hard strokes while my lips sucked hard against the lace, her nipples hardening underneath as I struggled not to bite through the fabric.

I wanted it off, all of it. I wanted her naked, stretched out under me so I could watch her. Or on top as she rode me, that would do too. Not that I was giving up what I had now for either of those options, our hips finding a rhythm as we gained speed.

"Max." Her nails dug into my skin, the marks they'd leave on my shoulders not a fucking problem for me as I sucked on her nipple harder. "I'm going to come."

As much as I loved hearing it, it was unnecessary, her body telling me everything I needed to know as her pussy clamped around my dick before the explosion of tiny pulses moved down my shaft. Even if I'd wanted to, I couldn't hold out, my body continuing to move as it pumped into her hard. The wave rolling through me so overwhelming, I had to grip the road case she was sitting on so I didn't lose balance.

"Just like old times." I laughed, my mouth moving back to her lips. "But I'm still going to have you in bed when I get you home. We're not even close to being done."

"Good, because I meant what I said." Her arms wrapped around me, as she looked me in the eye. "I want all of you, Max. I'm in love with you."

To say I'd imagined the moment I finally told a woman I loved her very differently, would be a lie. Truth is I'd only ever had one thought about it, that the woman on the receiving end would be Beth. I didn't care that it wasn't over a candlelit dinner, or watching the sunset—the two of us finally coming to our senses was as special as it got.

If she wanted grand gestures with flowers and jewelry, I'd

give her that too, but one thing was for fucking sure, I wasn't waiting a single moment longer not telling her how I felt.

"I've loved you for as long as I can remember." I brushed the hair from her face. "I just wasn't smart enough to tell you. I love you, Beth. I've always loved you."

It honestly pissed me off that I'd waited so long, so much time wasted while we tried to find ourselves. But as angry as it made me, I couldn't hate the process entirely. That we were here, finally together was worth every last kiss we'd ever had. All of them fucking history as I vowed to never make the same mistake again.

"Take me home, Max." Beth smiled, seeing her happy making me feel like a fucking gladiator.

"Anything you ask, sweetheart." I slowly pulled out, needing to get us both clothed and out of the club ASAP.

I didn't even give a shit I had barely spoken to the band since getting off stage. They'd live. My only concern was giving my girl exactly what she'd asked, which lucky for me was exactly what I wanted too. The two of us, out of here.

"Whoa!" The noise reverberated off the walls, our private sanctuary breeched. "They weren't kidding. You're huge."

Enter Jules, her timing fucking perfect—or not as the case may be—to see me standing with my dick in my hand. Her eyes peeled back to maximum capacity as she openly stared.

"Jules!" Beth pushed down her dress covering up what little had been showing. She didn't need to worry though; Jules had been too busy looking at my dick to notice she had also been flashing skin. "What the hell?"

"As you were people, don't let me disturb you." She waved her hands around, big-ass grin on her face.

"Peep show's over." I pulled up my boxers, the fabric covering my dick doing little to convince her apparently, her eyes still glued to my junk. "And you shouldn't be back here." My jeans were next on the redress.

"Yeah, well considering what the two of you were doing—" Her hands flying back and forth between Beth and I. "— I wouldn't say anyone is in a position to throw stones."

"So you've seen it." Beth jumped off the road case her feet landing heavily on the floor. "I hope you sleep better for knowing." And call me crazy, but she didn't sound anywhere near as pissed as I'd assumed. Can't say I'd be so cool with it if the situation was reversed; no one was getting the pleasure of seeing her naked if I had anything to do with it.

"Oh, I will. That's freaking impressive, Beth." The conversation continued, apparently my participation not needed. "I can't believe you held out on me."

"I can't believe you came back here." Beth planted her hands on her hips. "We need to set some serious boundaries, probably starting with not staring at my boyfriend's dick."

"I wasn't staring, my eyes were blinded. Like an eclipse." Jules unsuccessfully tried to hide her smirk.

"Um hello?" I waved, everything tucked away. "You ladies realize I'm still here right? Both me and my cock."

I wasn't embarrassed. Couldn't give a fuck. And not that I wanted the bastard to have its own Tumblr account, but I couldn't give a rat's ass who saw my dick.

"Well yeah, it's not like that equipment of yours could ever *not* be noticed." Jules raised her hands, taking a step back. "No wonder micro penis left you wanting, how did you get *that* all the way in?"

Hold on. Talking up my dick was one thing and not that I had any intention of pulling it out and giving everyone a refresher, but it was what it was. She'd seen it, big deal. But who the hell was this other cock—word choice completely intentional—we were talking about? And yes, I knew how fucking conceited that made me sound and I still didn't give a shit.

"Who the fuck is micro penis?" I waited, not really sure I wanted to know.

"The gym guy." Beth added, looking at me expectantly like those words should mean something.

"Nope, still don't know who we're talking about."

"The guy from the restaurant." Beth's final explanation filled in the blanks.

Bingo. Now that asshole, I knew. And I wasn't sure if I should be annoyed that he and his cock were getting a mention or freaking ecstatic that it had earned him the name micro penis. I was purposely avoiding the fact that he'd slept with her; the thought of him even touching her making my skin itch. I wouldn't be that asshole, the possessive meathead who was delusional in thinking she wouldn't have been with other guys. But it wasn't something that I wanted in my mental space right about now. Clearly it hadn't gone well, and thank fuck for that silver lining.

"So talking about dicks is a regular thing?" Another revelation, who knew?

Beth's "no" drowned out by Jules' "yes."

"Okay." I laughed, amused as hell. "So, maybe we can move on to non-anatomical related topics like," I pointed to Jules, her appearance still unexplained. "What are you doing backstage?"

"I asked the band and they hadn't seen you, so I figured I'd check here." Her head bobbled excitedly, the words faster than they needed to be. "No one stopped me. If it was such a restricted area, there should at least be a sign."

"And you just had to find us, urgently." Beth didn't bother trying to hide the sarcasm, the smile still on her face. "Couldn't have waited until we got back."

"You made such a big deal about wanting to kill me for standing you up at bowling." Jules rolled her eyes, sporting a matching grin. "I was trying to expedite the process."

"Considerate of you." Beth nodded. "I'm still pissed about that."

"Just so you ladies know, I'm still here." I waved my hand, the reminder obviously needed. "And as much as her tactics were questionable, I think we both can agree it was a good end result." I pulled Beth against me, my lips landing on her neck.

I also found it incredibly hot knowing this whole exchange was happening while her panties were in my pocket. Not going to lie, I wasn't in a hurry to hand them back, the idea of her walking around without them making me hard.

"Fine, I'll concede." She threw her arms up in defeat. "End result was good."

"Aw, I'm so glad. I had a terrible night, you guys." She rubbed the back of her neck, easing it left and right. "Barely slept a wink waiting for you to come home."

"Well, for future reference, don't wait up." I grinned hoping that whatever BS had been holding us back was now in the past. There wasn't going to be a night I was without Beth. Not if I had anything to do with it.

"Hey, why are you guys back here? Something we should know?" Joey rounded the corner, his arm slung around Kenzie's shoulders.

"Beth and Max were having sex." Jules stepped in, not giving either of us a chance to reply.

"Really?" Joey smirked, the bastard looking to me for confirmation. "Interesting."

"If you are looking to embarrass us, you're wasting your time." I shrugged, not regretting a thing. Could have done without the end of show reveal, but other than that, I was pretty pleased with the night's turn of events. "I'm not making apologies for being with my girl."

"No apologies necessary." Jules beamed, fucking thrilled beyond measure.

"There more to this story?" Kenzie asked, clever enough to see they were missing something.

"Jules happened to walk in, before everything got squared away." I went the diplomatic route, figuring my cock had gotten enough airtime tonight.

"Oh? Ohhhhhhhhh." Kenzie's eyes widened in recognition. No further explanation needed.

"I swear if I have to hear about this guy's dick one more time." Joey ignored my leave-it-alone eyeball, making it once again the topic of conversation. "Mine is so much more impressive, seriously. I just don't understand."

"Ahh, babe. Yours is perfect." Kenzie laughed, her hand rubbing circles on Joey's chest.

"Okay, can we move on now?" I shook my head wondering if I should be flattered or appalled. "We should probably go back into the club too; Rus and Angie are probably looking for their rhythm section."

"Well, if the show's over, I might head home." Jules nodded, her entertainment for the night over. "I'm assuming you guys are leaving together?"

"You assumed correctly." And if the words hadn't been enough, my hands around Beth said everything that needed to be said.

"Okay then crazy kids, enjoy. I'm out of here." Jules waved, ready to make her exit. "Beth, good luck with the anaconda."

"Mine's bigger," Joey called out, the moron not able to resist a parting shot.

"Can we really stop talking about my dick?" And who thought those words would be coming out of my mouth a second time, let alone at all tonight. That fucking Facebook page had a lot to answer for.

"Fine, we'll never mention it again." Beth giggled, her head resting against my chest.

"We'll meet you out there." Joey tipped his chin goodbye as he moseyed back to the hall, all talk of my cock shelved.

"So is this weird?" Beth asked, her nose scrunching up as she gave me an adorable smile.

"What? Us?"

I mean it really could have been anything. The public fornication, my subsequent flashing, the bizarre backstage conversation—but there was only one thing that I cared about right now. And it wasn't anything on that list.

"Yes, us. Together again." Those big brown eyes looked at me and she could have asked for anything at that moment and I would have agreed. Need me to take a long walk off a short pier? I have no problem getting wet.

"It's the way it always should have been."

I kissed her, not because I wanted to reassure her or myself, but because I needed to. My mouth needed hers, my body needed hers and I was done pretending it didn't. Whatever happened outside of the bubble didn't matter; this was the only thing that made sense. And no matter what the future threw at us, there wasn't a chance in hell I'd let it slip away. I'd been given a second chance and the only way I'd give her up is having her pried from my cold dead hands. Even then I'd find a way to hold on. Losing her again—not an option.

# Twenty-One

# Max

**I**t was probably the end of the world.

Or one of the planets was in retrograde, causing a massive cosmic disturbance in the force because there was no other reasonable explanation. Angie—our lead singer, who didn't let anyone even breathe in her son's direction—asked Beth and I to babysit. Excuse me while I recover from the shock.

Beth had offered in the past, but I'd chalked it up as sweet but never gonna happen. Not because Beth wouldn't have totally rocked the babysitting gig, but because there was a better chance of me shopping at the Gap than Angie agreeing. Well break out the polo shirts and khaki pants because the impossible happened.

Jase had wanted to take Angie out for a special dinner to celebrate her rebooted baby mama status. Considering the last time she had cargo onboard, she spent more time in the bathroom rather than at a dining table, I wasn't sure it was a great idea. But who was I to judge? Enter the request of hey-can-you-and-Beth-hang-with-Zack-for-a-few-hours? Yep, they needed to say it a couple of times just so I was sure I hadn't hallucinated the whole thing.

Beth had been excited to do it. Happy to help out and spend some time with me and junior Jase. So, it was all systems go as we arrived at Casa Irwin and knocked on the door.

"Okay, we shouldn't be more than a few hours. It's just dinner."

Angie gave us both a hug and welcomed us inside. The look on her face telling us she wasn't as cool with it as she was pretending to be, but I wisely decided not to point that out. I preferred to keep both my balls exactly where they were, thank you very much.

"You don't need to worry, we've got this." Beth alternated between hugging Angie and then Jase. "He's going to be fine and we'll have a great time."

"It's fine, babe." Jason rubbed his wife's back. "He's going to love it." The idea looking like it had been more *his* doing.

"You have our numbers and the pediatrician's number is on the fridge." Angie continued to fuss, the possibility of her relaxing probably not going to happen.

"Angie, we've got it." I nodded my head, reaching out to her arm and giving it a squeeze. "Don't expose him to light or water and whatever we do we won't feed him after midnight."

"Ha ha, asshole." Angie folded her arms in front of her chest, not amused. "And it's not funny." She gave Jase a poke in the chest who was trying unsuccessfully to hide his grin.

"Babe, everyone is going to be fine. Seriously." He pulled her into his arms trying to get her to relax. "Now, let's go say goodbye to Zack so we can make our reservation."

Zack was chilling in the playroom, his fat little fingers pushing a train along a wooden track as he chatted to himself. In other words, he couldn't give a fuck that his folks were heading out for the night, Angie's stress being completely self-induced.

"Bye, little man." Angie wrapped her arms around the kid, smothering his face with kisses. His little arms and legs wriggled trying to get loose. "We'll be home soon, and Uncle Max and Beth are going to take care of you while we're gone."

"Okay, Mama." Zack smiled, the announcement not rating as high as the train track in front of him.

"Be good, kiddo." Jase hiked him up off the floor, Zack squealing as his dad flipped him upside down. "Listen to what you're told and when it's bedtime, no arguments."

More shrieks as Jase blew raspberries under his chin and then lowered him to the ground. Zack giving both his parents a wave before returning to his train.

"We're cool, Angie. Go, have a good time." I nodded to the door, wondering if Jase was going to literally have to drag her out. "He'll be fine."

"Alright." Angie hesitated, her knuckles whitening as they fisted by her side. "We should go." I'm sure she said it more for her own benefit than anyone else's.

Jase probably guessing it was better to get it over with, threw a hand around his woman's waist and led her to the front door. The second goodbye happening just before they finally left.

"So, what do you want to play?" asked Beth, scooting down to his level.

"You're pretty." Zack reached up and touched her face, the little guy proving how smart he was by that statement alone.

"She sure is buddy." I joined the two of them on the floor. "You trying to steal my girl?" I tucked him under my arm in a bear hold. "You're cute, so I'll overlook it this one time." The kid erupted into giggles.

"Maybe we can make cookies for dessert? Would you like that?" Beth stood up, big grin on her face as she watched me wrestle with the kid.

"Only if they are chocolate chip," I added, lifting the little dude with me as I straightened up. "Oatmeal cookies suck."

"Suck!" Zack parroted, his little fist waving with conviction.

"Fine, chocolate chip it is." Beth shook her head, not comprehending how offensive oatmeal was to a cookie. I mean seriously, why bother? "But you need to watch your mouth." She jabbed a finger between my lips while trying to hide the smile.

Probably some sound advice. It would only take one random *fuck* and this little exercise would end badly. And there was no way I wanted for the kid's first cuss word to be courtesy of yours truly.

"Noted." I flipped Zack upside down as we made our way to the kitchen.

Angie had given Zack dinner before she left, so we figured a little dessert was cool. Then it was going to be a story and bedtime and Beth and I were going to get a pizza. Chill in front of the television. Possibly make out. Have to admit, the idea of getting to second or third base with the babysitter was sort of hot. And if I could take care of that little fantasy after the kid was safely in dreamland, what was the harm? Sounded like a win to me.

Beth took charge in the kitchen. Carefully explaining each of the ingredients to the little guy before letting him put them in the mixing bowl. She was so good with him, the process taking three times as long because of Zack's assist, and yet she didn't lose her cool once. Nope, just kept going slowly and allowing him to help every step of the way.

Man, I had it bad for this girl. Looking at her with that little boy and it wasn't hard to imagine her with one of mine. Straight up, I'd always figured I'd eventually have kids. Like down the line, when I was older. But watching her be so sweet with him and I could easily move that schedule to within the next few years. Ring on her finger, a dog—the whole nine yards. Yeah, that was a good plan and one I fully intended on making happen as soon as the time was right.

Cookies went into the oven, and Zack and I offered to clean up. Seemed fair since Beth had done most of the work with the baking. And it also gave me the opportunity to keep an eye on the kid so he didn't mack on my girl when I wasn't looking.

Not sure why Angie had been so worried, but her kid was awesome. Remembered his manners when asking for a second cookie and didn't give us any lip. He may have grumbled a few times when we told him it was bedtime, but after sweetening the deal with one more cookie and an additional story, he gave us no extra trouble. This parenting stuff was pretty easy if you asked me, absolutely no problems at all.

After making sure his teeth were brushed and his pajamas were on, we tucked up the little guy into his bed and said goodnight. The idea of some alone time with the babysitter probably excited me a little more than it should, my dick already starting to take an interest and we hadn't even ordered the pizza yet.

The delivery guy earned his tip. Our pie was delivered hot and within the thirty minute window the tagline had promised. Then with a couple of sodas—no booze while on kid duty—we camped out in front of the television and enjoyed our dinner. Best. Pizza. Ever.

And as much as I enjoyed watching her devour her slices, I could think of a better use for her mouth. My lips agreed as they moved in without notice.

My arms wrapped around her, pulling her closer as my tongue got where it wanted to be, the kiss moving past the hi-how-are-you-stage to let's-get-it-on. I didn't stop, my hands taking a little wander down to the front of her shirt, my fingers curling around one of her perfect tits as I continued to fuck her with my mouth. The bulge in my pants already rock fucking solid.

"What if he wakes up?" Beth pulled away glancing to the doorway, no noise coming from anything but us and the television.

"We'll hear him if he gets up. I'll be very quiet." My lips moved to her neck as my hand moved to the other tit. I didn't want to play favorites, both of them equally spectacular.

"Max, we shouldn't." She half-heartily protested, her mouth telling me a completely different story as she kissed back.

"Just let me play a little." I tried to negotiate, needing to touch her just a little more. "I'll stop before it goes too far."

Probably not the smartest thing to have come out of my mouth, but to be honest, I wasn't thinking straight. I wasn't thinking at all, with my dick clearly running the show, but as much as it had bad idea written all over it, I couldn't make myself stop.

While she didn't agree, she didn't stop me either, my hand sliding underneath her bra as she moved into my lap. Our mouths fused as she used my hard-on to give her what she needed, the rocking back and forth enough to make me want to blow my load.

We should have stopped. Enjoyed the make out session for what it was and looked forward to some serious sex once I'd got her home to my bed. But all the confidence my dick had had earlier—*we'll totally stop before it gets too far*—was completely MIA as I struggled to keep my voice down.

"Did you hear something?" Beth's head snapped back, her lips puffy from my mouth, my hand still up her shirt.

"Nope, didn't hear a thing." I shook my head, my eyes watching her tits heave up and down with each breath.

"Max, it might be Zack. We need to stop." She untangled her arms and pulled back on my lap, straightening her top.

I could have cried, my balls so tight I wasn't sure they weren't going to explode as my dick throbbed in my pants. "Okay, Okay." I cursed under my breath, needing a minute to commiserate before I could stand.

"We should check on him." Beth lifted herself out of my lap and climbed to her feet. "Just to be sure."

"Yep, just give me a minute." The bulge in my jeans not going anywhere despite us calling time out. "You stay here, I'll go."

The hall was still dark as I left the living room and climbed the stairs. Zack's bedroom door was still closed, not a peep coming from it as my head poked inside the room.

"What the fuck?" I flung open the door, the glow of the nightlight revealing an empty bed, the child that was supposed to be in it not in the room.

"What's wrong?" Beth raced up the stairs, her footsteps echoing off the walls as she met me at the door. "What the hell?" Her eyes got wide as they looked at the empty bed, the kid still missing.

"He has to be in here somewhere; it's not like he can disappear into thin air." I threw on the light and started searching. "Check the closet." I got down on my hands and knees to see if the little guy was playing hide and seek under his bed.

"He's not here." Beth looked around panicked. "How can he be missing? He was right there." She pointed to the mussed up sheets, no clues as to where he'd gotten to.

"Start going through the rooms. If he'd gone out the front

door, we would have heard the deadlock and there's no way he could have climbed out the window."

I might have seemed calm, but deep down I was a hundred percent losing my shit. The idea that we let something happen to the kid played in my head like a bad dream.

"Zack," Beth called out running through the upstairs rooms. "Zack, sweetie where are you?"

I took off down the stairs, figuring we needed to divide and conquer. Jase and Angie's house wasn't small, so it was going to take more than a few minutes to do a search. Kid wasn't big either, so could have easily wedged himself behind the drapes or into a cupboard, the list of hiding places literally endless as I moved from room to room.

My pulse raced as I checked bathrooms and the laundry, freaking out that he'd gotten himself into trouble while we'd been—yeah, if something happened I was probably not going to forgive myself.

"He's not here," Beth called out, taking the stairs two at a time as she met me in the study, the room deserted as she turned on every light in the house.

"Zack, buddy." I opened doors, each room turning up nothing. "Come out, little man, you're not in any trouble, but we need to make sure you're okay." I made my way slowly to the kitchen.

Empty.

Every fucking room, empty.

How could we have lost a human? Did he evaporate into thin air? Logically, I knew he had to be somewhere but I couldn't stop the worst-case scenarios looping around in my brain. This was so not good.

"Zack!" Beth screamed, her voice carrying down the hall as she double checked the rooms I'd just been in. "Come out and I promise you can have another cookie."

We stopped hollering; just hoping to hear something that would give us a clue. Then finally we heard it—a muted groan just barely audible.

"Kitchen." My head whipped around, turning to the direction of the sound. I swear I'd checked it before and came up empty, not that I cared now if it meant we found him.

"Zack, where are you?" I looked around the kitchen, the room no different to the last time I'd been in there, my head ducking under the counter as Beth checked under the table.

"Ughhhhh." Another groan, the noise coming from the walk-in pantry.

"In here." I pulled open the door, the little guy sitting on the floor curled up with a face full of cookie crumbs.

"Hey." I dropped to my knees thanking God we'd found him as Beth joined me in the tiny space. "You gave us a bit of a scare." I pulled him in for a hug, my silent *thank fucks* remaining unspoken.

"I don't feel so well." Zack clutched at his stomach the empty plate of cookies beside him a big fucking clue as to why. "I'm—"

He didn't finish his sentence, his mouth opening and blowing chunks all over me in the process.

"Shit." I tried not to gag, the stench jacking up my nose making me want to hurl too. My shirt covered in vomit as the kid started to cry.

"Oh God." I covered my mouth, my stomach retching wanting to do its own eject. The cough I was unable to suppress playing havoc with my gag reflex as I tried not to think about tossing my own cookies. It was going to be a close call.

"No, no it's okay." Beth grabbed a dish rag, the tiny piece of fabric doing jack shit to kill the fucking smell or the mess that was on the two of us. "You're okay." Her reassurance fell on deaf ears as the kids launched into full water works.

"Let's get out of here." I tried to stand up, my foot hitting a patch of spew pitching me back against one of the shelves. "God damn," I gritted out through my teeth, my shoulder bouncing off the edge before I went down on my ass, thankfully not landing on the kid.

"You're okay." Beth pulled him out of the pantry, the kid crying hard either from my yelling or the fact I'd almost made him a pancake. Spew freaking everywhere as I tried again to fucking stand up.

You know that scene in The Exorcist where the chick's head spins around and a stream of pea soup shoots out her mouth? Yeah, double that and you were in the neighborhood of what we were dealing with. He wasn't even that big, how he could have produced so much vomit was still a freaking mystery.

"It's all good, Zack." I bit down on my lip to stop from cursing as I climbed to my feet, my shoulder screaming from pain while I stuffed down the urge to dry heave.

"Let's get you cleaned up; we're going to make it all better." Beth took control of the situation, sitting him on the counter while she pulled off his jammies. The kid still hiccupping as she grabbed another tea towel and wiped down his face. "See no need to cry."

No need to cry? I begged to disagree, my puke filled shirt sticking to my chest as I grabbed paper towels and tried to mop up the chunks. Yep, this was going so well. *And fuck you, universe*, my metaphorical finger flipping off karma; my punishment, obviously, for insinuating the parenting gig was a cakewalk.

"I'm just going to get some towels and run a bath." Beth

looked over at me, my fruitless exercise of trying to clean up abandoned as I peeled off my shirt. I wasn't even going to bother. The idea of being shirtless preferable to the spew I'd been wearing. "Can you stay with him until I'm ready?"

"Yeah, of course." I walked over to the counter, tossing the shirt in the garbage as Zack's sobs started to taper off. "It's going to be fine, Zack. We're just going to clean you up and then it will all be over."

I don't know who I was trying to convince, because shit was most definitely *not* fine. But I needed him to stop crying, so at this point I'd stand on my head if it would get the job done.

"Un-cle Max." He sucked in a breath, snot dripping out of his nose as he tried to talk. His hands reached for me as the tears looked to start again.

"No, no." I grabbed him off the counter, praying to God Beth would walk in any minute. "No need to cry." I cradled him close to my chest hoping the jiggling wouldn't bring on spewfest round two.

"Potty."

He probably didn't need to say it, the stream of warm pee traveling down my stomach enough of a hint that he needed a bathroom. Could have used the memo a few minutes earlier so there'd been time to get to said bathroom.

"Are you kidding me?" I laughed, the top of my jeans now soaked. I mean seriously? Clearly it wasn't enough that I'd had been covered in spew. No, I needed to stink like a fucking urinal too.

"What's happened?" Beth came running back, the fucking towels redundant. "Is he feeling sick again?"

"Nope, hopefully we're done with the bodily functions though. There's only one left and I'm really not down with that."

And fuck me, what a freaking mess. I still had no idea where he was storing all of it, the volume of shit—thank God not literally—coming out of him still baffling the hell out of me.

"Oh, you had an accident. It's okay." She wrapped a towel around Zack, the kid still howling.

Again, *okay* not a word I'd use right now.

"Why don't you get him taken care of and I'll try and clean this up." The floor, the inside of the cupboard—I was going to need a mask and some holy water just to get through it.

"Are you sure?" Beth hesitated a beat, my earlier performance not convincing her I'd be cool. Had to admit, I wasn't so sure myself.

"It's fine." I said as much for my own benefit as I did for her. "I've got this, go."

"I'll be quick." She nodded, taking the Zack bundle towards the bathroom. Hopefully keeping whatever else was inside of him where it belonged.

Great.

The kitchen looked like a war zone, and I was nowhere near ready for battle.

Deep breaths.

I could totally do this.

Grabbing a stack of paper towels, I attacked the mess, breathing through my mouth so I didn't contribute to it. It really was amazing how far it had managed to spread; if we could just harness the kid's ability to *throw* for good rather than evil we'd have a World Series pitcher on our hands.

I finished up grabbing a bucket, a bottle of Clorox and a mop and if anything had ever lived on that floor it was fucking dead now. The place spotless by the time Beth had come back down with a clean, freshly PJ'd Zack.

"Wow, you did a great job in here." She surveyed my handy

work, Zack hiding in the crook of her neck.

"You didn't do too badly yourself." I nodded, the little guy peeking up at me from under his arm. "You feeling better little guy?"

"Sorry, Uncle Max." His bottom lip started to do the wobble.

"Ah it's okay." I gave him a big grin. "Probably shouldn't have eaten all those cookies, huh?"

In all the excitement we hadn't heard the front door. Jase and Angie back from their hot date came home to a house that was lit up like a Christmas tree, doors open left and right, but at least their floor smelled lemony-fresh.

"Oh my god, is everything okay?" Angie rushed into the kitchen, Jase following close behind.

"*Someone* got out of bed and ate a few more cookies than they should." I started to explain, Zack shoving his head back under his arm. "It didn't end well for my shirt."

"Zack, you know you aren't supposed to eat at bedtime." Angie hauled him into her arms. "You get a belly ache every time. Now let's get you to bed."

After a round of *goodnights,* Angie and Beth took a sleepy Zack back to his room where hopefully he'd stay.

"This your new direction? Topless maid?" Jase laughed. "Am I supposed to tip you? I think I have a fiver in here somewhere." He leaned up against the counter, thoroughly amused.

"Yeah, laugh it up. You're going to have two of them running around here soon." And if that had come out of one little person, I could only imagine the damage two could do. "I'm getting you both a case of bleach for the baby shower."

"And I wouldn't have it any other way." He puffed out his chest, proud of his growing brood. "Dude, did you piss yourself?"

"Don't even, Jase. It's not been a good night." I didn't bother explaining, there was really no point. It wasn't going to change the fact that I was still standing in someone else's pee.

"Well, thanks. We owe you." He held out his hand.

"You don't owe me shit." I clapped his hand with my own. "It was our pleasure." Well mostly, I was hoping if there was a next time it could be without the evac of bodily fluids.

"And you might want to hold onto that girl of yours."

Ha! He wasn't telling me anything I didn't know.

"Don't worry about that." I nodded, the intention well beyond just holding onto her. "I have no intention of letting her go."

**T**hings were great.

Better than they'd ever been.

We'd even survived our babysitting disaster. The night proved to be more of a challenge than either of us had thought. Lesson learned, put the cookies on a higher shelf next time.

He'd been so incredibly sweet with Zack though, and that just made my heart squeeze a little bit more.

Max was recording most days, Black Addiction was anxious to get back into the studio and work on the new album. They pulled long erratic hours, the whole process exhausting but necessary if they were going to put out another album before the end of the year. Angie was also pregnant, which complicated things a little, the timing of their album release important if she was going to be able to promote it before her next baby was born.

Monday to Friday I had class, so while I missed him, the days didn't seem so bad. We'd call during breaks though, flirty messages—anything to keep the connection. And even though both of us were tired, we were making it work. The last few weeks had been the best of my life and I'd take sleep-deprived and deliriously happy over rested and baseline mediocre.

The nights were the best.

I would sneak up to his apartment—he'd given me a spare key—and wait for him to come home. Sometimes I'd attempt to make dinner, or he'd pick something up on the way but they always ended the same way. Me with him in bed. It didn't matter how tired he was or how early he had to get up the next day. And if I happened to fall asleep in my own bed, I'd be woken up by a text message and Max Reynolds at my door. Being apart was something Max wouldn't accept.

It was a good system. It meant he was both the last and the first thing I saw every day.

I loved it.

I loved him.

And I couldn't be happier if I'd tried.

The *undercover* gigs had been sidelined having fulfilled their purpose. Besides, most people had clued up so the last couple had needed extra security just to deal with the extra crowd. But occasionally I got to see my own private show. Max happy to pull out a guitar and go through some of the new material while I laid in bed, his bass being benched for a six-string guitar on those rare times. My eyes would close listening to him sing, and I felt every single note he played.

Those words we'd avoided for so long—I love you—we said them as much as we could. We were that couple you hated, the ones who's loved-up displays made you want to puke. But I didn't care, and had no plans to stop.

The press attention was a little harder to deal with. It wasn't unexpected but you were never really ready for it until an extra-long zoom lens was pointed at your ass. Thankfully Max had an indoor gym, which meant my ass didn't look too bad. It also solved the problem of traveling to my new gym that unfortunately was further away than my old one, the one I needed to replace because of the micro penis debacle.

I hated the intrusion. When we dated before Max hadn't been famous, so I'd never had to worry about whether someone was going to rifle through my garbage. Or checking to make sure when I left the apartment I was photo ready. Sure, I could have easily just slummed it, let the photographers have a field day with photos of me in sweats, but I hated knowing those photographs would be out there forever. A quick makeup application was a small price to pay.

It seemed everything we—and therefore by virtue, I—did was newsworthy. Even my school had been getting some attention, with reporters itching to get the inside scoop. It had been a great disappointment that I wasn't A: a groupie or B: a gold digger, so I'm sure they were hoping that at the very least they could uncover something halfway decent. If they were looking for dirt—they'd be waiting awhile. I had nothing.

"Beth, can you see me in my office?"

It was rare for Mr. Ryan James to make an appearance at my classroom. Even rarer for him to request a meeting with me at his office, our principal a little old school in his approach, believing very much in the chain of command. If things were escalated up to him it could only mean bad things, which is why when he knocked on my door at four in the afternoon, I knew it spelled trouble.

"Sure, I'm just finishing the planning for tomorrow." I looked up from my desk, hopefully not with the fear I was feeling radiating from my eyeballs. "I'll be there in just a minute."

Not good.

This was soooooo not good.

It would have been smart to wait until after our conversation before I started freaking out but of course, I wasn't smart. Instead I was running through every possible scenario on what could warrant an audience with the big dog. Max and my newfound celebrity status, being the most obvious.

As I'd mentioned before, the school was no stranger to celebrity or what came with it. Photographers were often stalled by the huge black gates that lined the perimeter of the school and all faculty were well rehearsed with the typical "no comment," should a reporter come knocking.

Not that any of the parents had complained. A couple even congratulated me, giving me a nod of approval. Our public appearances were documented with glossy photographic evidence to match so there had been no point denying it.

But with my personal evaluations having always been extremely positive, I had no idea what else it could be.

Well I guess I was going to find out.

I quickly packed away my laptop, smoothing my skirt as I stood. My hands ran nervously down my thighs as I walked to Mr. James' office. It didn't matter how old you were, going to the principal's office still sucked.

Once I got to his door I faced another dilemma. Did I sit outside and wait to be called, or did I walk in with my shoulders back, trying to radiate confidence? It was something I debated for a good five minutes before knocking quietly on his door and poking my head into the doorway. It was a compromise and one I'd hoped would work in my favor.

"Mr. James, are you ready for me?"

"Ah, Beth. Come in." He waved over his desk, the old mahogany artifact he worked on probably as old as the school itself. "Please take a seat." He gestured to one of the leather chairs sitting opposite him, my ass lowering down slowly trying to avoid the inevitable creek.

Patricia, our vice principal, was also in attendance; her smiling face and bullet proof hair not giving me the comfort it usually did. They were showing a united front. Awesome.

She nodded as I situated myself in my chair, my smile back hopefully not conveying the what-the-fuck I had rolling around in my head. I wasn't holding my breath, though; it had been hard enough for those words not to shoot out of my mouth while I waited.

"I suppose you're wondering why I've called you here." His fingers tented in front of him as he leaned back in his chair. "I must admit, I was a little surprised to be receiving the call."

Great. Whatever it was, it didn't look good. A pat on the back and a *well done* probably not the reason for today's meeting. Patricia's appearance also spelled trouble, and the fact she hadn't said anything was also worrying.

"I'm sorry, Mr. James, but I'm not really sure what call you are referring to." A call? Did someone tip him off on my overzealous use of Post-it Notes?

"I'm assuming you are familiar with Mike Warren?" He leaned forward in his chair gauging my reaction.

I blinked back with almost utter shock.

*Micro penis?*

Well, I guess if you were going by the name on his birth certificate then I was familiar with *Mike Warren,* but I preferred to use my own title. I felt it had been justly earned.

"Umm yes?" I wasn't sure how to answer it exactly, I knew him but anything other than that was a stretch. "Mr. Warren was a member of a gym I used to attend. I wouldn't say I know him very well, we're not friends if that's what you're asking." Technically, the last time I'd spoken to him had been when I power walked out of his apartment. The thanks-for-nothing muttered out of my breath while I vowed to never see him again.

"I see." His eyes darted over to Patricia, an unspoken dialogue seeming to transpire between the two of them. "Well, this is a little uncomfortable for me to mention, which is why I wanted Patricia to sit in with us." The mystery of her appearance solved. "But I wanted to speak to you privately before anyone else is involved." He took a moment, clearing his throat. "Was the nature of your relationship with Mr. Warren violent?"

"I'm sorry, what?" There was really no other response, my brain needing a crash cart over the arrest that statement just induced. Where to even start? I'd say the first misnomer was the word *relationship*, as in, we didn't have one, let alone one that was violent. I couldn't help but look around to see if this wasn't some elaborate joke and I was being punked.

Any minute now.

"Mr. Warren has alleged that you had a relationship of a sexual nature and—" another uncomfortable throat clearing, "you liked to get physical."

Okay, now it was just bordering on funny. Surely this was too ridiculous to even be true.

"I'm sorry, Mr. James, but I'm not following." I tried not to laugh because I didn't want to seem disrespectful. "Assuming we did have a relationship, I'm not sure that has anything to do with my ability to do my job. Or why it's anyone else's business."

If I could go back in time and kick my own ass for poor choices, he would be the number one on my list. While I still had no idea why my faux pas in the dating world was relevant right now, I would happily save myself the trouble and the lost orgasm.

"Beth, you are one of our best teachers." He blew out a long exhale. "The kids love you, as do the parents and you are very well respected among the staff." I waited for the *but* as he took a breath. "I know you have recently been linked to that rock star but I need to know if there is any truth to this rumor."

"Max is my boyfriend." I nodded, still wondering why any of this was relevant. "We're dating." A quick internet search would have confirmed that even if I hadn't. "But I still don't understand how who I am currently or have dated in the past has any bearing on my ability to perform my job?"

"Mike Warren has spoken to the press." Again a pause, more unspoken eye ping-pong between him and Patricia. "I have a friend on the board at The Times, so naturally with the nature of the story he felt compelled to reach out to me. It's a rather detailed article, Beth. It alleges that you and he had a rather aggressive sexual tryst in the past. From his account it wasn't a good separation and that you were obsessive and had violent tendencies."

"Are you serious?" I coughed out, unable to keep my mouth shut a minute longer.

"Naturally, matters such as this are taken *very* seriously." Mr. James nodded. "It will be in tomorrow's edition. Parents, staff members and of course our board—it will be out there for all to see. So, unfortunately, I have to ask. Did you have an abusive relationship with Mr. Warren?"

"This is insane." I giggled, the complete hilarity of the situation unable to be contained as I laughed out loud. "Have you *seen* him? I'm like a third of his size; I couldn't sexually assault him if I tried." At least not without a ladder and some serious amounts of duct tape, even then I'd struggle.

"Beth, you haven't answered the question," Patricia interjected, shifting uncomfortably in her seat.

"No, it didn't happen. Not like that." I struggled to maintain calm, the professional exterior starting to crack the longer the interrogation went on. "Not that any of that matters though, apparently anyone can print what they like."

"So, then you didn't have a sexual relationship with him?"

And there it was. The micro penis knew there was no way I could deny the hook up. Because we had actually *had* sex. Consensual, boring, missionary position sex where I faked an orgasm and then left.

There was no doubt surveillance footage of the two of us at the gym, possibly some of me entering his apartment. So even if I wanted to lie, I couldn't. Nope, the only thing I could do was give my account of what happened in that bedroom which wasn't much. Which of course was at odds with his fictional version, not only sounding wildly embellished but highly incredible. Come on, me abuse him? Was he high?

"I think my personal life is under enough of a microscope, I'm not answering questions which are honestly offensive."

"You have to understand that I'm between a rock and a hard place." My nightmare continued. "What you do behind closed doors is your own business of course, but allegations of violence are not something we can ignore. We are answerable to our parents, Beth. And I'm sure they will have questions about whether it's appropriate if someone with that kind of lifestyle teaches young impressionable minds."

This couldn't be happening. It just couldn't be real. Some guy I'd basically had a one-night stand with was holding me to ransom. The allegation? Was he trying to insinuate that I beat him up or that I liked to get kinky in the bedroom? Or both?

"I refuse to be bullied by him or by anyone else." My anger rose with each passing second. "What he is alleging is an out and out lie. But even if it were true, I never would act inappropriately towards my students. I love my job, I love those kids and I would never, ever do anything to put them at risk."

"Beth, please." Patricia tried the diplomatic approach, my outburst threatening to continue. "We're not debating your sincerity, but that doesn't change how this looks. And supporting that *particular* lifestyle is not in line with the school's core values."

"Are you kidding me?" My butt flew off the seat as my feet hit the floor. There was no way I was going to remain calm, chances are I'd already lost my job so why bother holding back. "How this looks? This is my life, my livelihood and my name that is being slandered. My parents and grandparents are going to read that."

I had been prepared for having some asshole tell me I looked fat in my jeans, or that I wasn't pretty enough to date someone famous. Hell, I was even ready for the gold digger remarks if they so happened to come my way. I didn't care what they said; I would take all of it if that was the price of being with Max. My family knew who I was, my friends did too, and that was enough. But this, this was something entirely different. This was waaaaaaaaayyyyyy beyond what I was willing to take on. The allegations, that the people I loved would have to hear about me—it was more than I could handle.

"Beth, perhaps you should take a day or two leave." Mr. James shook his head, the words hanging in the air between us.

"Are you suspending me?" *Please don't cry, please don't cry.*

"Unfortunately, that is up to the board to decide. There will be an investigation to see if there has been some impropriety, but ultimately it will be their decision. The clause on your contract regarding personal conduct would be what is debated. I'm sorry, Beth, but I think until we work through this you should take some personal time."

I felt like the floor had been pulled out from under me and I was free falling into a black abyss. In an instant, everything had changed and I had just a few hours left before I lost everything I'd worked so hard for. Everything I loved.

"Call your friend at the paper, tell him it isn't true. Please, Mr. James, this is my life." I hated that I was begging, but what choice did I have? I couldn't just lie down and have it all ripped away.

"I already suggested he ask the editor to do some additional fact checking before running it, but there is evidence to support . . . I'm sorry, there is nothing else I can do."

I didn't run. By some miracle I was able to hold it together as I slowly walked out of the room. They wouldn't see me cry, they wouldn't see me fall apart; no one would get that satisfaction.

There were no slammed doors, no dramatic exit. Just a quick message to Jules that explained that I'd left without her and I was gone.

Not willing to deal with the subway, I hailed a cab, my façade cracking with each mile until I got to my apartment. I was so desperate to get away from everything and everyone, I completely ignored Ben's hello as I strolled past him in the foyer, the metal doors of the elevator closing before he had a chance to say anything else.

It was when I was finally inside my apartment and in my room that I finally let go. My body shook uncontrollably as the tears I'd been holding off for too long unleashed, my tangled arms and legs collapsing into a heap on the floor.

I thought about calling him, asking him why he was doing

this to me, but deep down I guess I knew. For whatever reason he wanted to hurt me. Whether it was for money, or fame, or maybe because I'd never called him back—but me calling him now wouldn't solve anything. It would just give him a front-row seat to watching me crumble and I wouldn't give him that.

Everything ached, every single part of my body and soul hurt, and I continued to cry. The stream of tears unable to stop as I sucked in jagged breaths that felt like my chest was tearing apart.

My solitude lasted only thirty minutes, Jules coming home soon after and knocking on my door wanting to know why I'd ditched her.

Instead of telling her the truth, I gave her a lame-ass excuse that I had a bad headache. Not a lie considering my head was pounding, my sobs smothered by crying into a pillow.

I didn't know why I was crying. I knew it solved nothing. I knew that if I wanted to fight this, I needed to get myself together and not be the mess I currently was. But at that moment, all the sense in the world didn't exist in my head. I couldn't make myself stop.

"Beth, what's wrong? I can hear you crying," Jules called through the door, my refusal to open it still standing.

"I'm just sick." I lied, curling my body into a numb cocoon.

She would find out soon enough. Everyone would and everything I'd worked so hard for would be gone too.

It didn't matter I was innocent. I'd seen schools let teachers go for something as trivial as a racy Facebook pic, a sex scandal? Bye, Felicia.

"Beth, open the door." Max banged so hard on the wood, the whole wall shook. I assumed Jules and her big mouth was responsible, his knocking not the *hello-can-I-come-in* kind.

"Max, I'm not feeling well." I barely lifted my head from my pillow, the tears miraculously stopping a few minutes before. "I'll call you tomorrow."

Or not. In any case, by tomorrow I wouldn't have to explain, so there was that.

"If you're not well, then open the damn door and we'll get you a doctor." His voice boomed through the door.

He sounded mad, and I hated that, but I was too involved in my own misery to really give it the attention it deserved. I guess that made me a shitty girlfriend. Just another thing to add to an already overwhelming list of crap I was dealing with.

"It's not that bad, please just give me a break tonight." I tried so hard, but those tears that had stopped, started again. And no amount of trying made my voice sound steady. "I promise I'll call you tomorrow."

"Open the door, Beth."

"Please Max, I just can't."

It would have been easy to open the door and curl into his arms. Pretend that the problem didn't exist. But it did, and part of me was worried about how it would all play out. Max had enough drama in his life. He didn't need mine too. Not to mention how awesome it was going to be to have his girlfriend branded a whore.

"Either you open it or I'm kicking it in but one way or another this door is history," he threatened, his fists thumping hard against the wood.

I didn't move, wrapping my hands around my head, not willing to deal with the decision. It was finally made for me a minute later with a huge crack, jamb-splintering at the edge as the door flew open. His threat hadn't been idle, his heavy boot no match for the feeble lock.

"What the fuck?" Max's eyes traveled over the length of my body, clearly not liking what he saw as they widened. His knees sunk onto the floor beside me, genuine fear clouding his beautiful brown pools. "You need to tell me what the hell is going on, Beth."

I'm sure I looked hideous. My face red and puffy from crying, my hair a mess. It's not surprising he looked scared; I'd be scared too if I saw myself.

"I can't."

I hated myself.

Hated that I was so defeated.

Hated that I had fallen into a heap.

Hated that I hadn't been stronger.

But as much as I hated all of those things, what I hated most was that other people I loved were going to be hurt because of something I'd done.

"Did someone hurt you?" He pulled me into his arms, his hands sweeping over my body trying to find the answers I wasn't giving him. "I swear to God if someone fucking touched one hair on your head, I will kill them."

Just like the door, that wasn't an idle threat. I didn't doubt for a second he didn't mean it. That he would risk his own ass for someone he cared about. It's one of the reasons I loved him, his kind and selfless heart.

"Max, you can't kill people just because they hurt me." I tried to smile, the effort coming up short as my mouth refused to curl.

"Who the hell was it?" he demanded, his fingers pushing the hair off my face. "I swear to you, their life is over."

"Max." It hurt to force myself to look into his eyes. "It's not what you think."

"No?" His face reared back in disbelief. "Jules called me hysterical, saying you've been holed up in your room and won't talk. Then I have to break the door down just to get in, and my head can't even process what I'm seeing. I'm losing my fucking mind right now, and every single possibility is worse than the last."

Whether I wanted to confront it or not, I needed to tell Max. It was either that or the man went on a murderous rampage. I was going to have enough bad press; I didn't need to cause any additional headlines.

"I had a meeting with my principal today. His friend works at The Times and called him about a story that is running tomorrow." My chest expanded and I let out a long shaky breath.

"Okay . . ." Max nodded, waiting for me to go on.

"That guy I was seeing before—" And I use that term loosely because he really wasn't a man as far as I was concerned. "He spoke to the press. About me." I continued, filling in the blanks about his crazy accusations, Max waiting patiently until I finished. His jaw tightened as I told him of lies, my penchant for beating up men and my *apparent* obsession. "None of it is true, but apparently I'm newsworthy." The air rushed past my lips as I let out another long breath. "It's not the kind of image that a teacher should have, so . . . there is going to be an investigation."

"Are you fucking kidding me?" Max's voice bounced off the walls. "The asshole couldn't cope with rejection, so he tells some dumbass reporter you smacked him around and were obsessed with him? I knew you said his penis was small, but clearly he had no balls either."

It was an honest assessment; he didn't have any balls, but his lack of testicular endowment didn't make this shit any better.

"Max, this is serious." My hands scrubbed the front of my face. "I work with children. Any allegation sexual in nature could end my career. This isn't just about getting back at me. This is something else altogether."

"Where does he live, Beth?" Max lifted off his knees trying to stand.

"You can't go down there." I grabbed his arm forcing him back down. "He is probably just waiting for you to show up, hoping to get an assault charge out of the deal as well. You need to let me deal with it."

Not that I had been doing such a good job *dealing* with it so far, but it was still my mess to clean up. I didn't want to be that girl who fell into a heap, someone who needed a man to fix things. And as much as I wanted him to make it all go away, I knew that it would forever not sit right with me. I needed to do this, for me.

"So, I'm supposed to just sit on my fucking hands while this asshole threatens you? *Tries* to fuck you over?"

"Yes."

He rose to his feet, his tightly coiled muscles twitching as he came to full height.

"God, what I wouldn't give to be in a room with him." Max paced around the room like a caged animal, his fists white knuckled by his sides. "Five minutes, that's all I'd need."

It was hard enough dealing with my own turmoil, but having to watch what it was doing to him was too much. I hated it. I hated all of it, and it confused me so much.

He shouldn't be here.

With me.

In this mess.

"Please Max, I can't keep it together and be worried about you too." I guess it was the night for begging as I got off the floor and faced him. "I'm not strong enough to do both."

"Listen to me." He pulled me into his arms, my head resting

against his beating chest. "You don't have to worry about anything, especially not with me. I'll give you my word that I won't lay a finger on him, but I'm calling our lawyers. What he's doing can't be legal."

"Okay."

It was a small concession and it was easier to give in; I was too exhausted to keep fighting. I didn't expect lawyers could do anything, but I wasn't going to talk him out of trying. Hell I'd be willing to try anything at this point. Or so was the rumor.

And the press was finally going to get their dirt.

I guess it's what he felt I'd deserved, I'd hit him where it hurt—his ego, his pride, and he would reciprocate.

Hitting me where it hurt me the most.

And hurt it did.

# Twenty-Three

# Max

I'd never been so angry in my life.

Even after all the shit Phil had put us through. The fucking trouble with the police, multiple girlfriends, and the shit with Alison. Nothing came close to the rage I felt when I thought about that smug piece of shit doing this for no other reason than to hurt her.

I wanted to hunt him down and strangle him, watch the breath leave his body as he looked into my eyes so he knew I was the cause. That he could never mess with what was mine.

But I'd said I wouldn't touch him, and I'd sooner strangle myself than go back on my word.

I hated it. Being motherfucking useless while the feeling moved across my skin like a rash. One way or another, I was going to need to find a loophole. That asshole was going to get what was coming, and his fifteen minutes of fame wasn't it.

"Okay Beth, this is just a contract stating you are retaining me as your lawyer." Rebecca, Black Addiction's flashy new legal eagle, laid out the pages on my dining room table. "I've already got my secretary on the phone setting up a call to the paper's legal team. The Times won't go to the presses until after eleven p.m. That gives me a few hours to convince them how bad an idea it will be if they run it."

Unlike the POS who was our first lawyer, Rebecca Cardwell was brilliant. Smart woman who was absolutely fearless, and didn't bat her heavily made-up eyes when I told her the deal. Nope, just got into her fancy BMW and met us up in my apartment, her iPhone glued to her ear as she walked in the door.

"Do you really think you can stop them?" Beth looked over the papers before putting her autograph where it mattered. "They don't seem too interested in my side of the story. No one has called for a comment."

"I'm sure as hell going to try." She barely took a breath as she gave us the rundown in her thick Brooklyn accent. "And they're not interested in your comment because it gives them plausible deniability. This isn't a court hearing, so the burden is different. If presented with a story that is supported by evidence, even if the evidence is bullshit, they can turn around and print a retraction slash apology later. They still moved units and who the hell cares about the mea culpa on page three, two days later. It's in the gossip section; their reporters are bottom feeders. They aren't going to be winning critical acclaim, so they will go for sensationalism every time."

Like I said, barely took a breath.

"Okay." Beth nodded, putting not only her faith but her future in the hands of a stranger. "Let's do whatever we need to do."

What we needed to do was put the asshole six feet under, but *apparently* that wasn't an option. So, while Rebecca C was going the legal route, I hadn't given up the hope of exacting some old school justice of my own.

*The dickless wonder* was going to find out first hand exactly what happened when he went after what was mine. A bruised ego was going to be the least of his problems.

"What are you thinking about?" Beth's fingers moved against my arm, Rebecca double barreling with a cell phone on each ear.

"Nothing. I don't want you to worry, okay?" And wasn't that the fucking truth. I was going to do whatever I needed to so I never saw her like that again.

My day had been textbook standard. In the studio, laying bass tracks down and working on the album. The reward for my efforts was going to be what it always was.

Beth.

So when Jules called me, bull-in-china-shop hysterical, I had my ass in a car heading Bethbound before the reverb had fully rung out on my deserted E string.

Lots of deep breathing, new age positive thinking BS had transpired on that ride, not to mention a few broken traffic laws as well. My mind absolutely exploded with worst-case scenarios. And make no mistake, seeing her like that on the floor when I kicked open her door destroyed me even more.

She hadn't said the words, but the heat that was on her was partly my doing. Not intentionally of course, but that didn't make it any better.

One of the *perks* of dating me. Not only did you get the relationship, but you get the bonus commentary from an asshole with a zoom lens. That POS who'd dated her, never would have come after her if it hadn't been for me. And whether it was because she'd given him the cold shoulder and his delicate sensibilities were hurt, or he was looking to line his pockets with green, I'd put that target on her back.

She was so quiet. Her hands pressed between her knees as she sat at the table like a living corpse. Her eyes so vacant it scared the fuck out of me.

"Alrighty." Rebecca lowered both her phones, giving us a tight smile. "Seems The Times aren't as attached to the story as first thought, imagine that. Article is dead in the water. That's not to say he isn't going to try and shop it elsewhere, but we've got some time to work on our offensive. You would be surprised how persuasive a defamation case can be, and if it doesn't, I'll have him in court so often his favorite color is going to be legal-pad yellow." Each sentence shot out with barely a breath in between, it always astounded me she didn't pass out when she spoke. Rapid-fire dialogue aside, she was damn good at her job. Case in point, Beth was no longer tomorrow's click bait.

"Thanks, Rebecca." I stuck my hand out, the words not conveying half the gratitude I was feeling. "You're awesome."

"No need to thank me, that's what your billables are for. We're not completely out of the woods, but his hand is off the trigger for now." She gathered her notes, shoving everything into an oversized bag that probably cost as much as my car. "I'll keep you both posted."

"Thank you. Really, thank you." Beth nodded, her feet unsteady as she stood.

"Don't mention it, it was a low blow and I hate assholes." Rebecca gave Beth a nod as she got ready to leave.

Beth stayed on her feet as I walked Rebecca out. The goodbyes at the door were as quick and efficient as most of her meetings, her exit happening a few moments later.

"I love you." I wrapped my arms around her and pulled her close. The words weren't new, but I needed her to hear and believe them. No matter what happened, that wasn't changing.

"I love you too," she mumbled into my chest, it sounding too much like a goodbye for my liking.

"If you are thinking about running, you need to forget it." I lifted her chin, her dark eyes still glassy from earlier tears. "I'm not letting you this time."

There were some things that were non-negotiable. Her walking out of my life was one of those things and I wasn't going to let her give up on us either so best she knew that now.

"I don't know what to think." She shook her head, her mind clearly having considered it.

"That's fine," my thumbs mopped the edges of her eyes, "you don't have to *know* right now, as long as it's not running."

"I could still lose my job. Everything I've worked so hard for." She conveniently sidestepped, avoiding the subject.

"And you're wondering if it's worth it. Being with me." I couldn't help but lay it on the table.

Fuck, I didn't blame her if she thought it was too much trouble. Hell, I'd probably want to bail on all of this too if I was her. Didn't change the fact I wasn't going to let her. Or give her an alternative that I wasn't part of.

"Come on, Max." She pulled back and I hated the distance she was trying to create. "You have to at least entertain the idea that maybe there was a reason we could never stay together."

If it had been any other girl I might have agreed with her. Cut my losses and bailed. It would probably be easier and a lot less heartache for her. But not *this* time, not *this* girl—she was wrong and together was absolutely the only way we needed to be.

"You know what, there was a reason and it had nothing to do with fate." My fingers curled around her waist. "We didn't fight for it, Beth. And I'm fighting for you now. I'm fighting for us now."

If I believed for a second that she seriously wanted out, I

*may* have been able to walk away. I say *may* because it still would have been a shit fight. But assuming we agreed it was for the best and it would make her happy, I would have walked out the door even knowing there was a piece of my heart that forever would be missing. But I knew she didn't feel that way, and her words might have said she was confused, but her eyes told me different. She loved me, she wanted to be with me and the only reason she was considering something else was because she was scared.

"I just need time to think." Her hands raked through her long brown hair, keeping up with her avoid.

"You can have all the time you want, but it will be with me by your side." It was killing me to be this close and feel the distance between us. It's like what we worked towards was eroding and I was digging in with both hands trying to keep it together. "You're my past, present and future, Beth. So if you're out, then I don't have anything left."

"I love you." The tears she'd been fighting pooled to the surface.

"Then that's all I need to hear right now."

I wasn't delusional. And I knew that *I love you* wasn't a commitment to stay. Or that everything would be okay from here on out.

But for tonight it was enough.

●●●

"You sure about this?" Joey jumped into the passenger side of my car, his hand tapping on his knee as I started the ignition.

"You know I am."

If I'd have told you the only thing that had been on my mind last night was Beth, then I would be lying. And while I'd spent most of the time watching her while she tossed and turned in my arms, I hated that anyone would even think to hurt her. I promised her she wouldn't have to worry, and I meant every word.

"If you've changed your mind, I can do this alone. No hard feelings." My hand hesitated on the gear stick, knowing how quickly it could all go bad.

Joey had a wife and a kid; that alone should have been enough of a reason to sit this one out. But when he heard what went down, he'd been the first one to ask me what did I need. The man beside me more of a brother than the biological one who shared my last name ever was.

"Don't get soft on me, dude." Joey smiled, tipping his head to the windshield. "You know you aren't doing jack alone so put your foot on the gas and let's do this."

My first instinct had been to track the son of bitch down and beat the living shit out of him. It had been my second and third instinct too. Actually, it had been the only plan that seemed to make sense, letting it go, wasn't happening. The not killing him promise I'd locked myself into caused a problem, which meant I'd have to get creative.

So while Beth slept, my iPhone and I got comfortable. A few well-spent hours were all I needed to lay down the framework, the asshole proving to be completely stupid as well as having no sack. Awesome. Thanks a lot, douchebag; you saved me a whole heap of trouble.

It had killed me to leave her in my bed. Her eyes barely opened as I kissed her goodbye, nodding her head as I promised I would see her soon. Then I had gotten into my car and driven to Joey's. He knew what I was doing and also knew why, and it had been his idea to ride shotgun. It was more than

I'd be willing to ask, but in the end I didn't need to, and for that I honestly loved the guy.

Angie and Rus were aware of the situation. I'd given them both the rundown as well as making it clear that as much as I loved the band, my first priority was Beth. I'd gotten no resistance from either of them, both of them at my back if I needed. Because that's the way it had always been, and no amount of fame and money was going to change that.

"You think he's going to show?" Joey stared out the window as we pulled up to the gym.

"Yep." My thumb tapped impatiently on the steering wheel. "He's predictable and not smart, so I'd say we're going to have no problems."

Mike Warren—or piece of shit, as I liked to call him—was a creature of habit. He liked to get a green juice from *Beets* around the corner, and then spend a couple of hours in the gym.

And as much as I would have liked to pretend the CSI had been difficult, I'd gotten his daily routine with zero effort courtesy of his Twitter account. Every check-in and Twit-pic of his boring existence was just waiting for me to see. But it wasn't just his fucktard poser gym photos that were featured. Nope, there were links to his family, where he worked—every single detail of the moron's life hashtagged for convenience. @Asshole #YouAreADumbFuck.

After that it was just a few well-placed emails, and all I had to do was wait.

Annnnnnnd there we were, right on schedule, the douchebag sucking his wheat germ, kale and whatever juice as he walked down the street. Time to get out of the car and give him his surprise; we didn't want to be rude and keep him waiting.

"Hey." He lifted his hands defensively the minute he'd spied Joey and I. "You touch me and I'll sue."

"Awww, he's worried we'd hurt his pretty face." Joey laughed, waiting for me to take the lead.

"We're not going to lay a finger on you." I leaned up against my 'Vette, wondering what the hell Beth had ever seen in this guy. "But we are going to talk and you are going to listen."

"Sure, I'm happy to hear whatever you have to say but my time is worth money, boys." Smug bastard grinned. So green it was, good to know. "How much is she worth to you?"

I was seriously having issues with not touching him.

No, for real. If my fist was to *accidentally* connect with his face that surely wouldn't count. I mean, he was literally begging for it.

"She's worth everything, but I'm not paying you one penny."

It wasn't an issue of money. If I knew that giving this guy a couple of grand would take care of the problem, then I'd happily open my wallet. I gave little fucks about the size of my bank account. But it didn't take a brain surgeon to know this dumbass wasn't going to be content with a one-time money pay off, nor did I like being extorted. Call me sensitive. I also preferred to neutralize this piece of shit rather than sweep him under a carpet; it was the old Bronx mentality that was hardwired to my DNA despite my new zip code.

"Well, then I think you are wasting your time. There are lots of people who are more than happy to pay. Your lawyer can throw up as many roadblocks as she likes. But photos don't lie."

Beth had mentioned he had some kind of proof, but she had assumed it was surveillance footage, witness accounts that put them together. Turns out that he wasn't just a garden-variety opportunist, but also a grade-A pervert who liked to take a couple of happy snaps. The nature of the photos was yet to be determined but I assumed they weren't of his microscopic dick.

Again, I struggled to keep my feet nailed to the floor, the asshole pushing his luck on how willing I was to allow him to keep breathing. My patience running out by the second.

"Here's what's going to happen." I fought the urge to shove the cup he was sipping on like a douchebag up his ass. "You're going to delete those photos and you're going to give Beth your heartfelt apology. You're going to get down on your fucking knees and beg she believes you're sincere and then you are going to say goodbye and crawl back under whatever rock you crawled out from under."

"Ha, why would I do that? I know you can't do shit." Fuckface smiled, no fucking clue about the shitstorm about to rain down.

"Really?" My grin matched his as I eyeballed him. "Pretty sure your boss, Cooper, feels differently." I pulled out my phone, the screenshots I'd saved displayed so he could get a clearer picture of what I was talking about. "I'm wondering if he is aware you fucked his underage niece last year at the staff Christmas party? Statutory rape stings like a bitch, dude. Not a lot of work out there for child molesters."

"She was eighteen." He paled, his eyeballs widening like he couldn't be sure. "And you have no proof I slept with her."

"You really are a dumb fuck." I barked out a laugh. Seriously, how this man was able to think and breathe at the same time was still a fucking mystery. A few clicks here and there and I was able to get all the recon I'd needed, he even made it easier for me, his profiles wide open.

"Her date of birth is on her Facebook profile, which you probably should have checked *before* you tagged her in your *threesome life goals* post." I scrolled through my camera roll, screenshots illustrating my point. "Also the photo of the two of you on your buddy Braxton's couch doesn't do you any favors. I'm sure you remember the one, dated the day after your original post." Screenshot. "Even with your shirt over her head, it doesn't take a lot of detective work to see they're her tits in your mouth." Amazing how the smug ass grin was no longer plastered across his face. I was just getting warmed up too.

"Social media, man." Joey shrugged, his eyes looking between my screen and the dickhead. "It really is the downfall of society."

"So true." I nodded with as much sympathy as I could muster. "But I'm glad to see your mom, Celica, is embracing the digital age." Her Facebook profile front and center on my screen. "It's good to be able to connect."

Mention of his mom made his head snap up, predictably he didn't want mommy dearest finding out about what kind of asshole she'd raised. And we were just getting started.

"Who else did we find, Joe?" I gave my chin a stroke, the grave we were digging about to get a little deeper.

"Dude, like everyone." Joey pulled out his own phone and started scrolling through the names we'd compiled. "Uncle Pete, your cousin Steve, Aunt Jackie, your brother Tom." He paused, looking up from his phone. "He looks like a serial killer, by the way, so you might want to watch out for him. One day you'll be out chilling and next minute you end up in a barrel behind his garage. It happens. Oh and PS, your sister Alice has a nice rack."

"You-you can't do this," douchebag stuttered, all the fucking confidence he'd been radiating mysteriously MIA.

"Actually, we sort of can." I laughed as he wriggled around like a worm on a fucking hook. "And it's pretty fucking wonderful how easily we can get everyone together and give them a big cyber hug. Don't you think your fam would be really interested to know all this stuff? Joey and I are pretty concerned citizens; the public service alone would be our pleasure."

"She told me she was eighteen." He continued to shake his head like saying it again would somehow make it true. He really needed a new tune; the one he was singing was getting old quick.

"Yeah, close but just not close enough." The fact not changed regardless of his ignorance. "Incidentally eighteen or not, you really are a disrespectful fucker. You have a sister, you should definitely know better."

"What do you fucking want?" He raised his hands in surrender, all talk of monetary compensation forgotten in his moment of defeat.

"I told you what I fucking *want*." I got up in his grill, my fists so tight my fingernails were cutting into my palms as I kept them glued by my side. "Whatever photos you have are fucking gone, and then you're going to grovel like the worthless meatbag that you are. And you better be fucking convincing, or I not only tell your family everything, but I will destroy you. All of that shit, was done in one night. Imagine what I can put together when I have some time on my hands. You were worried about me taking a swing? Dude, you'll be praying for me to end your life."

This was as big a compromise as I was willing to make.

The urge to beat the ever-living shit out of him hadn't passed. And if I saw the fucked up grin of his one more time Joey was going to have to hold me back, deal or no deal. But my point had been made.

No one fucked with what was mine. That wasn't going to change whether I was playing a stadium or whether I was broke, working at Staples. And if anyone else had similar ideas, they would have the same fucking fate.

I loved that girl and it was about time to show everyone exactly how much.

As another unanswered call went to voicemail, I continued to ignore my phone.

While the news story hadn't run as previously planned, my sudden absence at work had been noticed. A substitute had been called to take my classes, while staff and parents were informed I had taken some *personal* time.

Jules fed me details—something I hadn't asked for—claiming complete ignorance while being my inside man.

Most had assumed my rock-star boyfriend had whisked me away on a romantic trip, while others whispered that I was probably pregnant. Because, of course, those were the only plausible reasons why I was no longer in the classroom doing my job. The fact that the establishment had taken the right from me based on hearsay and innuendo couldn't possibly be to blame. No of course not.

I wasn't proud of how I'd dealt with it. I was still grappling with my emotions and how I'd responded, annoyed I hadn't been stronger. But the shock had knocked me off my feet, and it made me question everything. That someone I'd barely known could take so much away from me scared the hell out of me. I'd been naïve, and I had more than learnt my lesson.

Max was right about one thing.

My first instinct was to run.

Not because I didn't think he was worth the trouble, but because I was scared that I was going to lose everything—Max included. I figured it was easier to bail out early than to have it taken from me. And the last thing I wanted was to be anyone's burden. I loved him too much for that.

Turns out he didn't give me a choice.

And maybe that is what scared me the most. That he would one day regret his decision.

He'd kissed me before he left, he seemed reluctant but I knew he had work to do. They had an album that needed to be recorded and I couldn't ask him to drop everything or put his life on hold just because mine was in the toilet. Besides, he'd already done so much. Holding me, loving me—not once asking for anything more than I was able to give.

I forced myself to shower, go downstairs to my empty apartment and put on some clean clothes. I might soon be unemployed with no prospects, but I wasn't going to totally give up on life. And it was while I was there looking at the bed I hadn't slept in that Max had called, asking if I could meet him at a nightclub in midtown.

A *nightclub*.

In the middle of the day.

Sure, that wasn't weird.

I thought by virtue anything that had the word *night* in its title wasn't operational during the daylight hours, but hey, crazy shit happened all the time. Who was I to judge? And it's not like I had a good excuse not to go, my daily schedule was completely clear. It was probably going to be that way for a while too, so other than the venue being slightly questionable there really wasn't a reason not to.

Maybe it was a band thing? Wanting to test out the music on a stage through a PA or something? I mean, maybe that happens, right? Or what if he bought the club? Deciding that just being a highly successful musician wasn't enough, so he should invest in property too? It would make sense, the two industries sort of overlapping. And he'd recently bought the penthouse he was now living in so maybe he was expanding his portfolio.

So, with wild and differing theories running in my mind, I made my way to the address he'd given me, a small boutique club in Midtown that had a big red closed sign on the front door.

It was while I was debating whether to knock on the door or call Max on the phone that the dark wooden door swung open. A mountain of a man who stood seven foot tall and at least four foot wide answered the door.

Gulp.

I looked down at my phone to make sure I had the right address.

"Hi." The big burly guy with a man bun smiled. "You must be Beth."

"Ummm, yes I am." I put out my hand wondering if offering a handshake made me appear lame or business like. Probably lame but I had other problems to worry about, like what the hell I was doing here.

"Pleased to meet you, I'm Dom." He returned my handshake, his hand surprisingly gentle for someone with that many muscles. I had fully expected to have a bone or two crushed in the exchange so was pretty pleased to have all my wiggly fingers whole.

"Hi, Dom."

I'd hoped it was his name and not his job title. Maybe I had been presumptuous in thinking I knew what kind of club this was. And if this was Max's way of being funny—ha ha invite the girl who was accused of kinky, wild sex to a sex club—I was going to kill him.

"Come in, I'll get Max for you." He stepped aside so I could squeeze past, my feet stepping into a small foyer with still no clue as to why I was there.

"Hey, sweetheart." Max appeared a few minutes later, his lips on me before I had a chance to return his greeting. "I would have come and picked you up, but I was in the middle of something."

"It's no big deal." Making my way to the club by myself the least of my worries. "Is there a reason you asked me to meet you here?" Not that I didn't appreciate the distraction from my misery, but the question needed to be answered.

"I didn't want an audience." He took my hand, taking a step forward; the door leading to the main part of the club still closed. "I need you to trust me and walk through that door."

This *was* totally a sex club.

"Max, I trust you. I do, but I need to know what I'm walking into. It has nothing to do with trusting you." I kept my feet in place not moving any closer towards the door. "With the stuff that has gone on in the last twenty four hours, I can't handle any more loss of control. I need to be in the driver's seat."

"I promise, you will be all the way," he said, giving away very little. "You don't like the way it is going, you walk out the door. Come with me, Beth. I'll be with you the entire time."

If I ever was going to take a massive leap of faith, it would be now. And even though I had no idea what was waiting for me on the other side, Max had made it clear that I wasn't doing it alone. What was the worst that could happen?

I nodded without trying to over think it; my feet taking a few tentative steps until he pushed open the door.

The lights were on, illuminating the entire place so I had barely stepped foot inside when it all became clear. Mike was there, sitting at one of the empty tables with Joey sitting beside him. And every single ounce of oxygen housed in my lungs expelled itself in one giant rush.

"What—" *is he doing here?* I couldn't finish the sentence, my chest hurting as I struggled to breathe.

"Beth, he won't hurt you." Max steadied me, his hands on my waist holding me upright. "He does have something he needs to say though."

I didn't hear the words right away, too busy wondering why Mike was here and what he could possibly say that I wanted to hear. Not gonna lie, I was also surprised he was still breathing after Max's reaction last night. He'd obviously showed a ridiculous amount of restraint.

"What?" Again the sentence not completed, the *do you want* left hanging, he didn't deserve more.

"I'm sorry about what I said to the press." Mike's knee jigged under the table. "But I won't be saying anything else to anyone so . . . I'm sorry."

I wasn't an idiot, I was well aware his sudden need to apologize had been coerced. While Mike was sitting with no visible marks or bruises, I didn't expect he'd come to the realization all on his own.

"You're sorry?" The words sounded just as ridiculous coming from my mouth as they'd had from his. "You tried to ruin my life."

"I didn't think about it that way." He shook his head, clueless to the hell I'd had to endure at his hands. "You pissed me off, okay? You were all about me and then nothing. One date and then you took up with *him*." His eyes moved to Max. "How is that fair? I can't compete with a fucking rock star, so I figured if I was going to have to be shoved to the side, might as well make some extra cash in the process, no big deal."

"Me and you not being together had nothing to do with him. You were a terrible date, and I just didn't want to go out with you again." I felt Max's fingers tighten on me, and I wasn't sure if it was to stop himself from punching him or to comfort me. Probably a mix of both. "And even if I had been so shallow, it doesn't justify what you did."

"Yeah, well." He shifted uncomfortably in his seat. "I think it did."

"Tell her the rest," Max spat out, obviously knowing more of the conversation than I was hearing.

"The reason why the paper was willing to run the story was I had photos. Of you. It was enough to prove your identity and our relationship, and that's all they really wanted to know. The other stuff they were happy to take my word on."

I couldn't speak, first that my privacy had been violated and secondly that a paper cared so little about the *actual* facts they were willing to take unsubstantiated half-truths.

"Just a couple of snaps while you were taking your top off. Nothing too graphic," he qualified, like any part of that had made it any better.

Was I supposed to cheer he hadn't taken a full frontal nude shot? Or that he hadn't videoed the whole thing? I didn't need to worry about Max killing him anymore; I had my own murderous thoughts to deal with.

My feet seemed to move of their own accord, placing me directly in front of him. And while my legs had been on autopilot, my arms decided that was a good system too, my hand slapping him so hard across the face my palm stung.

His head snapped back either from shock or the contact, the action and the sound not as satisfying as I'd hoped. And there I was thinking the worst thing about him had been his small penis. It was actually compensating for the fact he was a HUGE dick, an opportunistic creep and just a shitty human being.

Joey, who had been sitting silent up until now, shifted in his chair. "You want us to hold him for you so you can smack him around?" His head nodding to Max who'd magically re-appeared by my side.

"He's not worth it." I squeezed my hand shut; the throbbing in my palm feeling like it had its own heartbeat. "Where are the photos?"

"They were on my phone." Mike coughed out. "But they are all gone. There aren't any copies."

"You expect me to believe that?" I tried not to laugh because the man was clearly a freaking moron if he expected his word to count for anything.

"I don't know, but it's the truth." His eyes widened in an effort, I assumed to convey sincerity. "They are all gone, and I need you to understand how sorry I am. For all of this."

Oh, he sounded sorry, but I doubted it had anything to do with me.

"What do you need, Beth?" Max asked, his hand moving slowly to my back. "Nothing is going to change what happened, but what can we do to make it better?"

I hadn't expected the question and honestly didn't know what the answer was. Of course I'd thought about it. Lighting him on fire would have been a good start, but I really couldn't see myself as a murderer. Maybe we could just set him on fire for a little while, make him a little charred? No, as much as I wanted him to hurt it still wouldn't change anything.

"You're going to pay the rest of my outstanding gym fees and find a different place to work out." The seemingly ridiculous demand came out of my mouth without proper thought. At least I was practical; there was no reason why I should have to cover the cost.

"And then you are going to pretend you never met me. If you see me on the street you will turn around and walk the other way so I never have to deal with your existence again." Out came another demand, wishing I had the ability to literally repel him within a five-mile radius.

"You are also going to write a letter of apology to my principal, apologizing for slandering my name and my reputation." Not that it would fix anything but I still wanted him to admit to my boss what a douche he'd been.

"Anything else?" Max asked, his arms wrapping around me as Mike nodded in silence.

"I want him to leave; I never want to see him again."

Mike stood up, Joey keeping his eyes on him as he moved. "I'm sorry. I'll take care of it and you won't hear from me again."

"I'll help him find the door." Joey got onto his feet. "In case he gets lost on the way."

I wasn't sure if it was to remind Mike of my terms and conditions or stare him down a little more, either way I was thankful for the privacy it gave us. The room empty as the footsteps echoed and finally faded.

"You have something on him."

It was either that, or Max and Joey had cut off one of Mike's fingers. It was obvious he wasn't the caliber of human who would just wake up on his own and be decent. And he seemed to have all his digits, so it must have been some convincing argument they'd been able to pull. Something the lawyer hadn't been able to do.

"Yeah, I counted on him being like every other piece of shit who posts every second of their lives online." He nodded coming clean with no other prompting. "I had to go back through a few months, my eyes almost bleeding from the amount of gym pictures the asshole posted, but eventually I got what I needed." He turned me around in his arms and kissed my forehead.

"I don't want you getting into trouble over me." I hugged him tightly against my chest, the consequences not something I wanted to think about. "If he goes to the cops . . . extortion is still a crime last time I checked."

"Trust me, he won't go to the cops," he said with so much confidence I had no choice but to believe him. "He has too much to lose. He won't be a problem, Beth. Not anymore." He planted another kiss on my forehead.

"You already knew that before I got here, didn't you?" Whatever he'd dug up was obviously compelling enough to get him down to a club for a private confrontation with me. So my appearance was probably not needed. "Why bring him here?"

"It was really hard not to hurt him, Beth." Max shook his head, the strain starting to show on his face. "Watching what he'd done to you, it took everything I had not to take a baseball bat to his head and work on my swing."

This wasn't something he had to tell me, I'm sure if we'd been back in the Bronx and something like this had gone down, it might have been his exact reaction. But he had so much to lose now if he did, money could only get you out of so much trouble. Assault still carried heavy penalties the last time I checked.

"You would have been arrested and charged. I don't think Angie and the band would have been able to continue if you were in jail."

"You think the threat of jail or losing my career was the thing that stopped me?" His brow furrowed confused like those reasons hadn't been good enough to stop him. "Fuck that, you would have been worth losing my freedom over; hell you'd be worth losing my life over. I didn't touch him because I promised you I wouldn't and I wasn't breaking my word."

I stood in silence, his words flooring me; he was so sure, no hesitation on what he would have done. Never had I seen anyone so fierce and determined, so positive on what they would have given up just for me.

"Beth, as much as I wanted to fix it, this wasn't about me." He tilted my chin, his eyes focusing on mine. "It was about what *you* needed, what *you* wanted and I knew that the only way this would work was on your terms. It was your right for this to play out your way. Not mine, not his—yours."

My life had been shattered yesterday. My heart had ached beyond measure and I didn't think I would ever get over it. I'd felt violated and vulnerable, but mostly weak. Out of control in every aspect. And here was a man who had no guarantees I would stay, handing me back the pieces and helping me put it back together.

Without. Asking. For. A. Thing. In. Return.

He put me back in control, my hands steering us forward even though he had no idea of the outcome.

"You did all of that for me?" The lump that formed in my throat was threatening to undo me.

"Yes, and always. Even if it meant losing you." He gave me a tentative smile. "I knew it was a risk; that you might come down here and hate me for this, but if it gave you some peace then it would be worth it."

The lump in my throat was no longer the problem with my

eyes suddenly having trouble staying dry.

"I don't deserve you." My head rested on his chest. It was too hard to look at him, feeling so unworthy.

"It's the other way around." He laughed as he played with my hair. "But I'm not dumb enough to lose you on a technicality."

"I don't know what to say." My leaky eyes ruining the front of his shirt, my stupid tear ducts completely out of control. It had been the general theme for the last day or so, and I wasn't expecting it to change anytime soon.

"You don't have to say a damn thing; we've always found our way back to each other. It's where we both need to be."

"I love you." The words spilled so easily from my mouth it was like they had always been spoken. With what I was feeling, those three little words didn't seem enough.

"Good, because I love you too." Max laughed. "This time it's forever, Beth."

My heart pounded, as I looked at him. "You sure about that? Forever is a long time."

He didn't hesitate.

"And still not long enough to be with you."

# Twenty-Five

# Max

**D**om Hudson was a guitarist from back in our old 'hood. He had been tight with Kenzie, Joey's wife, and he'd proven his loyalty in more ways than one. When shit had gone south with Kenzie and Joey, he'd been there through most of the shit, so we knew he was the real deal. Not afraid to roll up his sleeves to help out his friends, getting dirty not a problem for him either. It was also an asset that in recent times he had taken a break from grinding his axe to become the promotions manager for his uncle's club. It had been one of the places we'd done our surprise-we're-really-Black-Addiction gigs when we were playing undercover. And if Kenzie trusted him, then Joey did. A phone call later and we had our own private meet and greet set up. It kept us away from the prying eyes of the press who struggled with non-of-your-business types of situations. Mike aka micro penis, or as I preferred to call him dickless wonder, had been more than accommodating with allowing me to choose the venue. No surprises there.

I was being a hundred percent truthful when I told Beth that keeping my hands to myself hadn't been easy. I'd have ended him and then turned myself in to the cops with no questions asked, no fucks given either if it meant she would be okay. But instead of doing what I wanted, I did what was right. And in this instance, it meant being a man and letting my girl decide what she wanted.

Took a hell of a lot more balls than beating his face in, I can tell you that.

That slap she'd given him probably was more gratifying to her than anything I could have done, and that was what it was all about. Even when she'd assumed she had been falling apart, I knew how strong she was.

She had always been fierce; there weren't too many women who would have been cool for me to walk in and out of her life like an asshole. I'd marveled at how awesome it had been, stupid in not realizing what I had potentially been throwing away. She was far better a person than I could ever be, and whether she saw it or not, she was a gladiator.

I would do what I did all again in a heartbeat for the woman in my arms. Having her tell me that she loved me and we were going to be together, well that was a fucking prize I'd only hoped to win.

"You guys making out or am I cool to come back?" Joey's face poked through the doorway, his smile a hint he'd at least heard some of our conversation.

"You have the worst timing in the world, dude." I pulled my lips reluctantly from Beth's mouth. We had just been enjoying our non-verbal celebration of douchebag making his exit, the *I love yous* leading into more show than tell.

"Bullshit, I could have totally picked a worst time." He grinned, the rest of his body stepping into the room. "Where did Dom go?" He looked around noticing the dude in question hadn't returned. "Big Foot need an understudy or something?"

"I'm right here, loser." Dom pushed open a door, ignoring

Joey's usual insults about the guy's size. Honestly, he was huge, so I understood Joey's fixation.

"Hey man, thanks for the space." I threw my hand out there, waiting for his to clap against mine. "And for keeping it on the quiet too."

"Not a problem." He nodded before moving his attention to Beth. "You cool? My brother in law works for the IRS and would love to give him a colonoscopy."

"Thanks," Beth smiled, my other arm around her keeping her close. "Let's rain check that for now."

"Offer's there." Dom shrugged, his massive shoulders rolling as he moved. "He might have some problems getting into a few clubs in the near future too. I hear crowd control is a big issue these days." Big-ass grin tossed our way as well as the freebie. He, like the rest of us, couldn't stand disrespectful assholes.

"Nice work." I gave him a quick nod. The additional grief the POS would be receiving courtesy of Dom's network making me happy. "We'll be out of here in a minute or two, let you get back to work."

"Take as long as you need." He gave his knuckles a crack before picking up a clipboard on the bar. "I'll be in my office, just shut the front door on your way out." A few steps later, and he was gone from the space.

"You know, for a big mofo, he's pretty agile." Joey nodded to the closed door of Dom's office. "I always expect more Fe Fi Fo Fum."

"You're lucky he's got the patience to match his shoe size." I laughed, giving my girl a squeeze. "You want to get out of here, sweetheart?"

"Yes." She nodded, her arms untangling themselves from mine as she walked over to my buddy. "Thanks, Joey." My BFF treated to a hug courtesy of my girl.

"No thanks necessary, babe." Joey returned the hug. "We take care of ours, and your dude has been there for my ass more than I care to admit. Family first, always."

He was right on the money about that. It wasn't about keeping score either. One of the boys or Angie needed something, there'd be no questions asked. But they'd had my back too, every single one of them pulling through whenever I needed. It's what a family did, and we'd always been more than just a band.

"He's right." I waited patiently for Beth to return to my side. "Like it or not, you're part of this now. And everything that comes with it."

Her face lit up, the smile she gave me making my world turn. "I think I'm going to handle that just fine."

•••

As far as work was concerned, it had been a wash. Rus and Angie were cool with having a down day, so instead of heading into the studio, we said our goodbyes to Joey, and Beth and I headed back to my apartment.

It was good to see the smile on her face as some of the tension eased out of her, but I wasn't living in fantasyland thinking it was smooth sailing from here on out.

She was still unsure of where she sat on a few issues, her job being the most obvious. It wasn't about her being on personal leave either, assuming they dropped whatever bullshit investigation, AKA witch-hunt, and allowed her to come back, why would she go back after they'd treated her like that? If it were up to me I'd be flashing them deuces and telling them to peace out; their handling of the situation not cool. I didn't give a fuck what the rumor had been, you circle your wagons and you stand beside your people until you have some facts. But as strong as my opinion was on the matter, I was behind her whatever choice she made. She wouldn't get any lip from me.

"So, what are you going to do?" The pressure I hadn't applied was coming thick and fast from her roommate. "There is nothing to investigate. No scandal, you should be able to come back, right?"

Jules had knocked on my door the minute she'd gotten home from class, partially to find out the 4-1-1 and partially to tell us they had already started to take odds on whether we were having a boy or a girl. The general consensus for Beth's leave, she was knocked up.

"I don't know if I want to go back." Beth's pendulum of should-I-stay-or-should-I-go kept swinging. "I would hate to leave my kids, but I hated being backed into a corner. Part of me really doesn't want to be there."

"But you can't leave, what will you do?" she persisted, her insistence starting to piss me off.

I knew Jules meant well, heart in the right place and all of that, but she was going to be giving Beth zero grief on this.

"She can do whatever she wants. There are other schools, or she can couch surf for a while. But whatever she decides, we're both going to support her, you hearing me, Jules?"

"Whoa, dude." She gave me a handful of settle down I wasn't interested in hearing. "If you weren't totally staring me down, that alpha shit would be so hot right now." She fanned herself for effect.

"Are you hitting on my boyfriend?" Beth laughed, ignoring the fact I was rolling my eyes at the BS being tossed my way. I had learned pretty quickly that acknowledging it only made it worse.

"No, but I'm freaking shocked you aren't dry humping him right now." Jules nodded as if to agree with her own assessment.

"Do I need to remind the two of you, I'm still here and can hear every fucking word?" I waved my hand like a fucking loser in my own house. The conversation took a left turn onto a what-the-fuck tangent.

"Like we could ever forget you're here." Beth smiled, her hand resting on my chest.

"Although, if you really wanted to remind us, you should take off your shirt. Just sayin'." Jules' eyes following Beth's hand action, her smile getting wider.

"I'm not taking off my shirt." At least not right now; later when Beth and I were alone it would be another story. "Nice try though. Now, let's refocus on what's important, a job doesn't define you or at least it shouldn't."

I didn't usually pull the Confucius shit, but in this instance it was valid. Beth was an amazing woman with a huge heart. She'd always wanted to be around kids and teaching was what made her happy. It wasn't the other way around.

"Honest to God, I am no happier playing a stadium than I was playing a bar with two bucks in my pocket. Sure, shit is easier now. I don't have to worry about money and the success feels great, but if it all goes away tomorrow I would be okay with it."

Perhaps that came out wrong, like I didn't give a shit what she did or that she shouldn't be pissed that her hand had been forced. She should be livid, and I absolutely cared, but what I was trying to say—albeit badly—was that she should do what made her happy, the location wasn't what was important.

Thank Christ, I wasn't a fucking career counselor, because I would suck at it.

"Max is right," Beth announced, failing to clue me in on what she was giving me props for.

"Awesome." I clapped my hands together happy I'd helped in some way. How exactly? I was still none the wiser. "About . . ." I waited for enlightenment.

"That I'm not going to give up teaching. I love it, but I'm not going to be forced to stay because I'm afraid I won't find something else. There are other schools, and I am damn good at what I do."

And fuck yeah, we'd made progress. Some of that bravado I knew she had was peeking through again. Jules looked like someone had kicked her puppy, the realization that they weren't going to be working together sinking in. I guess there was the other issue of living arrangements that I was going to bring up too. As in, I wanted her out of her apartment and into mine.

I hadn't mentioned it yet because shit had been crazy enough without me adding to it, but make no mistake, it was coming. Deep down I think Jules knew it too, which is why she was bummed about the job.

Jules stayed a little longer, but didn't try and change Beth's mind. Then she said her *see ya laters* and went back downstairs. She hadn't asked if Beth was joining her, rightly assuming she wasn't.

"She's disappointed." Beth curled up on the couch, the funk of the earlier conversation hanging in the air. "I get it; I just want her to know it's not personal."

"It's not your responsibility to make it okay for everyone. It's good to care, but it's also cool to be a little selfish sometimes too." She did not have to take ownership for other people's feelings. That was for everyone else to do.

"I feel guilty." She bit her lip, her body fitting perfectly against mine as I sat beside her, her head resting on my shoulder.

"About what?" My hand moved slowly up and down her arm.

"Well, we wasted a lot of time in the past." She snuggled in deeper, her voice vibrating off my chest. "Trying to do the right thing but in the end it really wasn't, not for either of us."

"Don't think about the past, none of it matters now."

"No, I know but I mean that I want different things now."

"And what is it that you want?" Because let's face it, whatever she wanted was pretty much hers. She wanted the Taj Mahal, I'd find a way to bring that son of bitch to her, brick by fucking brick.

"You," she said quietly.

"You already have me." I laughed, not a single part of me left unclaimed.

"No, you said forever and I want to know if you meant it."

"Of course I meant it, I'm not going anywhere."

"Make love to me, Max."

"That's one thing you'll never have to tell me to do. I'll volunteer every time."

**W**hen I'd moved to Manhattan it had been for a fresh start, not because my old life had been bad, but because I thought I could make it better. Turns out I'd left out the most important part.

The world could fall apart around me, and as long as I had Max it would all be fine. Not because he was my hero and he would save me, but because he was beside me, holding my hand and making me stronger. And that was *better* than a hero.

"Beth."

My name had never felt so important as did it when it came from his lips, his hands moving against my skin.

"Max." My body arched against his, feeling the friction between us, and still not being close enough.

We'd moved from the living room to his bed. The journey took us a little longer than usual as we walked blindly to his room. We couldn't stop touching each other, and if I wore a bruise or two from a rogue doorjamb then it would have been worth it; my lips constantly on him until my back hit the mattress.

He didn't need me to tell him what I wanted, his hands got busy stripping each layer of clothing off my body as his mouth kept mine occupied. The pile of clothes on the floor a testimony to his multitasking while I lay naked underneath him.

"God, I love looking at you." His fingers trailed along my bare skin, the tingle following close behind.

"I want to look at you too." My eyes dipped down to his still-clothed body, the undressing part having been extremely one sided.

"That I can do." He pulled off his shirt and tossed it to the floor. His talent for making things disappear again proved to be outstanding, refusing my help as he pulled off each item one by one.

It had been slower than when he'd had his hands on me, each inch of flesh he unwrapped making it harder for me to resist. He wouldn't let me touch though, moving just beyond my reach as he continued his show.

Finally there was nothing between us; his body hovering over mine as he took his hard cock in his hand and stroked it slowly, my eyes mesmerized as my fingers reached out on their own accord. This time he didn't fight me, my smaller hand slipping under his, then gliding up and down tighter under my touch.

"That feels good." He grinned; his hands now free to do other things.

It didn't take too long for them to find a new purpose, his mouth moving to my breasts as a finger plunged into me.

"Yes." My hand gripped tighter, needing a minute to stop just to absorb the sensation.

He inserted another finger, moving them deep inside of me before sliding them out and slowly lifting them to his mouth.

His lips closed around them as he sucked.

"You taste amazing." He licked what was left off his fingertips before unpeeling my hand from the death grip I had on his cock. "As much as I enjoy you jerking me off, I want to go down on you more."

Funnily enough, I agreed with this. His mouth covering my pussy as his tongue plunged into me, my hips bucking against his mouth.

It was maddening; the slow lick against my clit and then a slide inside, the rhythm unpredictable as he constantly changed tempo. My fingers pulled at my nipples, my body feeling like it was going to explode.

"I want to taste you too." My body shifted on the bed, angling myself so his cock was in reach. His eyes widening as my tongue got close enough to lick the head.

"Fuck, Beth." He shifted to his side, giving me better access while he could continue to keep his mouth on me. That access wasn't wasted as I wrapped my lips around his dick and sucked hard.

Max mumbled against my core, the vibrations feeling amazing as he refused to stop. The encouragement reciprocated as I sucked him further into my mouth, my hands joining in.

It was like a switch had been flicked, his body jacking off the mattress, pulling himself from my mouth. My hand struggled to maintain a hold as his powerful body pushed against mine.

He was beautiful, the raw sexuality emanating from every pore as he stalked above me. Each muscle perfectly defined like it had been chiseled from stone.

"I didn't want to stop," I protested, my hand reaching for him and hitting the hard cords of his abs, my fingertips trailing along the ridges.

"We aren't stopping." His knees split my thighs apart as he settled in between them. The mattress compressed under his weight as his fingers trailed up my skin as he looked at me with hungry eyes. "But I'm going to be inside you first, then if you want me to come in your mouth, I'll give you that too."

He didn't ask, his cock entering me in one swift movement, pushing so deep inside of me I gasped at the invasion.

"I need you, Beth." He slowly slid out before plunging into me again; my core tightening around him overwhelmed by the sensation.

"God, that's tight." His mouth dropped to my neck sucking me. His fists punched into the mattress underneath, his strong arms flexing as they supported his weight. My body caged, completely filled by him as his hips bucked against mine, slow and steady.

"More." I scrambled to get closer, wanting more of him as I felt my body ignite.

Slow and steady was abandoned as he leaned back onto his knees and grabbed my legs, thrusting hard as he gave me all I could take.

It didn't take long, my fingers pulling against my nipples as with one last heave I came apart in a rush. My body pulsed against his as I writhed on the mattress, his finish coming soon after as he exploded into me.

Our breaths were out of control as he collapsed beside me, his arms rolling me to my side so we would stay connected. His fingers moved against my clit as another orgasm started to build.

"Max." My eyes slammed shut as once again I splintered, this time without warning as the wave overtook me. My body completely boneless as it shuddered beside him, his hand refusing to stop.

"God, I love feeling you come." His mouth moved slowly up the back of my neck, soft kisses in their wake. "Every time is no less fantastic than the last."

"Well, it's not like there is a shortage when you're around." I laughed, my body still tingling as his hand started to slow. "I thought you said you were going to come in my mouth?"

"Yeah, if that's what you want, I'll give you that later." He pressed his lips against my throat. "There wasn't a chance I wasn't coming inside of you first."

"I like the way you think." My body shuffled closer against him, not wanting the moment to end. "I wish we could stay like this forever."

I wasn't sure if it had just been a thought or I'd said it out loud, knowing eventually we would have to face reality and everything that came with it. It was easy to get lost in the bubble.

"We can be like this forever." He lifted his head, whispering in my ear. "You are my forever."

• • •

It only took me a few days to get my shit together and hand in my notice. It was bittersweet. Even though the school year was almost over, I decided not to go back. I didn't want to subject the kids to any more upheaval, the substitute teacher agreeing to see them out through the rest of the year. I sent them all a huge card and cookies for them to share, the goodies hopefully softening the blow. It wouldn't be long before they'd be saying goodbye for summer break and all thoughts of me would fade. I'd never forget them; the time I spent with each little person staying with me long after the years ended.

Jules was sad but she understood, happy that the nightmare was finally over. I even got a written apology from the principal, with them apparently *sad to see me go.* Surely they couldn't be surprised? Either way, I was done and felt better for it.

So, after applying for a bunch of teaching positions for the coming school year, I had a whole lot of time on my hands. Just days filled with not a lot of anything. But I was okay with it, happy even, because strangely it had worked out for the best. It also meant I got more time with Max.

He was still putting in ridiculous hours in the studio. Gone for hours and hours while they tried to finish the album. But no matter how tired or how long his day had been, he always made time for the two of us when he got back.

And whatever happened in the future, he had to be a part of it.

There was no going back.

It was only a matter of time before I told Jules I was moving out. It made sense; I was hardly ever in my own bed anymore. She'd seen it coming, her lack of surprise evident when I'd come home to pack up my things and she'd overtaken the use of my closet.

"Just so we're clear, you guys aren't going to leave the building, right?" She helped seal up one of my boxes. "Because if you decide you want to buy a house or some shit, I'm gonna put a hex on you both. You're going to give me abandonment issues."

"I promise you, we're going to stay right here. Just a few floors up and you can visit anytime you want." I slung my arm around her.

It was hard to leave our cozy little space. She'd been an amazing friend and one who had accepted me in all my incarnations and never asked for anything other than friend-ship. We'd always be close.

"Good. I want some weekends too." She grabbed another empty box and started filling it. "Maybe like every third Friday as well."

"Jules, you can't negotiate me like a custody agreement." I tossed a pillow at her head; her arm deflecting it before it could find its mark. "Anytime you want to see me, just call."

"Can we talk about how big his dick is?" She speared me with a sideways glance, the topic of Max's penis size not having been mentioned in a while.

"No, we cannot." I shot her down with no room for debate.

"I assumed, but I figured I'd try." She shrugged, my response not a surprise. "By the way, in case I haven't said it, I really like him. And as much as it sucks for me that I'm losing a roommate, I'm really happy for you."

"Awww thanks, Jules." All efforts to pack up my room tossed to the wayside as I wrapped my arms in a hug. "I really like him too."

"Yeah, I can tell. Don't get me wrong, you seemed happy before, but since you guys have been together, it's like . . . I don't know, something else."

She didn't need to say the words; I knew exactly what she meant.

He didn't make me happy.

I'd been happy before.

He made me whole.

# Twenty-Seven

# Max

**I**'d never been comfortable in a tux.

It felt like a straightjacket, the collar buttoned up too tight. But as I stood in the church, waiting for the ceremony to start, I put all of that shit out of my mind and focused on what was important.

Family.

The music started; heads turned to the back waiting for the bride to make her entrance and my mom had already started crying.

"She's stunning." Beth squeezed my hand, Alison doing the slow walk to Rusty who was waiting at the end of that aisle looking like he'd just hit the lottery.

I guess in a lot of ways he had, and lightening had struck more than twice with each of us finding our slice of happiness. And as for me, I was the luckiest bastard of all.

The album had been finished. We'd all agreed it was some of our best work yet and were beyond excited to get it to where it mattered. Our fans. They were the reason we got to live our dreams every day of the week and we wouldn't dare give them something that wasn't worthy of their love and support.

And with the free time we all had in front of us, Ali and Rus decided not to bother messing around anymore and make it legal. The two of them preferred a small private service with just a few family and friends. And I had to admit, as the two of them stood up at the altar—no bells and whistles, no bridal party—even I got a little choked up. It was everything a wedding was supposed to be, just about them, and the only way I would have been happier was if it had been Beth and I saying those words.

I hadn't pushed the issue, knowing she already had enough on her plate with the job search. She'd also recently moved up a few floors as well; her new address matching mine, so there really wasn't a reason to rush.

But I wanted it.

I wanted to put a ring on her finger more than I cared to admit. The need to make it permanent almost unreasonable. But for her, I'd wait. Wait as long as I needed to, because we'd already proven no amount of distance or time would ever keep us apart.

Ali dabbed at her eyes as she made promises to Rusty in front of all of us, Rus barely getting his words out when it was his turn, and we'd all cheered when he finally was able to kiss her. And there were no fucks given that my folks or his were standing in the front as he claimed her mouth like there was no one else in the room.

"You going to let him manhandle your niece like that?" Joey grinned, his beautiful wife and daughter beside him.

"Yeah, I couldn't think of anyone better for the job." I nodded my head watching how deliriously happy she was with one of my best friends.

Ironically, my asshole brother—and her father—was

noticeably absent from the celebrations, her mother's invitation also getting lost in the mail. But my folks had more than made up for those two oxygen thieves' shortcomings, welcoming Ali in as the family she'd deserved to have.

"Mama, hungry." Zack, Angie's kid yanked at his mother's skirt. The promise of cake too much to take now that the service was over.

"Soon, baby boy." She patted his head, Baby-daddy Jase scooped his son up onto his shoulders to hopefully keep him entertained.

"Got any cookies?" Dan, head douchebag and sometimes bass player for Power Station, snickered over my shoulder. The big-ass grin he was wearing spelled out exactly where he was going with it. "Maybe we should give the kids a snack."

I should have known that our little babysitting *incident* had filtered through to the Power Station camp. Apart from Jase being Angie's other half, they were also the owners of our record label and had become some of our closest friends.

"Yeah, if anyone looks like they are going to puke or take a piss, I'm out." I discreetly flipped him off.

And that took some talent, because not only were my parents sitting in front of us, but we were surrounded by little people; their eagle eyes sure to pick up Uncle Max being rude.

Man, things had changed.

And we all were a long way from the Bronx.

It would be easy to sit back and reminisce, the people around me giving me a crazy trip down memory lane, but we still had a reception to get to.

"You want me to drive?" Beth leaned casually against my ride, her voice dipping seductively as she held out her hand for the keys.

"Sweetheart, I love you, but I don't want you killing my

'Vette. When was the last time you drove a stick?" I pressed up against her, the fancy tuxedo pants not doing shit to hide the hard-on underneath. "But I can give you a lesson later if you like." And I wasn't necessarily talking about the car.

"I know how to handle a stick, Max." She moved her hands up my arms and it looked like we were on the same wavelength.

"I love you," I whispered against her lips. "And in case I didn't tell you before, you look beautiful."

It probably wasn't cool to say, but as gorgeous as Alison had looked, it was Beth who knocked me on my ass. Flawless, in a simple dress that clung to her body like a sheath, she'd turned more than a few heads when we walked in. And didn't that make me feel like I was ten feet tall knowing that it was my arm she'd been on.

"Thank you." Her fingers straightened my tie. "You look pretty good yourself. I like you in a suit."

"Yeah, well get a good look because it will be awhile before you see me in one again." I pulled at the collar of my shirt, more interested in getting out of it than getting back into it. "It's only because I love Rusty and Alison that I'm wearing it."

"Oh, I think maybe we can find a reason for you to wear one again."

With all of Black Addiction married, there were only two occasions in the future I could think of where the monkey suit was needed. One would be my funeral, although I was really hoping that when I went for the big dirt nap someone would cut me some slack and bury me in a pair of jeans. The other was marrying Beth. And because I didn't want there to be any misunderstandings as to which she meant—I really hoped she wasn't thinking about the first—I wanted her to spell out *exactly* what she meant.

"Oh really?" I brushed the hair off her face, my eyes nailed to hers. "What did you have in mind?"

"May-be." She hesitated but only for a second. "You and I could do something like this?"

Sounded pretty clear to me and I was fucking thrilled beyond measure at this latest development.

"Beth Hart, are you asking me to marry you?"

It was the first time either of us had said the word, even though I'd been thinking it for a while.

"Yes."

"Then you would make me the happiest man alive." I kissed her forehead, my heart feeling like it was about to explode in my chest. "I want you to be my wife, Beth. I need you to be my wife. And if we could convince the preacher to marry us now, I'd do it in a heartbeat."

For real, I didn't give a shit if there were a million people around or it was just the two of us.

"I want a wedding, Max." She smiled, her teeth playing with her bottom lip. "It doesn't have to be big but I want a day that both of us remember."

"Anything, it will be whatever you want it to be."

She wanted a fucking three-ring circus and the biggest reception she'd ever seen, then I'd be calling in the Ringling Brothers. Didn't matter how much it cost or what I had to do, it would be exactly how she wanted it. And I wasn't stopped at the wedding either, I was determined to make every single one of her dreams come true.

"What about you? What about what you want?"

That smile of hers slayed me. Every. Fucking. Time.

"I've already got what I want."

And I'd spend the rest of my life making sure I'd never lose it again.

When that once in a lifetime happens, you need to hold on to it. Wrong time, wrong place—it was all bullshit.

The only thing that mattered was the right person, and I'd found that years ago.

"**Holy shit, not only do you get the big dick but you got** a huge ring too." Jules pulled my hand into the light. "Wowza, does your hand cramp under the weight?"

It was taking a little getting used to, but I would soon be Mrs. Max Reynolds, the Cartier diamond on my finger apparently necessary.

"I tried to tell him it wasn't necessary." I unwrapped Jules' death grip and regained control of my hand. "But it wasn't worth the battle."

It had been exactly two weeks since Rusty and Alison's wedding, the day of our unofficial engagement. Seeing him dressed in a suit and being so happy for them got me caught up in the moment. The words had come out of my mouth before I'd even really given them proper thought, asking him to marry me felt like the most natural thing in the world. I hadn't even considered the possibility of him saying no, something that could have been a real downer given we still had to sit through the reception. Thankfully, he said yes and I was saved from the most epic letdown of all time.

"Girl, I mean this in the nicest possible way. But fuck you." Jules folded her arms across her chest, the pie I'd gotten from the *nice* bakery remaining uneaten in front of her.

Despite me moving in with Max, we still saw each other all the time, Jules spending almost as much time in the penthouse I was now living in as she did in my previous home.

"Yeah, totally valid." I eased back into my seat, unable to argue that my life wasn't pretty fucking spectacular at the moment. I'd even secured a new teaching position for the end of summer, the glowing recommendation I'd been given from my ex principal no doubt helping.

"What's valid?" Max's hands brushed off the hair from my shoulder, his lips kissing my neck. He'd been stealthy in his entrance. I hadn't even heard the front door open or him walking into the room. "Hmmmm is that the nice pie?" He looked down at the dessert sitting on the kitchen table.

"Don't even think about it, Reynolds." Jules picked up her fork, pointy bits out and brandishing it as a weapon. "You already took my roommate and my best friend; I'll fight you to the death for the pie."

"Fine, fine. Enjoy your pie." He laughed conceding defeat with very little effort. "But I'm going to need a minute or two with my future wife."

I didn't have a chance to protest, his hands pulling me from my chair and into his arms. Not that I would have resisted; being wrapped up in Max wasn't something I passed up.

"Go," Jules groaned, her forked hand waved at us. "You both make me sick."

I wanted to tell her I didn't care what she thought, that I was deliriously happy and wanted the world to see it, but Max didn't give me a chance to respond. His mouth sealed mine, his desperate hands pulling me close against his body.

I knew that kiss.

It said everything without uttering a single word. His lips and tongue dominated mine and I relished in its possession. It made me feel loved, desired and secure all at the same time, and so powerful that I could drive a man like Max as crazy as I did.

"I missed you," he whispered when he finally released my mouth, his lips lingering along my neck while his hands showed no signs of letting go. "Touring is going to suck." His smile curled, his beautiful face lighting up.

"Or . . ." I resisted the urge to tell him how much I would hate it too. That I'd curse every mile that separated us and live for the days I'd get to join him. "We can have all kinds of fun with Skype and cell phones. I've been practicing my heavy breathing."

"This would be the first time one of us is leaving, but we're staying together." Max's eyes darkened, his grip tightening slightly. "New territory for both of us."

"I'm not worried." I gave him my best smile. "We always found our way back to each other; clearly we belong together."

"Right." Light kisses landed on my forehead. "And every opportunity I have, I'm going to fly you to wherever the band is or I'll fly back. Fate or not, I want you in my bed as often as possible."

"Do you think all of this was fate? Like this is how it was all supposed to end up? You, me, the band?" I looked at him, feeling that I really didn't need him to answer. While I never believed there was anyone else driving my own destiny, I couldn't deny that sometimes the universe had a way of making sure the right people ended up together.

"This is exactly how it should be," he answered, not an ounce of hesitation. "I knew for sure the minute I stepped on stage with Rusty, Angie and Joey that it was going to be for keeps. I knew that we'd find a way to claw our way in, and even if it took a lifetime, we'd eventually make it." He took a breath before brushing his lips gently against mine. "And I know with the same amount of certainty that you are my forever."

"It seems a little greedy that we get everything we want." A tiny, almost microscopic piece of doubt crept in, the words flying out of my mouth before I had a chance to stop them.

"Our happiness isn't taking from anyone else—there is enough to go around."

He was right. And far smarter than anyone gave him credit for. He, the band—they'd done what made them happy knowing that everything else would fall into place. Where as I had assumed I needed to *make it* first, the happiness coming from my success. I now knew how wrong I'd been.

Rather than worrying about if the glass was half full or half empty, I should have been appreciating the beauty of the glass.

And now that I saw it, my glass was flawless.

To keep up to date with all T Gephart's

news,

appearances
and releases,

please subscribe to her mailing list at

http://eepurl.com/bws5Av

# Acknowledgements

Thank you to my family Gep, Jenna, Liam and Woodley—you will always be my heart even if mine were to stop beating.

Thanks to my amazing extended family and friends. It doesn't matter at which station you joined the crazy train, you're on it now and I am forever grateful.

Special thanks to amazing my beta team who have to deal with my missed words and sometimes muddled thoughts. MK, Maz and Danielle—your feedback is invaluable. Love your work, ladies. Professional, super quick and constructive, you are a rare find!

A million thanks to Jules. Dude. I can't even right now. All I know is that we were meant to meet and become friends. We need to get together, eat pie and hang out more. Don't ever forget how awesome you are.

Thank you to the authors who inspire me and support me. I was a reader longer before I was a writer and I'm privileged to be among you. Lili Saint Germain, JB Hartnett, Monica James, Skyla Madi, CJ Duggan, Lilliana Andersen, Rachael Brookes, JD Nixon, Natasha Preston, Kirsty Mosely, Jane Harvey-Berrick, Ker Dukey, LA Casey, Jill Patten, Tillie Cole, Andie Long, Abbi Glines, Chantal Fernando, Helena Hunting, Christina Hobbs and Lauren Billings, Penelope Louleas, Jay Crownover, Kim Karr, SC Stephens, Joanna Wylde and Kylie Scott—and to anyone I've left out, you all rock.

Hang Le—your work is stunning, and yet it's only a fraction of how beautiful you are both inside and out. Ninja hugs for life.

Special and extended thanks you to the bloggers and blogs who have and continue to support me. The incredible effort you go to with shout outs, shares, likes, comments, teasers and reviews help us keep writing. Don't think for a second you aren't appreciated or valued, I see it all and it warms my heart.

Thanks to the T Gephart Entourage, you are awesome.

Thanks to my Penny and Angela #UnimpressedCat

Thanks to my editor, Nichole Strauss, from Perfectly Publishable. You are more than just an editor, thank you for all that you have done especially with this book. Texas is so far away but I hope you feel my hug, thank you.

Thank you to my proofreader Rosa for picking up pesky mistakes.

As always, thanks to Max Henry from Max Effect for her spectacular formatting.

And last but not least, a HUGE thanks to my readers. You have allowed me to live inside your hearts and minds, and for that I will be eternally grateful. Thanks for coming on the journey with me.

# About the Author

T Gephart is an indie author from Melbourne, Australia. T's approach to life has been somewhat unconventional. Rather than going to University, she jumped on a plane to Los Angeles, USA in search of adventure. While this first trip left her somewhat underwhelmed and largely depleted of funds it fueled her appetite for travel and life experience.

With a rather eclectic resume, which reads more like the fiction she writes than an actual employment history, T struggled to find her niche in the world.

While on a subsequent trip the United States in 1999, T met and married her husband. Their whirlwind courtship and interesting impromptu convenience store wedding set the tone for their life together, which is anything but ordinary. They have lived in Louisiana, Guam and Australia and have traveled extensively throughout the US. T has two beautiful young children and one four legged child, Woodley, the wonder dog.

An avid reader, T became increasingly frustrated by the lack of strong female characters in the books she was reading. She wanted to read about a woman she could identify with, someone strong, independent and confident and who didn't lack femininity. Out of this need, she decided to pen her first book, A Twist of Fate. T set herself the challenge to write something that was interesting, compelling and yet easy enough to read that was still enjoyable. Pulling from her own past "colorful" experiences and the amazing personalities she has surrounded herself with, she had no shortage of inspiration. With a strong slant on erotic fiction, her core characters are empowered women who don't have to sacrifice their femininity. She enjoyed the process so much that when it was over she couldn't let it go.

T loves to travel, laugh and surround herself with colorful characters. This inevitably spills into her writing and makes for an interesting journey - she is well and truly enjoying the ride!

Based on her life experiences, T has plenty of material for her books and has a wealth of ideas to keep you all enthralled.

## Website:

http://tgephart.com

## Facebook:

www.facebook.com/tgephartauthor

## Goodreads:

www.goodreads.com/author/show/7243737.T_Gephart

## Twitter:

https://twitter.com/tinagephart